COMBATANT

COMBATANT

THE KACY CHRONICLES™ BOOK 3

A.L. KNORR
MARTHA CARR

DISRUPTIVE IMAGINATION

This book is a work of fiction. All of the characters, organizations, and events portrayed in this novel are either products of the author's imagination or are used fictitiously. Sometimes both.

Copyright © 2017 LMBPN Publishing
Cover copyright © LMBPN Publishing

LMBPN Publishing supports the right to free expression and the value of copyright. The purpose of copyright is to encourage writers and artists to produce the creative works that enrich our culture.

The distribution of this book without permission is a theft of the author's intellectual property. If you would like permission to use material from the book (other than for review purposes), please contact support@lmbpn.com. Thank you for your support of the author's rights.

LMBPN Publishing
PMB 196, 2540 South Maryland Pkwy
Las Vegas, NV 89109

Version 1.06, October 2022

The Oriceran Universe (and what happens within / characters / situations / worlds) are Copyright (c) 2017-22 by Martha Carr and LMBPN Publishing.

From A.L. Knorr

For anyone who ever wished they could fly.

From Martha

To everyone who still believes in magic and all the possibilities that holds.
To all the readers who make this entire ride so much fun.
And to all the dreamers just like me who create wonder, big and small, every day.

THE COMBATANT TEAM

JIT BETA READERS

Joshua Ahles
John Ashmore
Kimberly Boyer
Kelly O'Donnell
Larry Omans
Paul Westman
Nicola Aquino
Alex Wilson
Tim Bischoff
Sarah Weir
Thomas Ogden

If we missed anyone, please let us know!

CHAPTER ONE

The heels of Jordan's boots clicked against the hardwood floor of the foyer. There was a squeak as her toe depressed the loose floorboard. The sound of a crackling fire drew her to the parlor. It was an inviting sound, a comforting sound, given the maelstrom that whipped the leaves of the trees outside and threw pellets of rain against the glass of the windows.

Jordan paused in surprise. A strange dog was curled up on the carpet in front of the fire. A Greyhound, if she wasn't mistaken—a racing breed with long limbs, powerful shoulders, and a long spine. He was curled into a ball with his back to her. White speckles dusted his ginger fur, and the fire threw his shadow long and soft against the carpet. The bones of his spine made a row of low mounds down his back. He was thin, this dog. *The hallmark of his breed,* she supposed.

The dog sensed Jordan's approach and lifted his head, facing away from her, ears cocked. He got to his feet, slowly, stiffly, and padded in a small circle to face her. His jaw and mouth were dusted with gray; his once bright hazel eyes were milky with cataracts. A scar carved its way down the side of his face, just in front of his right ear. He had the noble face of the Greyhound breed, fine and sleek. As they looked at one another, Jordan gasped.

This Greyhound was her father, Allan.

The fire blew out.

A wisp of smoke drifted from the blackened logs and disappeared up the chimney. Outside, the gale of wind and rain screamed on like a coven of vengeful witches. The shadows of the room turned blue and cold. These were the evil, creeping shadows that lurk where light does not live.

Jordan shivered. "Dad?" She took a hesitant step forward.

The Greyhound crossed the room on stiff hips and a limp. Jordan came to her knees, her heart pounding and her mouth with distress.

"Dad, don't leave me." Jordan's voice trembled, and her eyes pricked with tears. She put her hands on the dog's withers. The Greyhound drew close and lifted a paw, resting it heavily on her knee. He whuffed out a sigh.

The Greyhound's mind whispered to hers: *I'm tired, Jordy. So tired.*

"Dad, no. Don't give up." A tear tracked its way down Jordan's cheek. "I'm coming for you."

The Greyhound's pink tongue licked the skin of Jordan's chest, just under her left collarbone. She put her forehead against his. He licked her again, his tongue warm and slow.

"Dad, don't leave me."

He licked her again in the same place, just above her

heart. But moisture ran from the lick, up into the hollow of Jordan's throat, against gravity. The droplet turned cold and spilled over her neck and into her hair. Jordan noticed only then that the hair at the nape of her neck was damp. She shivered.

"Jordan." The Greyhound spoke in a woman's voice, making her start.

Jordan flew awake like a small bird at the hoot of a Great-Horned Owl. She was panting, her neck wet, her eyes darting from side to side. *Where am I?*

"You were dreaming, Jordan." The whisper came from a dark shadow bent over her. It was accompanied by the pressure of a warm hand on her shoulder.

The sounds of the gale were real. Rain drove and whipped across the portholes, the creaks and groans of wood shifting and timbers rubbing against one another cleared Jordan's memory. Another cold drop struck her below the collarbone and ran into her hair.

The ship.

She was still on the ship. It had been a dream. *Just a dream.* She exhaled in relief.

One of her wings jutted out awkwardly to the side. Her feathers trailed in the water that slid across the wooden boards of the cabin floor. The other wing she couldn't feel, it had gone numb beneath her.

"Are you okay?" Eohne whispered, sitting in the hammock next to Jordan's. "You were mumbling."

Jordan wiped at her wet neck as another droplet fell from the ceiling and hit her just above her heart. She sat up, and three ratty old blankets fell away from her shoulders. "I dreamed my dad was a dog." Jordan yanked her trapped wing from underneath her body, wincing as the blood rushed back into it and made the whole appendage tingle.

Eohne's shadow was still as the Elf absorbed this. "How curious."

"A racing animal," Jordan explained, wiping her wet neck and chest with one of the blankets. She realized her face was also wet, but this moisture had come from her eyes. She swiped at them and the smell of moldy fabric made her pull back with a moue of disgust. "But the dog was old and stiff. His racing days were over."

"Hmmmm." Eohne made a contemplative sound.

The two women swayed back and forth with the rocking of the ship.

"Where's Toth?" Jordan asked, searching for the Nycht.

"Up on deck."

"In this weather?" Jordan pushed the pile of blankets aside and put her feet on the floor. She felt around in the dark for her boots. The floor was damp, downright splashy in some places. Vertigo swallowed her as the ship lurched and she gave a groan. "Nevermind, I get it."

Jordan pulled on her boots and fumbled around her hammock for the long-sleeved leather jacket Eohne had purchased for her before they'd left Maticaw. Jordan loved it. It was specially made to accommodate her wings, lacing up underneath them so they could be free, yet keeping her back warm. Best of all, it was lined with something fuzzy and soft. Jordan hadn't wanted to ask what kind of animal fur it was, if it was fur. She'd worked hard to reject Eohne's buying her the jacket, but the Elf had insisted. Where they were going, it was going to be cold.

"Do you think we're getting close?"

"We are. The fog is growing thick; that is a good sign, under the circumstances."

"Creepy," Jordan muttered, putting her arms into the jacket's holes. The fabric draped over the tops of Jordan's wings, and she turned so Eohne could lace the back of it closed above and below them. Jordan fastened the metal clasps that ran up the front and instantly felt warmer. She laced up her boots next.

The two women swung in the hammocks as the ship's nose took a dive into a trough, sending their stomachs lurching. Loud voices from the deck of the ship yelled commands in a foreign tongue. Heavy footsteps ran overhead, waves slapped the hull, ropes were yanked and sails hoisted. The whole cacophony blended together in a tense soundtrack.

"Care to move somewhere more solid?" The Elf's voice was strained as she gestured to a wooden shelf at the rear of the hold. It might have been used for storage, but it was currently empty. Eohne grabbed one of the blankets from Jordan's bed and got up.

"Absolutely." Jordan's stomach flopped over as they staggered across the floor. Muscles in her back complained at having slept in a swinging hammock for several hours. She marvelled at how sailors could sleep in such uncomfortable beds for months at a time.

Eohne spread the blanket on the shelf, and the two women sat with their backs to the rear-wall, facing the bow of the lurching ship. The steps leading up to the deck were directly behind them. A couple of empty bottles rolled across the floor as the women settled themselves back and grasped the posts on either side of the shelf to help keep still.

The ship tilted and swayed. Jordan loosed a groan from deep in her gut.

"The Captain said this part of the Rodanian Sea is always rough. It'll pass."

Jordan turned her head away from Eohne and covered her mouth with her fingertips, wondering if she was going to lose her last meal. She breathed deep, and the nausea eased. She sat back, letting her head fall on Eohne's shoulder. The Elf rested her own head on top of Jordan's.

"Tell me again," Jordan croaked. "Please? It'll take my mind off of vomit."

"Tell you…"

"About the rickshaws. I want to be thoroughly informed before we get to Trevilsom."

"The Rakshaaks?"

Jordan grunted in agreement. "I can never remember the name."

"Trevilsom Prison sits on an island surrounded by a dangerous sea," Eohne began, her voice soft. The Elf lifted a long, tapered finger and ran it in a straight line in the air in front of Jordan's face, from the top of her forehead to her sternum. The finger curved to follow the shape of Jordan's bent neck.

"Whoa!" Jordan's head snapped up; her vision had gone foggy. A misty cartoon scene opened before her: a large island, mostly rock, beneath a huge stone building with no windows—save for a few on the upper level. "How are you doing this?"

"We learn it young." There was a smile in Eohne's voice,

though Jordan could no longer see the Elf. "I haven't used Charra-Rae storytelling magic for a long time. To be honest, I wasn't sure I could still do it."

"Your skills are intact, let me tell you."

Small seabirds wheeled in and out of the clouds hovering over the scene in front of Jordan. "Everything looks like it's drawn by hand. It's like a moving painting." Jordan reached a blind hand forward into the scene, but she found nothing solid. Even her own hand was not visible. "Keep going." The lurching of the ship seemed to ease as Jordan's senses were occupied by the story.

"Over eight hundred years ago, the Kingdom of the Rakshaak giants was ruled by a selfish king named Keeriak."

A tall, bony, giant of a man, wearing long robes and a tall spiky crown, appeared on the battlement of the ugly castle. His shape wavered there as though it was made of colored smoke.

"King Keeriak was a supporter of Rhazdon, a treacherous Atlantean who had plans to dominate your Earth. Rhazdon faced all the other species in a battle for supremacy of Oriceran. Thankfully, he lost. The Prophets, including my ancestor, were the key to his defeat. Prophets still exist today to help ensure the treaty is upheld."

"This is the treaty that prevents people from traveling back and forth between universes?" Jordan didn't need to add that the treaty was only marginally successful at discouraging portal-hopping activities.

"That's right, but that's a story for another day. The island king was not only a follower of Rhazdon, he was also obsessed with finding the secret to immortality."

"Who isn't?"

The scene wavered and changed. A cold stone room with a fire of green flames crackled behind the king as he bent over a stack of mouldering books. As Jordan watched, the giant got to his feet, swept a glass off the table with a hand the size of a car tire, and threw the goblet into the flames. A splash of thick red liquid sizzled against the hot stones behind the fire and ran down in streams, smoking as it went.

"Keeriak's obsession took him abroad, to the port city of Maticaw."

Jordan watched the giant disembark from a huge ship, his enormous size making the dock sway and creak under his weight. Fish visible in the water beneath the dock darted away, and Jordan thought she could hear the little creatures squeaking in the background, 'Run for your lives! Swim away!' She chuckled at the cartoonish silliness of the story.

The giant lumbered alone down the streets of Maticaw, while magical creatures darted into shops and dove under benches to escape his baleful gaze and clumsy footsteps.

"How do you know all this?"

The giant stopped lumbering, his expression went from malevolent to vacant.

"My ancestor, a Prophet named Firohne, left a journal," came Eohne's answer. "I've read it front to back several times over. The Elves of Charra-Rae know this history like they know their own faces, because Firohne was given the forests of Charra-Rae as a reward for what he did. He was our pioneer, and as you know, Charra-Rae is our home even today."

"Where were your people before that?"

"We were part of the Light Elves' kingdom. We still bear some resemblance to them, but we've had eight hundred years to evolve our own magic."

"Okay, sorry to interrupt. Please continue. The king looks bored."

The king's face was relaxed and good-natured, not unlike an expression Eohne wore most of the time. As Eohne resumed the tale, the giant re-engaged and snapped back into character. His bushy brows slammed together, and his mouth twisted cruelly.

"Firohne sold King Keeriak an Elvish potion, which, when drunk and allowed to course through the king's veins at the passing of the full moon, would turn the Rakshaak King immortal."

The scene morphed into an indoor meeting between King Keeriak and a very handsome, chestnut-haired male Elf wearing satin robes. The Elf and the giant sat together, heads bent in serious discussion. Firohne's lips moved soundlessly and he reached into his cloak and pulled out a small vial. The greedy king snatched at the vial and threw a sack of coins at Firohne, who caught it with a secret smile.

"What the giant didn't know was that Firohne was part of the movement to stop Rhazdon and his cohorts from taking over Earth. The potion was a lie."

"Your ancestor was a treacherous Elf," Jordan murmured.

The cartoon Firohne made eye contact with Jordan, his face a picture of innocence. He said in Eohne's voice, "All for a good cause, my friend," before dissolving away.

"Keeriak took the potion back home to wait for the full-moon," Eohne continued.

A new scene materialized: Keeriak strode back and forth impatiently in front of that same crackling, green fire. A window in the background displayed a half-moon, and then a three-quarter moon as it waxed in time-lapse. King Keeriak grabbed the vial from the table as the moon popped into full. He tossed the whole thing, glass and all, down his gullet.

"King Keeriak died. Sort of."

Keeriak went stiff and his tongue flopped out of his mouth. His eyes turned into black buttons, and he fell over to the sound of a long, descending whistle. He crashed to the floor with the snapping sound of breaking branches. The king's shape remained still, and the room behind him wavered away and became a huge, dark tomb with large bearded heads of stone jutting from the walls.

"His people buried him and swore vengeance, but little did they know…"

A hole in the ceiling of the tomb where the king lay appeared and widened, showing again the passing of the moon.

"One week later, the Rakshaak King came back to a kind of half-life."

"Like a zombie," Jordan added.

Eohne's voice grew thick with drama. "Worse than your zombies."

The shape of the king blackened and thinned, his robes dissolved, revealing a long body with sharp angles, made more of shadow than any real flesh. The dead king slowly rose from his place in the tomb. His head was featureless and drifted above his shoulders, where, instead of a neck, a column of smoke held his chin suspended above the collarbones.

"So. Spooky." Jordan felt her flesh marble with goosebumps.

"King Keeriak became the first Rakshaak guard of Trevilsom, though it took him some time to turn all of his people." The bony giant made of shadows and smoke bumped his floating head on the stone ceiling of the tomb, making the head bounce like a balloon. As the giant made his way up the stone steps, he repeatedly hit his head against the ceiling. A hollow sound, like coconuts being knocked together, accompanied every bump.

"A Rakshaak leaks a toxic poison that contaminates any magic around it. When Keeriak emerged from his tomb, he addled the minds of his own people, and they became disorganized, confused, and unable to take care of themselves. They died soon after, becoming Rakshaaks themselves."

The Rakshaak King emerged from underground into streets full of giants, who made soundless screams and scattered before him. They fell away and dissolved into the same kind of tall, neckless creature as their former king. They each fell into step behind him until there were no living giants left—only an army of tall, dark, neckless wraiths.

"Trevilsom guards feed off the fear and confusion that they create, which is why the island became a place that everyone sent their criminals."

The vision of the army of Rakshaaks dissolved into another scene: a rowboat on the ocean carrying a devious looking little man, who was tied up in more rope than what would be needed to moor a ship. He was tossed from the rowboat onto the island, and the three oarsmen (the fat plumes in their hats waving goodbye) turned the boat around and sailed away. The little man jumped to his feet, ropes falling away, shaking his fist at the now distant vessel.

"Watch behind you, little man," Jordan said, her warning surprisingly sincere.

The little man whipped around, and his hair grew white in an instant. A Rakshaak approached, its dark lumbering shape crossing the land, and its long skeletal fingers reaching. As the moon swept by in fast-motion, the man's form slowly dissolved. The fog left over seeped into the Rakshaak. Its neck grew long as it absorbed the mist, the smoke lifting the head higher as it fed.

"That's a ghastly story, no matter how silly you make it look. Can I have my sight back now?" The scene dissolved, and Jordan's view of the dismal ship returned. She shivered. "If we get too close to one of the giants, we'll lose our minds and become Rakshaaks, too?"

"No, you wouldn't become a Rakshaak. Only the original giants became Rakshaaks, and they are finite in number and thankfully cannot reproduce, as far as I know. However, if you're in the presence of a Rakshaak, you'll soon become so addled that you won't be able to find your way off the island, let alone out of the prison. You'd stay there until you died, with the Rakshaaks feeding off your fear. They are motivated to feed and water the prisoners to keep them alive as long as possible, so they can continue to siphon their own sustenance from them. It's a nasty business."

"But you've got magic that will protect us from this toxic poison?"

Eohne nodded. "I invented it a long time ago, for a school project. It will work, but it will also decay over time." Eohne pulled her knees up into her chest and wrapped her arms around herself. "We have to get in and out of there quickly."

"My poor father. It's a good thing humans don't have any magic for them to leech and make him crazy."

"Yes, that's a good thing. But Firohne wrote of the effects the noxious magic has on humans."

Jordan remembered. "A coma. What else did Firohne write about in his memoirs? Tell me something that can help us."

The story had been entertaining, but now that the cartoon vision was gone, the reality of her father's situation set in. Allan was in grave danger. As a being that the Rakshaaks could not live off of, it would only be a matter of time before they simply discarded his lifeless form—— threw him into the ocean and left him to drown.

"Firohne wrote of the caves under the island being the only way to access the prison, and delay coming into contact with the toxic magic until the last possible moment. He said that a strong magical being could fight off the effects of the Rakshaaks and preserve their sanity for a time. If they were strong enough, they might descend into the tombs of the old kingdom and find the pools leading to the underwater tunnels."

"They'd have to be one heck of a swimmer," Jordan murmured.

"Yes."

"I wish Blue were here," Jordan said, rubbing her upper arms. "I miss the little guy."

"He can't come where we're going. You know that."

"I know."

"Do you think he'll do as you asked?"

"He'll do it." Jordan spoke with confidence, but she'd never asked Blue to do anything without her before.

Jordan had penned a letter to Sol, who by now would be frantic with worry. In a short message, Jordan explained Allan's predicament, told him who she was with, and revealed that they were going to Trevilsom to rescue her father. She hoped that Sol would take some comfort in knowing that Toth, the intimidating Nycht mercenary, and Eohne, the brilliant Elvish inventor and magician, were her allies. She didn't give him any specifics of their plan; there hadn't been time for that.

She'd tucked the letter into a cylinder, fastened it to Blue by way of a collar they'd acquired in Maticaw, and given the dragon instructions to return to the apartment on Upper Rodania. He'd even flown in the right direction, which was comforting.

"I think the storm is coming to an end." Eohne's words broke through Jordan's musings. It did seem as though the waves had lost some of their power.

Footsteps pounded on the steps behind them, and the women hopped down from the wooden shelf. The pock-marked face of a young sailor appeared, zeroing in on the Elf and the Arpak.

"Trevilsom approaches," he said. "Cap'n won't go much closer. Best get ready."

CHAPTER TWO

"There you are."

Toth turned from his place at the railing. His face was pale——quite an accomplishment for a man who already had the complexion of a Viking.

Jordan and Eohne stepped up to the railing on either side of Toth and leaned their elbows on the wood. They gazed out into the fog. The rough seas had calmed, and the ship's prow now cut through the smooth murky water.

"Nice view." Jordan's tone was laced with sarcasm. The horizon was shrouded by fog and the filtered light was flat and dim. She glanced at Toth. "Did you lose your breakfast?"

"In three installments," the Nycht groused. "Thank heavens the storm has eased. Strix are not meant to sail." He shot Eohne a glare. "I could have carried you to Trevilsom."

"I don't doubt it." Eohne's expression was mild. "But if you had, you'd have been so exhausted by the time we arrived that we'd have to abandon you on some rock and go on without you."

Toth grunted and stared into the water sliding by below them.

"Did Firohne write about how long the Rakshaaks wait before they give up on a human?"

Eohne shook her head. "I'd guess a week; he wrote that it took a week for non-human species to deteriorate to the point of being a food source for the Rakshaaks."

Toth voiced the fear that was burgeoning in Jordan's own mind. "They must have had humans on the island before. Why would they give him even a week's worth of time?"

"Firohne seemed to think that the Rakshaaks don't distinguish an Elf from a human, or a human from a Dwarf. They don't have much in the way of functional logic——they are more like radars for fear. If that's true, then they would give every prisoner the allotted week before keeping or discarding them."

Jordan took a shuddering breath. "Any idea how long my father has been on the island already?"

"I don't know for certain. I know that a ship left Vischer five days ago, and it's a two day journey by ship from Vischer to Trevilsom."

"So you think he's been there for three days?"

Eohne nodded. "That's my best guess."

The ship began to slow as sailors yanked on ropes and the sails shifted.

"Look." Eohne pointed to dark shapes off to the side of the ship, "we can't go much further. There are too many islands to navigate these waters safely."

"Correction," a voice made them turn. The captain they'd bought passage from in Maticaw had approached. "We can't go *any* further."

The sound of a heavy chain running out the side of the ship and the splash of the anchor backed the serious look on his face. "Best grab the railing."

They did so, and the ship lurched to a halt. Sailors stumbled forward, and Eohne slid into Toth, who slid into Jordan. Only the captain, who hadn't been clutching anything, managed to keep his footing.

"There's nothing here." Jordan peered through the fog at the surrounding waters.

"There's a small island just beyond the fog where we'll leave you." The captain took off his hat. "That is, if you still want to pursue this lunacy. It's not too late to change your minds. I can drop you off in Skillen, if you like?" The old captain, his brow lined with wrinkles, seemed hopeful that his suggestion would take root.

Toth shook his head. "Thank you, but we've got someone to rescue."

The captain nodded. "Good luck to you, then." He gave a signal, and a rowboat was lowered onto the water. Toth, Eohne, and Jordan joined two oarsmen in the dinghy and waved to the captain as they were rowed into the fog. The ship was rapidly swallowed up by the mist.

In short order, the rowboat bumped against a small barren island, and the threesome was helped from the boat. One of the oarsmen shook his head at them as they rowed away.

"Let's not waste any time," muttered Toth. "This place is eerie."

"Godforsaken," Jordan added. "Do your magic, Elf."

"A few things to cover, just briefly," said Eohne, raising a finger. "I know I've already said this, but I'd like to reiterate that we have to get Allan out of there as quickly as possible. I've made a compass that will lead us to him, and the shields should protect us from the toxic magic up to a point, as well as make us undetectable to the Rakshaaks. But we have to be off the island by the time the magic wears off or-"

"We'll never leave," finished Toth. "Got it." Toth peered into the murky water. "Caves." He gave a visible shudder.

"You're a Nycht," Jordan thwacked him on the shoulder. "Don't your kind live in caves?"

"Yes, high off the ground," Toth protested, hands out. "Not underwater!"

"I have a basic formula for underwater tunnels which I invented as part of my early training." Eohne was rifling through one of her satchels. "Sohne dropped a jewel into one of our deepest lakes and challenged me to retrieve it without getting wet," she explained. "I'll adapt that magic to send the tunnel not toward a precious gem, but toward a pocket of oxygen."

Jordan's fingers and toes were freezing, and her pulse felt light and fast. She and Toth were putting their lives into Eohne's hands. If the Elf's magic failed them, they would die. Jordan felt the desire to point out the obvious risks, but clamped her lips shut. The Elf didn't need to be reminded.

"So, to sum up," said Toth, "we tunnel our way to the cave system, climb out, following your compass to Allan, snatch his unconscious form out from under the noses of vampiric Rakshaak guards twice our size, and then fly to Rodania?"

"You make it sound as though you don't face hideous flying monstrosities on a daily basis." Eohne retrieved a sack, untied it, and peered inside. "I have seen what you can do to a full-grown harpy female."

A muscle flexed in Toth's jaw. "Harpies wield toxic claws, but they don't leak toxic magic. I am always fully in control of my mental faculties when I'm facing one."

"Well, you're right except for the flying to Rodania part. While you were rescuing Jordan from certain death back in Maticaw, I made a deal with a sailor named Thom—"

"How did you know I was facing certain death, by the way?" Jordan interrupted.

"You know that compass Eohne is going to make to help us find your dad?" Toth asked.

"She made one leading to me?"

He nodded.

Jordan gave the Elf an adoring look. "You are brilliant *and* gorgeous."

"Thanks. Can I go on now?"

Jordan nodded. "Sorry."

"Thom runs a regular delivery of goods to the east side of Lower Rodania. It's the closest civilized landmass. He'll pick us up on the west side of Trevilsom when we're ready." Eohne looked at Toth. "You'll only have to carry Allan for a short distance. And you," Eohne looked at her Arpak friend, "if you can manage it, will have to carry me for a short distance, as well. Think you can?"

"No problem." It wouldn't have mattered if Eohne had

asked her to carry a Cadillac; she would do her level best, if it was what was needed to rescue her father.

Toth raked a hand through his hair, standing the spikes on end. "This is madness."

"Yes," replied Eohne simply. "Now I need a moment's quiet, please."

Eohne produced an empty cup. She knelt and scooped up some seawater with it, then set it on the rock beside her knee. Next, she retrieved a coil of string, which she stuffed into her mouth.

Toth and Jordan shared a bemused glance and crouched to watch with interest. Watching Eohne work was like watching a street magician.

Eohne held the string in her mouth for several seconds to ensure it got a good bath in her saliva. She pulled out a small box, and something inside rattled. Eohne poured a gray crystalline powder into the palm of her hand. She deposited the wet string into the powder and mushed it around with her finger. She then produced a small glass cylinder. Pressing her thumb against the bottom of the cylinder caused a flame to burst from the top. She held her palm flat and touched the flame to the string. The string flared to a bright yellow, and a series of popping sounds made Jordan jump——but the string didn't burn, it only flashed brightly in the palm of Eohne's hand and slowly began to fade, looking much as it had before.

Eohne put away her Elven lighter, grasped the end of the string, and threw the rest of the string into the sea. Her body seemed to freeze. Her face turned upward, and her eyes took on a faint glow.

Jordan and Toth shared an uneasy glance. Eohne appeared to have fallen into a trance.

Toth pointed, and the two Strix watched as the string moved through the water, away from their small island platform. To Jordan, it moved as though a fish was attempting to swim away with it. A light source appeared, small and distant under the water. In the light of the blue glow, they watched as fish darted by, several of them alarmingly large. Waving fronds of kelp swayed back and forth, and the rock walls below them came into view. What seemed like shallow water on the surface was revealed to be water so deep, there was no visible bottom. The islands were long fingers of stone, reaching up from the depths to poke from the seas and strain toward the sky.

The blue glow traced the string all the way to Eohne's fingers. The Elf took a deep breath, and her eyes returned to normal; her chest rose and fell as though she was a little out of breath. She took her Elven lighter and touched the flame again to the end of the string.

There was a crack like the sound of thunder overhead.

A hole appeared in the water where the string had been, and thunder echoed from the tunnel. It was loud, but rapidly growing distant as the hole made its way to whatever caves Eohne had found, breaking and holding the water apart.

Jordan's mouth went dry as she realized what they were about to do. This was their path——the tunnel that would lead them to the caves under Trevilsom. Jordan closed her eyes and whispered a prayer for strength as fear threatened to overwhelm her. She felt Toth's hand squeeze her shoulder, and the terror passed, leaving only tremors along her spine.

Eohne stood and reached for their hands, and the three of them stood on the small island. The strange, wide hole in the water was just behind Eohne. The companions held hands, clutched and squeezing, and Jordan felt a burst of gratitude and strength come from the connection. She looked from one to the other.

Ready.

Eohne released their hands, turned, and with a graceful leap, jumped into the tunnel. She became a blurred shadow, as the tunnel curved away from their island and then passed out of view. It was like watching someone descend a transparent waterslide.

Toth gestured that Jordan should go next.

Jordan took a small torch from her satchel. Eohne had given them each a small Elflight torch, which they only needed to blow on to light.

"For you, Dad," she whispered, and leapt.

The underwater world became a blur as she slid along the surprisingly hard surface. Darkness closed overhead as she slid down the first sharp descent. The angle soon shallowed, and she was able to get to her feet and run. Her heart was pounding, and she gasped at the sensation of being on the edge of out of control. She braced her legs and found herself sliding, as though on some invisible skateboard.

The tunnel flattened enough for her to slow and light her torch. Jordan blew, and as the blue light increased, she gasped at the world that lit up around her. Schools of fish swam past the tunnel, and she caught a flash of long tentacles as some squid or octopus-like creature disappeared into a crack in a vertical stone wall. The tunnel wound its way between rough stone pillars, always descending. She looked back as Toth blew his torch alight. She could make out his bulky silhouette through the walls of the tube above and behind her. Eohne was somewhere ahead of her, out of sight.

The angle of the tunnel sharpened again, and Jordan lost her footing and slid. The underwater world whizzed by at a frightening speed. If the tunnel broke, there was no way she could surface in time to survive. She tried not to think about how many feet below the water's surface they now were.

Her breath echoed against the walls, and her hair slapped against her face. The tunnel flattened out again, and she got to her feet with trembling knees.

Toth slid up behind her, his legs braced like a snowboarder.

"Alright?" Toth's voice echoed like they were in a drainpipe. Jordan felt his hand against her lower back, and she took strength from his warm touch.

"It gets very dark up here." Eohne's voice echoed up to them through the tunnel as a light appeared ahead.

Toth and Jordan made their way along the tunnel, which was now flat enough to walk. Eohne was revealed, standing in the tube, when they rounded the bend. Her skin appeared to be blue in the underwater light, and her brunette hair seemed inky black.

Jordan gasped as a monstrous form drifted over Eohne's head. Something with long tentacles spiraled around the tube and passed into shadow. The path beyond the Elf was a yawning black hole.

"This is where we enter the caves." Eohne walked along the tunnel, and her footsteps echoed. A weighty blackness closed in around them. Even with their torchlights, they could only make out each other's forms. Their speed slowed as Eohne felt her way forward in the pitch dark.

"The tunnel climbs here. This will be a bit tricky." She bent and reached a hand down to feel the way the floor of the tunnel ascended. She put her light between her teeth and reached out with both hands, bracing herself on either side of the tunnel. She looked like she was suspended in space.

Eohne spread her booted feet and braced them against the wall, inching her way up the tunnel. Jordan thought she'd never seen anything so strange as Eohne's form monkeying its way up in the dark, her feet and hands bracing themselves against what looked like nothing.

The Elf reached eyeball-height and was able to move forward again. She looked back and down at her friends. "It flattens out again here."

Jordan's eyes were adjusting to the strange environment. She could make out cracks in the stone they were passing through, and sea vegetables as they swayed.

She took a leap up the tunnel, trying to follow her friend, but slid back down with a sound like the squeak of skin on glass. Her wings flexed and floundered, trying to keep her aloft, and for a moment, the tunnel seemed filled with feathers.

Eohne reached a hand down to Jordan. "Let me help you."

Toth put his arms around Jordan's knees and lifted her to where Eohne could clasp her hand and pull her up. She joined Eohne where the tunnel flattened, and turned to look at Toth.

The Elf and the Arpak held out their hands to him, but he only said, "Back up a little."

Jordan and Eohne backed along the tunnel to give Toth room, and held their torches up to light the way.

Toth took a running start. His wings shot forward and wrapped around his body, and his dewclaws caught against the curving surface of the tunnel, pulling him forward and up. He landed in a crouch, and his wings folded themselves away.

"That was cool. I wish I had dewclaws," Jordan whispered.

"Why are you whispering?"

"Because Rakshaaks?"

"They're still far above us," Eohne assured her, already a good distance ahead.

They continued in this monkeying fashion as the tunnel snaked its way through the caves beneath Trevilsom. Only the sound of their breathing accompanied the three travelers; the tunnels were deathly silent. A chill entered Jordan's bones in spite of her new jacket, and the sound of her teeth chattering echoed around them from time to time.

After an hour of halting tunnel travel, Toth's voice broke the silence. "Don't suppose you have any magic for keeping Jordan warm, do you?"

"Sorry," said Eohne over her shoulder.

"Y-you d-d-don't s-seem c-c-cold," chattered Jordan,

her body tense and stiff from the chill. She felt she might shatter if someone flicked her hard enough.

"I'm chilly," said Eohne, "but Elven bodies regulate better than those of Strix."

"Maybe better than an Arpak," countered Toth. "Nychts like the cold just fine. It's the wet we don't like."

"Shhh," Eohne said. "Listen."

They froze, ears perked. The sound of droplets splashing into water echoed through the tunnel from somewhere up ahead.

"We're close."

They picked up speed, eager to escape the unfriendly pitch black of the underground.

CHAPTER THREE

Jordan's head broke free of the tunnel, and she took a huge breath of dank, warm air. Eohne's hand wrapped around her wrist and helped pull her onto a cold rock floor on her belly. The slimy, springy sensation of moss squished under her hands and against her cheek as she caught her breath. Her teeth chattered, and her fingers felt numb with the cold. She took a sniff of the air and wrinkled her nose. It smelled like death.

There was an intake of breath as Toth surfaced behind her, and the sounds of grunting as he pulled the weight of his bulk, his armor, and his weapons out of the tunnel. The sound of his dewclaws raking against stone echoed in the spacious cavern.

A larger ball of white-blue light illuminated Eohne's face. "Wow, that's bright," Jordan whispered. She blinked and faced away to give her eyes time to adjust.

Eohne held the bright circle of light in her palm, lifted it to her lips, and breathed on it. The light floated into the air, illuminating the cave. "Too bright for the tunnel, but perfect for this cave," Eohne explained.

"Everyone okay?" Toth's voice was low. He got to his feet and helped Jordan up. They extinguished their torches and put them away, since the Elflight was floating overhead like a small moon.

"All good." Eohne was bent over the tunnel. There was the sound of water splashing as she collapsed it, which echoed through the cave.

"Here. Wherever here is," added Jordan.

"If I calculated correctly," began Eohne, crouched and drawing the string out of the underwater pool where the tunnel had been. She wrapped it round and round her fingers. "We're about eighty feet beneath the prison. According to the journal, the toxic magic starts just above the waterline."

Jordan's eyes had adjusted enough to take in her surroundings. "Whoa," she breathed. "This is a tomb."

The white-blue light of Eohne's light threw its glow out, illuminating huge wide steps covered in black moss.

"Look at the statues!" Jordan pointed at the massive stone sculptures of bearded men and imposing women.

"Yes, these would be the ancient Rakshaak kings and queens." Eohne finished raveling her string and tucked it into her satchel.

Jordan crossed the wet stone floor to look up at the two statues guarding the steps: two huge and handsome bearded men, each with their hands crossed, one resting on the hilt of a sword. The swords alone were twice Jordan's height.

"Do you think these are true to size?"

"I'd imagine so." Toth stood beside her, neck bent. "Those stairs weren't built for ordinary men, that's for sure." The steps leading up into the shadows beyond couldn't be climbed by an ordinary person unless they pulled themselves up using their arms.

The natural structure of the cave was broken in places by huge flat plaques, each with a bearded head protruding from its base, as though the dead monarch inside had tried to crawl out of the resting place and turned to stone. The plaques had the remains of writing on them, but time had worn most of the words away. Black moss filled in the deepest crevices of the faces: between the lips, in the holes where the eyes should have been, and within the curls of beards and folds of fabric. Eohne's light illuminated their foreheads, noses, and lips.

Huge weapons lay scattered on the floor and stood leaning against the cavern walls, rusted and broken. A sword with a missing pommel leaned against a plaque. It would take a man who was at least as tall as a harpy to wield it. The stone face above the broken sword glared down at the intruders, its eyebrows drawn down in anger and the lips twisted in a sneer.

Jordan shuddered. "Creepy. Feels like they're watching us." She looked up the steps. Her father was somewhere above them. "Paste first, then compass?"

Eohne nodded and pulled the bag of powder from her satchel. She dumped a pile of it into Jordan's hand and added to it the prepared fluid containing the Arpak's frequency. Eohne had collected both Jordan's and Toth's frequencies for this very moment before they left Maticaw.

"Mash it together with your thumb."

Jordan followed Eohne's instructions and watched as the paste darkened. Tiny particles reflected the light, like minerals would.

"Sorry about the taste," Eohne said. "This magic tastes like copper."

"Better than the smell down here." Jordan licked the paste off her palm, trying not to think about what she was eating. It stuck to the roof of her mouth and coated her back teeth.

"It'll take a minute to swallow. Take your time."

Eohne pulled out Toth's fluid and dumped the powder into his palm, repeating the routine.

"You have very strange magic," said Toth. "The Light Elves sing and flick their fingers or wave their arms."

"True," said Eohne, now dumping her own powder into her palm. "Our magic parted ways a long time ago and evolved very differently. But I trust the magic I make. Frequency is a language I understand; I don't have the kind of power in my voice that a Light Elf has."

"You might be wrong about that," replied Toth, thinking about how every time Eohne spoke, it felt as though someone had plucked a string that ran through his body. He licked the paste off his palm and let it dissolve in his mouth.

"Yuck" Jordan shuddered, swallowing the last of her paste. "That tasted like blood."

"Sorry." Eohne was mashing up her own paste. "My magic can do a lot, but I haven't figured out how to make it taste like honey yet." She licked her palm and began to work on it.

Jordan felt her ears pop and watched as a film formed

in the air around her. In the glow of the Elflight, it looked like a soap bubble was taking shape. The thin film stretched outward, looking first like a honeycomb, the holes shrinking as the edges met. Little popping sounds could be heard as the gaps closed. When the last of the edges came together, the film disappeared completely.

"Amazing." Jordan's voice echoed back at her softly. "This will keep the toxic magic from hurting us?"

"For a time, remember?" Eohne warned. "I've never been here before; I don't know how long it will last. It will wrap around you and stay with your body, but don't make big sudden movements or it could break. The shield is invisible, but as it deteriorates, you'll notice spots of dirt marring your vision. Eventually your sightline will become so obscured, you'll need the shield to break just so you can see."

"Let's get out of here before that happens," said Toth with a moue of disgust as he swallowed the last of the paste. He looked at Eohne. "Shall I carry you up?"

"I'll manage." Eohne eyeballed the massive steps. She tackled the first with fluid grace, jumping and hooking her hands over the edge. She pulled herself up and smoothly stood, ready to take the next one.

Toth and Jordan flew, their wingbeats echoing dully in the cavernous space. The Elflight floated in the midst of them, keeping itself between the triad. The path behind Toth and Jordan was alight, rather than the path ahead, so they could only move as fast as Eohne anyway. The Elflight ascended the steps like an apparition, throwing eerie shadows in every direction.

At the top of the steps, three hallways yawned, tall and

narrow. They led in three different directions. Eohne, barely puffing from her climb, produced a small disc, and her collection of vials strung together. Using the vial marked 'human' and the palm-sized disc, Eohne resurrected the small orange dot she had followed to find Toth in The Conca.

The dot slid to the right-hand side of the disc, directing the way. The threesome shared a look of relief. If there were no living humans on the island, the orange dot would not have appeared at all, indicating that Allan was already dead.

They proceeded down the dark hall, the Elflight illuminating the way. Row upon row of grave markers, much less elaborate than the ones below, sped by as they walked. Black moss wound between the cracks of the stones beneath their feet. The faces protruding from each tomb were smaller and less imposing than the ones below.

Jordan rubbed her eyes as specks of dust appeared in the air before her. "Already?"

"The closer we get to the Rakshaaks, the faster the magic will deteriorate," explained Eohne. "It will only get worse."

As if a command was given telepathically, the trio began to jog. Jordan's heart rate spiked, and not just from running; the speed at which their protection was wearing down was alarming. Already the specks of dust were making her wish for a windshield wiper.

The orange disc bade them to turn right two more times. There was a sudden end to the tombs, and a flash of dim light struck them as they passed by an empty one, its plaque cracked and falling apart.

Eohne held the disc up. The orange dot was telling them to go into the broken stone. Eohne pointed and shrugged. Jordan shared a doubtful look with Toth. *Eohne might pass through the crack quite easily——**she** doesn't have a giant set of wings.*

As though reading her mind, Toth's wings pressed inward and seemed to shrink, his dewclaws coming closer to the top of his head. Jordan did her best to mimic this, like pulling her arms tight against her side.

Eohne crawled into the space and Jordan followed, tailed by Toth.

The Strix had to turn sideways to fit but Eohne was able to pass through without crouching or twisting. The most difficult part was their footing; a pathway of rugged stones, broken plaques, and clumps of dirt.

Their fields had deteriorated to the point of dirty glass.

The light filtering into the crack was dull, but bright enough that the Elflight was no longer needed. Eohne put her hand behind her back, and the Elflight flew into her palm and disappeared in her fist.

Toth tugged on one of Jordan's feathers, and she paused to look back. Toth gestured to his ear and made a flat waving motion with his hand.

Jordan listened. There was the very faint sound of waves echoing through the crack. She nodded.

A tap on Jordan's shoulder pulled her attention to the front where Eohne had halted. The crack had come to an end. The light was coming solely from the right, and unsurprisingly, the orange dot directed them to the right. Eohne stepped out into a large square depression. Three large steps led up and out of the hole. The walls were cracked and lined with broken tile, and the floor was covered in the rubble of more broken tiles. The Elf and the two Strix squeezed out of the crack and into this strange, square pocket and looked around.

Jordan looked at her companions and mimicked a breaststroke. Toth nodded, and Eohne's brows shot up as she understood. They were standing in what had once been a swimming pool for giants. A huge crack connected the old pool to the hallway of tombs below.

Jordan took a step forward, and there was a loud snap as a tile broke under her foot. She froze and held her breath, shooting Eohne a look of horror. They became still and listened, breathless, each wrapped inside their own dirty bubble of protection. There was no sound, save their own breathing. It was unlikely this pool had been used anytime in the last five hundred years——longer, if the memoirs of Eohne's ancestor were correct. The Rakshaaks had no reason to be lounging poolside.

Convinced it was safe enough to move and feeling the anxiety of working against the clock, Jordan peered at the disc that Eohne held. The orange dot now directed them to move left. Jordan and Toth flew from the pool and waited as Eohne crawled out.

Eohne jerked her chin left to where a cluster of pillars obscured their path. The film of black specks seemed to thicken dramatically as they passed these pillars. Jordan's heart rate trebled in response; they needed to find Allan, now.

A huge dark shadow obscured the light ahead for a moment, and a big smudge of ruin appeared on Jordan's field down near her knee.

On the other side of the pillars was a tall, covered walkway filled with broken tiles and rubble. Slat windows let in a muted gray light. The orange dot directed them to follow the shadow that had passed.

As they caught sight of the giant striding down the hallway ahead of them, Jordan's hand flew to her mouth. The giant seemed to be made more of shade than any kind of flesh, even though its movements belied a heavy weight. The outline of the form was bony and long-limbed, moving almost gracefully. Long skeletal fingers trailed from the wrist joint, curling in and out, as though the giant was thoughtfully working something through. The head and neck were even more startling than they'd been in Eohne's cartoon story: the head floated above the shoulders on a pillar of dark, wispy smoke. The giant had no visible hair, only the curve of a perfectly smooth skull. Jordan's flesh iced over. She hoped the Rakshaak wouldn't turn around. The giant wouldn't be able to see them through their fields, but Jordan thought she might scream if she saw the thing's face.

The giant rounded a corner, and the trio followed at a distance, skirting the piles of broken tile and rubble as best they could. Fresh air that smelled like salt and sea blew through the hallway, and the sound of waves crashing told them they were close to the ocean——though well above it.

A turn down the next rugged corridor revealed a body lying on the stones.

Allan's body.

CHAPTER FOUR

Jordan gasped in horror. "Dad!" She tried to surge forward, but Toth's arm snaked around her waist and held her back. She strained against him. Her own voice bounced around her bubble of protection, echoing endlessly.

"Wait," Toth said into her ear. "You cannot help him if you break your field."

Allan was lying pale and inert. His skin was gray, his lips blue. He looked for all the world to be long dead.

"He's alive," Eohne said. "He's alive, otherwise the orange dot would not have appeared. It targets the nearest living human."

The words were only a small comfort to Jordan, as the triad watched the Rakshaak stop and look down at Allan's motionless form.

Jordan's heart was in her throat, and her blood was pounding in her ears.

"Slowly," Eohne instructed, and began to move forward.

Toth tentatively released the grip he had on Jordan, as though afraid she would bolt.

"What's it doing?" Toth whispered to Eohne.

"Probably trying to sense if Allan still might wake and serve as a food source for him."

It seemed the giant had come to a conclusion. The Rakshaak bent and grasped Allan's ankle with his long skeletal fingers. He lifted Allan upside down, letting Allan's head bump against the stones. The Rakshaak began to walk, dragging Allan behind him.

Toth barred Jordan's chest as she let out a moan of frustration, her fingers curled around Toth's forearm, squeezing. The three of them moved forward as one.

"What do we do now?"

A wind swept through the hall from a break in the wall up ahead. The Rakshaak casually dragged Allan's body to the break where he unceremoniously and without any warning threw Allan from the hole.

Jordan screamed and ran forward.

Toth cursed and bolted ahead of Jordan.

There was a loud crackling sound, like firecrackers going off, as their fields broke. The Rakshaak turned his shoulders toward them sharply just as Toth barrelled into the monster, and shoved him from the hole. The Rakshaak fell, his legs and arms splayed out in surprise as he grappled at the air, searching unsuccessfully for something to grab. The Rakshaak bounced off the side of a jutting stone with a dull *thud*, sending his body pinwheeling into the water.

Toth's wings pressed tight to his back as he dove after Allan's falling body. Jordan leapt to follow. A high-pitched scream sounded off in her brain, and her hands flew to her head as her vision went fuzzy. The world spun, and Jordan fought for control, her eyes locking on the blurred shapes below her.

Allan fell like a sack of rocks and splashed into the churning waves just as Toth reached him. Toth's wings snapped open and beat madly in an effort to keep from following Allan underwater, and the Nycht's arms and face were submerged as he reached for the man. Allan partially surfaced as Toth heaved on him, but with the field of protection broken, the caustic magic that permeated the island threw Toth into disorientation.

The waves churned and smashed against the stones, as though they wanted to jerk Allan from Toth's grasp and claim him as their own.

Jordan fought to focus properly. *Water is bad, air is good.* She repeated this like a mantra to help ignore the screaming sound echoing around in her head.

Toth floundered below her, losing the battle with the water. Swaying back and forth, his wings beat out of sync as a wave slapped over him and Allan. Both men disappeared under the surface—one limp, and the other flailing what seemed like more than one set of batwings.

Jordan dropped to the water's surface, her flight erratic and verging on out-of-control.

"Hand," she panted, reaching down to Toth. "Grab my-" she lost her words in the effort to stay dry and airborne.

A strong hand wrapped around her forearm, and her fingers locked around it, holding fast in a way she'd never held onto anything before in her life.

Forward, came a whispered thought around the edges of the awful screaming. Eohne's voice.

Away from the island.

Jordan pressed forward, heart pounding, teeth gritting, wings working. Dragging them to sea and away from Trevilsom.

The strange chain of human, Nycht, Arpak moved forward as Jordan heaved Toth and Allan's bulk through the water. Bubbles churned up in front of them. She tried to lift her cargo over them, but the weight was too much; it was all she could do to drag them and avoid the treacherous stones.

Foot by foot, they sliced forward through the salt water.

The screaming in Jordan's mind began to ease. She could finally hear her own breathing and the breathing of Toth below her. Her stomach clenched when she realized she could not hear her father's breathing. Stealing a quick glance down, she saw the gray face of her father, his head tilted back against Toth's shoulder, his eyes closed.

Toth's teeth were bared in a grimace of effort.

The space between the jutting stones widened, and the way became less treacherous. Jordan's mind cleared as the island grew small behind them. She became conscious of her body again—the ache in her wings, the stinging burn in her lungs. Still she dragged without stopping. She cast around and behind her for Eohne, but the Elf was nowhere to be seen. Mist had swallowed up even the island, so that the threesome was lost in a sea of dark water and fog. The haunting shapes of tall, sharp rocks, too sharp to stand on, loomed from the mist. Jordan dragged Toth and Allan around them, trying hard not to let them hit anything.

"Eohne," she tried to yell, but the name came out on a gasp.

Straight ahead, came a whispered command. *The way is far, but you are strong.*

"Jordan, I'm sorry," Toth panted.

She shook her head. It wasn't the time for words, and certainly not for an apology from the Nycht who had risked his own life for Allan's.

She shot Toth a look of pure adoration for what he had done. Toth's hair was plastered to his head, his temporarily useless wings were folded tight and behind him like a strange fin, helping to make Jordan's job easier.

Jordan's throat felt like it was icing over as she pulled for breath.

"Slow down." Toth coughed as a wave hit him in the face. "Conserve your energy," he spluttered.

But Jordan couldn't slow down. Everything in her was driving to pull Allan and Toth as far from the island as they could get. An empty sea was better than those screaming voices and nightmarish prison guards. Her heart hammered in its cage, throwing itself wildly around in her chest. Still she dragged, her wings burning.

Steer left, came Eohne's whispered voice. Jordan dragged the men to the left. *Now listen.*

Jordan's ears strained for something other than the sound of waves, her own heavy breathing, and pounding pulse.

The unnatural sound of water beating itself against a hull came faintly through the mist. Jordan aimed for it. Hope rose swift and sudden in her heart. *That'll be the sailor Eohne asked to pick us up!*

"Do you hear that?" Toth panted, heaving Allan higher on his shoulder.

A shape loomed from the fog. A small ship.

"Hey!" Jordan yelled, her voice cracking. That one short word seemed to knock the wind right out of her. She stopped trying to talk and focused on breathing.

Men's voices speaking rapidly in a foreign tongue sliced through the mist. Jordan pulled Toth toward the rear of the ship. A heavy net splashed into the water in front of her face, making her gasp and almost lose hold of Toth.

"Grab on!" cried a loud, strong voice from the deck of the ship. The silhouette of three men appeared over the ship's railing.

Toth tried to release Jordan's arm, but she resisted letting go. The state her father was in was making her irrational with fear for him.

"Jordan, it's alright!" Toth smiled up at her. "I've got him."

The reassuring smile from the Nycht, even while under desperate circumstances, buoyed her heart. Jordan released him.

Toth locked an arm around Allan and with the other, grasped the netting. He nodded to the men on the deck, and they began to heave Allan and him up out of the water.

"Mon dieu!" came a cry from one of the men.

Jordan hovered, flapping clumsily, watching as the men were safely brought on board.

One of the sailors held an arm out to her, beckoning. "It's alright. Come!"

With barely enough energy left to keep her aloft, Jordan let herself drift toward the rope ladder leading up to the crow's nest. She hit the ropes like a fly caught in a spider's web and clung to them, bouncing. Her wings went limp and her chest heaved but there was no time to rest. She crawled down the rigging, her muscles trembling with exhaustion.

Strong hands helped her to the deck.

"Is this man Allan from Virginia?" A sailor with a strong French accent braced his hands on both sides of her shoulders. It seemed he was almost bellowing into her face. His expression was clouded with concern.

"Yes, yes! You made a deal with Eohne, to pick us up." Jordan bent over as she rasped the words out, thinking she'd never been so weak and fatigued in her whole life. Even speaking seemed too much of an effort. But her father needed her. She straightened, gulping in air. She shared a look of relief with Toth, who snapped his wings out, sending a spray of water in every direction.

"Eohne? Who is Eohne?"

"The Elf from Charra-Rae." Jordan passed the sailor and made for where her father was being lifted from the deck and taken toward the stern. Toth held Allan's shoulders, cradling his head. "Where are you taking him?"

"Captain's quarters." The sailor followed her. "Wait. Who is this Elf? We know no Elf."

Toth and Jordan shared a look of confusion. *How can these sailors not know Eohne?*

"Where is she?" Toth's icy eyes scanned the fog, but it was useless. There was no horizon to search; everything was shrouded in mist. The Nycht's brow wrinkled with concern.

"I thought she'd be here." Jordan followed the men,

pushing her damp hair out of her face. Her whole body itched with salt. "I heard her voice. She directed us to you."

A sailor dashed ahead and opened the narrow door to the captain's quarters. "Put him on the bed."

"Where is your captain? He will know about Eohne." Jordan scanned the face of the sailor, taking him in properly for the first time. He was young, probably not much older than she was. His brow was furrowed with concern as he watched the sailors and Toth settle Allan onto the wool blankets. He seemed very invested in what was happening with Allan, for someone who they'd never met before.

"I am Captain here," the sailor said without any offence. "Marceau sent me to see what could be done for Allan."

"Marceau?" Jordan's mind whirled, and she felt dizzy as the ship swayed under her feet. "I don't know any Marceau. Was this pickup not arranged by an Elf? Tall, slender, long dark hair?"

The captain shrugged and shook his head.

Jordan squeezed through the men to get to her father's side. They moved away from the bulk of her damp wings, allowing her to sit on the edge of the small bed. Jordan put a hand over her father's forehead. He looked like death, pale and still, with his face relaxed, but his skin was warm to the touch. She pressed her fingers into his neck, and some of the panic eased as she felt the strong pulse there. She leaned her mouth close to her father's ear.

"Dad? It's me, Jordan. Can you hear me?"

No response.

The men around her seemed to hold their collective breath in anticipatory silence.

"Marceau said it could be too late." The captain's voice was soft. He addressed the other men. "Get us underway."

"Wait. We're missing someone." Toth made for the door and turned back. "Can you wait? While I go back and search for her?"

"Are you crazy? You wouldn't find a feroth freighter in this fog. If you stumble back into the vicinity of that island, it'll be over for you."

"We found you." Jordan looked up at the captain, pleading. "Please? We would never have made it this far without her."

"I'm sorry. We simply cannot wait."

"Go then," Toth said, going for the door. "I'll track you down. If not, I'll take Eohne on to Rodania," he looked over his shoulder at Jordan, "and meet you there."

Jordan's stomach clenched. The idea of being separated from Toth set her on the edge of panic. But they couldn't just abandon Eohne to her fate.

"Wait, let me see if I can hear her." Jordan kissed her father's brow and followed Toth onto the heaving deck of the ship, ignoring the bemused looks the sailors shared with each other upon hearing these words.

Jordan made her way to the prow and searched the fog and the waves. There was nothing but choppy seas and thick, impenetrable mist. She closed her eyes. *Eohne? Are you there?*

No response. Jordan felt the ship rise and fall under her feet, heard water splashing against the hull.

I heard you before. Talk to me. Where are you?

"Not to interrupt, but what are you doing?"

She turned to see Toth watching her, an eyebrow

cocked. She flushed. "I heard Eohne's voice. While I was dragging you. She directed me here. How else do you think we found this ship?"

Toth's lips pressed together. "But these sailors don't know her."

"I can't explain that, but how could she have directed me here if she didn't-—"

A thump against the hull made her pause and listen. The Nycht and the Arpak stopped breathing and strained their ears, then rushed to the railing and peered over. Gray and white-capped waves splashed against the hull in a relentless churning rhythm. A second thump from under the ship made Jordan and Toth glance at each other pensively.

"I hope that wasn't a sea monster."

A three-foot-wide bubble emerged from the waves, opening a tunnel like the one they'd passed through. The tunnel exited the sea at a sharp angle, and a voice echoed from its mouth, sounding like a person yelling from inside a well.

"Perhaps a rope?"

"Eohne!" Jordan leaned over the railing and peered into the tunnel as best she could. Relief flooded her already adrenalin-shot body. She heard Toth yelling for a length of rope behind her.

The Elf's pointed face appeared briefly, but disappeared again accompanied by the sound of skin squeaking against glass as she slid backwards. "Who else?"

Toth joined Jordan at the railing, and they were further accompanied by a bunch of sailors, crowding around them to watch. Toth lowered the rope into the tunnel. A couple of burly sailors grabbed the other end of the rope behind Toth and made ready to pull.

"Grab on!" Toth yelled.

Eohne was raised from the hole, clinging to the rope like a monkey. She looked pale, even for her. Jordan wrapped her up in a hug the moment her booted feet touched the planks of the ship. Eohne hugged her back, then released her and bent over the sea. The hole closed up with a splash.

"Allan?" Eohne scanned the ship.

"He's in the captain's quarters."

Eohne nodded, worry marring her brow.

The young captain made his way through the crowd of sailors. "Back to work, men. Get us underway!" He barked before stopping in front of the Elf. "You must be Eohne."

The Elf nodded. "Who are you?"

Jordan looked from one to the other. "I'm so confused."

"You're not the only one," said Eohne. "This is not the sailor I made the agreement with."

The young captain stepped back onto one heel and bowed with an elegant flourish of his hand. "Captain Segolan Torega of the good ship *Le Monarque*, at your service. The service my men and I provide for you today has been paid for by one Marceau-"

A grating, deep-throated, screaming roar in the distant fog interrupted his explanation.

Jordan's eyes flashed to Toth, and the two Strix shared a look of trepidation.

They both knew that sound.

CHAPTER FIVE

"What was that?" Captain Segolan scanned the fog for the source of the menacing cry, his brows almost lost in his hairline.

"Harpy." Toth and Jordan spoke together. Toth's voice was grim and deep, and Jordan's was full of dread.

The captain looked askance between them. "They exist?" His brown eyes scanned the sky and his hair lifted in the wind. The ship had begun to turn.

Jordan gripped the railing as the ship listed.

"I thought they were monsters made up to scare little children."

"They're very real, I can assure you." Jordan nodded towards Toth, who was checking that his weaponry was all present and buckled down properly. His leather armor was dark with wet, and his wings were still damp from the swim. "He fights them for a living."

"Thank God we have you, then." The captain clapped Toth on the shoulder.

The sound of powerful wings beating at the air made

the group go still. Faces looked to the sky, but the fog was so thick that nothing was visible but a veil of gray-white swirls.

A sharp, croaking cry carried clearly over the lapping waves, loud and threatening.

"That was way too close for comfort," the captain said. "Top speed!" he cried to his men.

"I don't suppose you have any crossbows or long-range weapons?" Toth cast about for just that. His wings snapped in and out in an attempt to dry them faster.

"We have only six guns. We're a cargo ship, not a man-o-war." The captain looked pensive. "Cannons are built for firing on other ships or defending a beach attack; they would do very poorly firing into the sky at an enemy we cannot see."

His words were choked off by another scream, this one further away.

"Is it leaving?" Captain Segolan sounded hopeful.

Toth shook his head, his body taut. Any weariness he'd displayed was replaced by a lethal focus. The mercenary had emerged. "Do not allow yourself to hope for that. When they find prey, they make concentric circles before attacking." He lifted an ear at another scream, this one closer than the last. "Pitch was too high for a female," he muttered, his lips barely moving.

Toth eyed the crow's nest and crossed the deck in quick long strides. The harpy's screams telegraphed its intention––an attack was imminent. Toth did not fancy protecting the ship from attacks that could come out of nowhere. He had to go out and meet the monster, make him sorry he ever thought about leaving Golpa, the caves at the north end of The Conca. Toth began to climb the rigging to reach the uppermost part of the ship, the best place from which to launch himself.

Something whirred overhead, mere dozens of feet above the ship. Its sheer speed dragged the razored sound across their ears. The ship was moving faster too, away from Trevilsom. The mist had thinned enough to make out the dark shape with pinioning wings. The harpy passed overhead, banked, and climbed higher into the saturnine sky. Sailors winced as it released another threatening cry. The piercing scream seemed to come from everywhere.

Layers of cloud boiled high over the expanse of churning waters as a barely visible shape circled back towards *Le Monarque*. Toth reached the crow's nest as the harpy once again disappeared where the fog thickened. The Nycht's wings snapped open and he leapt from the small balcony, catching at the air with torpid beats.

Jordan heard the sailors around her murmur with wonder at Toth as he gave a few experimental flaps of his wings. She narrowed her eyes at the Nycht as he climbed. Having seen him fight before, she thought that for all his obvious strength, his wings seemed leaden, almost clumsy. While he'd been there in front of her, the membranes of his wings glistened, and the dewclaws had small channels of water running down them. Jordan became keenly aware of how heavy her own wings felt. Her back and shoulders ached at the mere thought of launching herself into the air and working to staying aloft. The pit of her stomach felt heavy with dread; Toth was fierce and capable, but even he had his limits. How would he do against this harpy when he was clearly hindered?

Toth's hands suddenly glinted with drawn steel. With each beat of his wings, he climbed a little higher––but each foot of altitude cost the Nycht more than it would have.

Eohne reached out and took Jordan's arm in a firm grip. She brought her lips near Jordan's ear. "Can he do this?" The Elf's face was fraught with concern. She lowered her voice to a whisper, as though her speculation, if heard by the Nycht, would only serve to weaken him further.

"He threw up his food." Eohne's whisper became harsh and desperate. "And he's still *wet*."

Jordan's lips parted. She wanted to say yes; she wanted to tell Eohne how she had seen Toth take on a harpy twice the size of the one circling them now. She feared her voice would betray her, would amplify the fear she felt at the burdensome strokes of the Nycht's wings.

She cleared her throat. "He can do this."

But Eohne did not miss how the Arpak cast about, cataloguing the weapons she saw strapped to the sailor's belts. The question was written in the air between them. How would they help if Toth got into trouble? How would they fare against an aerial attack if the Nycht failed?

The harpy was closer now, and Jordan could see that this one was indeed smaller. She felt some relief at this initially, but as she watched it move with an easy and powerful grace, her relief evaporated. Shouldn't this harpy be tired from his flight this far out to sea? But he seemed fresh and vigorous, and his obvious vitality left Jordan feeling cold. Her jaw worked, her teeth clenching and relaxing. Her voice felt like a loaded spring ready to release a barrage of curse-words and epithets at the beast. *We only just escaped Trevilsom, and now this?* Her cheeks flushed with a high fury.

This harpy's body was sleeker, leaner, than any she'd seen. As it wove between the drafts of air, it seemed like a black blade slicing lithely through. A beam of sunlight penetrated the thinning fog and illuminated the harpy briefly, and Jordan caught a flash of red. Her fingers twisted on themselves, thinking at first there was blood; she realized that a bright, arterial, crimson crest raced down its bare crown and neck. And his gory looking beak inspired a different brand of terror than the female harpy had, with her rack of devil's horns. He gave another raptor's shriek and, with a tight spiral and cycloning mist, he dove at Toth with heart-stopping speed.

For a moment of pure panic, it seemed Toth did not see the predator coming.

Jordan and Eohne cried out a warning as one, and several sailors behind them joined in. Jordan's throat seemed to tear with the urgency of her scream. The beast extended sharp, venomous talons. At the last second, Toth's wings pinched inward, and he turned in an arcing barrel roll. One muscled arm shot up, holding a short sword angled back in a reverse grip. The harpy rushed into the gap where its prey had been only moments before, dragging its breast across the readied blade as it fought with surprise to arrest its momentum.

The creature gave a keening wail as its feathery chest gleamed with blood. There was a collective inhale from the ship, but celebration was strangled as the harpy's whip-sharp dragon's tail snapped downward. Toth, still working too hard to stay aloft, did not move away fast enough. With a tremendous crack, the Nycht mercenary was thrown. Sent cartwheeling through the air by the terrible strike, he seemed unrecognizable——nothing but a spinning tumble of wings and limbs on a downward trajectory.

Toth righted himself with heavy, frantic wing beats. His flaps were out of sync, but he came out of his spiral in a wide swoop, a stabbing spear in hand, his head darting about, his narrowed eyes seeking the enemy. Toth used his momentum, turning it to his advantage. His skill in the air seemed to defy the laws of physics, and there were murmurs of amazement from the ship.

Had the harpy been coming after Toth, his speed from the recovered spiral may have spitted the monster then and there. But the fiend was in no mood to take risks; not after learning his quarry had teeth. The harpy banked hard away from the recovering Nycht, making a meandering loop toward the ship. His flight now seemed relaxed, taunting, even arrogant.

Jordan said to no one in particular, "The harpy wants to tire him out."

"Are they that smart?" Eohne's tapered fingers gripped the straps of her satchels.

Jordan never took her eyes from the airborne pair. "They're that smart."

Eohne frowned. She'd already frantically inventoried her magic in her head, casting about for something to help the Nycht. But her brand of magic was slow and customized; she was more scientist than magician. There was nothing she could think of that would make his time against this predator any easier. By the time she'd invented something with the meager supplies she had, the Nycht could already be dead.

She added to the mental list she kept, the invention of some kind of weapon that could be used from the ground against an airborne enemy. As she watched the battle unfold above them, her mathematical mind listed off criteria: light and mobile, accurate, high-powered, rapid-firing.

The harpy's pace was nothing near the eye-watering speed it had displayed earlier, but it would reach them soon enough if Toth did not catch up. Jordan did not know which would be worse; the harpy descending on them as they clutched the deck or Toth speeding back to die, exhausted, on waiting talons.

Toth's wings pummeled the air in a frenzy to build up speed. With gathering velocity, he swooped low over the water and then picked up altitude. His path through the fog-churned air would intercept the harpy's languid flight.

The harpy gave an exultant cry, arcing high and then diving toward the ship. It streaked toward the deck, and sailors scattered. As the demon passed through the narrow space between the two fore-masts, his talons snapped closed over the hair of a young sailor, who dove to the deck with a yell. Someone threw a thin-bladed sword at the harpy, which arced uselessly through the air and splashed into the water beyond the railing.

The harpy peeled about in an acrobatic display of aerial prowess as Toth flew over the ship in pursuit. Sailors scrambled to their feet and ran to the other side of the deck, making the ship list. Eohne and Jordan were right there with them, hands gripping the railing, faces jutting out over the water, necks bent and creaking. One of the sailors produced a small brass eyeglass and brought it to his eye. He enjoyed only a momentary glance through it before it was snatched from his grip by Captain Segolan, who then brought it to his own eye.

The harpy struck at the air with a few climbing wing strokes, his body angling back toward the advancing Nycht, bringing the two in line for an apparent head-on collision. The black and red projectile seemed about to hit the Nycht in a deadly rush of talons, but then banked wide less than a dozen feet from Toth. He wound a tight loop around the mercenary, which Toth struggled to keep pace with; spearpoint following wing beats. The harpy skimmed close by Toth again, just beyond the reach of his deadly spear.

Again and again, the harpy rushed past him, over him, under him, around him, always a little closer, but never within reach. It made Jordan dizzy to watch. Each pass took a little more strength from Toth, and each time, his spear seemed a little slower in coming about. For his part, the harpy seemed to only be gaining speed—–each pass and bank propelled him as though he was riding a typhoon.

With a desperate lunge, seeming at the end of his strength and patience, Toth darted into the path of the spiralling harpy, spear outstretched. With contemptuous ease, the monster dodged the thrust and rolled over to lash out at the mercenary, talons agape.

Toth jammed the spear haft between himself and the harpy's claws. A dull knock reverberated through the air as the harpy hit the stout wood and locked his talons around it. For a heartbeat, the two spun upward, stuck in a lethal dance, wings beating in unison. Up and up they went, turning around the focal point of the spear like a kind of insane top.

With a clicking hiss that could be heard from the ship, the harpy flexed its talons, and the spear shivered in its grip. It suddenly snapped with a sharp retort. Splinters and the bottom half of the spear fell away. In Toth's grip was half a foot of jagged wood and the stabbing head. The harpy gave an exultant cry and snaked its toothed beak forward with a nasty snap into Toth's face. The Nycht reacted with lightning reflexes, shoving the broken haft of wood between the jagged ridges of the predator's beak.

With a throaty shriek, the harpy chomped down on the spur of wood and steel, jaws clamping. His fist working like a piston, Toth punched into the creature's exposed throat, once, twice, thrice. From the ship, the strikes were silent. Jordan heard Captain Segolan blow air out from between tight lips, and the surrounding men made sounds of appreciation at the display of tight-quarters combat. Jordan thought she saw money exchanging hands in the corner of her eye.

She wanted to slap the sailors for enjoying the show. Her friend was risking his life for everyone on board.

Toth kept up his barrage of strikes. Nycht and harpy wings worked in sync to keep the fighting pair aloft, while at the center, a deadly battle raged. A waft of harpy stench drifted to the ship for the first time, and the crowd groaned in a reaction of delighted disgust.

The harpy gave a choked warble as its crimson head rebounded with the punishment Toth was delivering. The half-shaft of the spear came free from the harpy's jaws, and he snapped at the air desperately. The hollow *click-click-click* of the harpy's beak closing on air was faintly audible to those watching. With a savage beat of his wings for momentum, the Nycht delivered a devastating uppercut with the deadly iron tip, nailing his opponent through the vulnerable fleshy wattle under his beak.

A collective gasp went up from the ship, followed by several streams of foreign words, delivered on tones of awe. The spearhead burst from the top of the monster's hooked-tooth beak.

The gargles and shrieks gave way to a low, liquid whine as the harpy floundered; wracked with pain, blinded by blood, desperate to escape the creature who had turned the tables on it so utterly. The harpy's once-graceful wings wobbled and spasmed, as his pierced, crimson head cast left and right.

Not to leave things torturously half-finished, the Nycht let the harpy drift below him then swooped down upon the back of the struggling creature. In his hand, a fang of steel glinted fiercely in the first real fog-penetrating rays of sunlight. He rode the beast down, and the pair began to spiral. His wings tucked tightly, Toth lay hold of the thrashing neck. The harpy's resistance was spastic at best, but Toth still had to avoid the harpy's head, which keened and swung every which way. At last his grip held sure, and the curve of steel journeyed across the harpy's throat, ending its suffering forever with a long, deep slash. Blood now fell in gaudy streamers rather than in wind-tossed speckles. With a casual caution, Toth released his quarry and let the monster fall, his own wings stretching out to catch his weight and lift him.

In his dying moments, the harpy recovered his lost elegance and aerial grace. With ribbons of life draining away, the fiendish raptor began an easy roll seaward. Tail corkscrewing behind it like a pennant, wings curling inward as though embracing itself in a final hug. The once mighty predator spun around and around like a dancer as it plummeted. It seemed a kind of climax to the performance, that elegant mortal dive.

Triumph lay with the weary Nycht who watched his foe plunge, lifeless, into the churning sea. For a moment, not far from the ship, Toth was caught in a vignette stark and clear enough for all to see. His sharp-edged batwings, finally dry, gracefully flexed in and out. His face, too far away to see the expression clearly, was downturned to the sea. His silver hair caught glints of sunlight. Ribbons of blood wrapped both forearm bracers and fists, dripping from his knuckles. The broken spear had gone beneath the waves with the harpy, but the shorter curved blade was held loosely in one hand, its duty done. The smooth bellows of Toth's wings could just be heard above the sound of the waves, licking the hull of the ship. Even the sea, it seemed, had paused to take a breath in acknowledgement of the moment.

The high exultant scream of a seabird jolted everyone from their reverie, and a jubilant cry of men's voices went up from the ship, loud and amazed. Feet stomped and hands clapped vigorously as the sailors applauded Toth's impressive performance and success.

Jordan and Eohne looked at each other, their faces a torrent of relief. Jordan thought she might burst into tears as emotion surged through her. Relief, exhaustion, worry for her father, fright, all caught her in a thicket of feelings. Eohne's own emotions were not so different from Jordan's, and the Elf threw her arms around her friend, squeezing her tight in a damp hug. Jordan felt the Elf laughing against her torso and joined her, her vision misting up as her eyes filled with moisture.

They turned to watch Toth descend to the ship, seeming to ride on the wave of his ovation. Though he'd been triumphant, his face was pale and drawn with concern. Jordan knew, watching as the sailors parted so Toth could land on the deck, that something was still dreadfully wrong.

CHAPTER SIX

The moment Toth's feet landed on the deck of the ship and his wings closed up, the sailors rushed him. Toth found himself jostled and slapped, his bloody hands pumped, his shoulders gripped enthusiastically and shaken with excitement. Questions in three or four different languages barraged him from all sides. Toth's face was pale and bluish circles had formed under his eyes. His expression did not reflect the jubilance of his congratulators.

Jordan watched the Nycht withdraw and shoved the sailors aside.

"Let him be," she barked, making Eohne blink at her with surprise.

The captain hollered orders and the crowd broke as the sailors jumped back to business, cheeks pink and smiles wide.

Toth's shoulders drooped with exhaustion and relief. He looked down at his bloody hands, the curved blade still dripping, then cast about for a way to clean himself.

The captain drew the Nycht's attention to a bucket of

seawater sitting on the deck at the foot of the fore-mast. The young man's eyes followed the mercenary with an expression akin to worship. Toth crossed the deck and cleaned himself and then his blade, slipping it back into its sheath.

Jordan waited until Toth had stood and stretched his back before she asked, "Are you okay? The tail, the way it hit you. I thought––"

"Hit my armor," Toth murmured.

"I have never seen anything like that." The captain's voice made them turn. "I can offer you a king's ransom to join my crew––" His words were silenced by the look in the Nycht's ice-gray eyes. Captain Segolan cleared his throat and gestured to the door leading to his quarters. "I'll have someone bring you food and water. Please, use my cabin to rest and collect yourselves."

"Thank you." Toth made for the cabin, seeming like all he wanted in the world was to be out of view for a handful of minutes.

The captain nodded respectfully. "If there is anything else I can bring you, please ask. I am at your service." He gave a little bow and turned away.

"Wait," Eohne stopped him. "Who are you? Why are you helping us?"

"One of my friends and business partners met your man Allan in some godforsaken prison in Vischer." The captain gave an easy shrug, but Jordan's eyes shuttered closed with horror. The man continued. "Seems he either felt he owed something, or he was moved to assist in some way. Marceau asked me to see what could be done about freeing Allan."

Eohne and Jordan took this in.

"How exactly were you planning to free him?" Eohne wanted to know.

"Cannons," he said with complete and utter confidence. "Then swords."

Eohne's dark eyes stretched wide. "Do you know nothing about what guards that place--" She blew out a breath. "Nevermind. It's over now. Did you happen to see any other ships on your way? Specifically, a fishing sloop?"

Captain Segolan's mouth turned down doubtfully. He shook his head. "Nothing on our way from Rodania, but who knows what lurks in that fog; it was dense enough to gather in a pot for stew." He neared the women, looking from one to the other. "I think you are both tired. We have a full two-day's journey to Rodania. We can talk again. Please, refresh yourselves. Nothing but the best I can offer will do for Marceau's friends." He gestured to the narrow cabin door Toth had already disappeared through.

Eohne and Jordan thanked the captain and left him to the business of sailing. They found Toth perched on a stool, his threaded fingers propping up his chin as he stared at Allan, thoughtfully. He looked up as they closed the door.

Eohne made directly for Allan. "Do you mind?" she asked Toth, nearing the bed.

Toth got off the stool and made way for the Elf in the small space. Eohne bent over Allan, finding pulse points, lifting his eyelids, listening to his chest. Toth and Jordan watched apprehensively. Eohne whispered words into Allan's ears, pinched his earlobes. The man did not respond.

"Tell me you can help him?" Jordan's voice quavered and she hated the weak sound. She wished she sounded strong, the way Toth and Eohne were strong.

The Elf straightened, lifting the satchels from her body, and setting on the bed. She face Jordan. "I have not dealt with this before." The Elf's face was serious, possibly even angry, but Jordan felt that this anger was directed inward.

Jordan's lips parted, but no words came.

The Elf took the Arpak's cold hands. "I promise you that I will work day and night to figure it out." Eohne lifted Jordan's hands high between them, stepping close and pressing the Arpak's hands flat between her own, as though leading her friend in a prayer. "I vow not to leave his side until he wakes."

There was a moment of silence as the unthinkable words filled the space between them.

"Or dies," whispered Jordan.

"That's not going to happen." Eohne's words were fierce, and her eyes turned pleading. "Please forgive me. I am at fault."

Jordan could not think of how to react to this. Her teal eyes drifted down to her father's pale, still form. Her mouth flattened into a grim line. "Just save him."

Eohne turned away and began to rummage through her satchel as Jordan watched. She retrieved strange looking tools, vials, and mysterious objects. She paused to look over her shoulder at the Arpak. "I need time. My magic is not fast."

"Give him what you gave me when I was getting sick at The Silver Pony," Jordan suggested.

Eohne shook her head. "That was different."

"I can help. If we could get it down his throat––" Jordan paused when she felt Toth's hand on her elbow, and allowed the Nycht to draw her away.

"Let her work," he said quietly.

Jordan crossed her arms over her chest. She went to peer out the small porthole near the captain's desk. She stood there for a long time, and Toth watched her watching the waves. Eventually, Jordan let loose a long sigh and sat in the captain's chair.

The trio was interrupted by a sailor wearing a dirty apron, coming to deliver mugs of ale, a jug of water, salted meat, and slices of dry bread and cheese. He attempted some polite conversation but soon gave up, discouraged by the sullen Strix and the Elf who was focused intently on the man in the captain's bed. The sailor dismissed himself.

Toth beckoned for Eohne and Jordan to come eat. Neither woman had much appetite but they knew they needed their strength. They ate slowly, forcing themselves, never breaking the silence.

The ship gently bobbed on the waves. The mist had cleared and blue sky and gray water seemed to stretch endlessly in the view from the portal.

Jordan finally tired of working over the problem of her father's state in her mind. When Toth finished eating, she pinned him with a look. "You were awfully grim when you landed after your fight." It was a statement, not a question, but her expression was an invitation.

Toth leaned against the ship's hull and faced Jordan. "It's the harpy."

"What about him?"

Toth lowered his voice so as not to interrupt the Elf. "His presence this far out to sea is unprecedented."

"How do you know that? You live way inland at The Conca."

"Yes, but I've had occasion to battle them off-shore. I have fought harpies for a decade now; I'd like to think I know something about them. They don't fight over the sea because there is no point. They don't want to lose their meal to the ocean."

Jordan was nodding. "Blue and I were attacked by two of them just north of Maticaw, just off-shore. They kept trying to herd us over land."

The Nycht paled upon hearing this. "That cocky young Arpak let you travel to Maticaw from the north by *yourself?*" Toth let loose a stream of unflattering epithets.

Jordan put up a hand. "No, he didn't want to let me go. I insisted."

"He didn't try hard enough," Toth said harshly, raking a hand through his silver hair.

"I also had Blue."

Toth gave her a withering look. "Blue is no defense against two harpies."

"You'd be surprised––" Jordan shook her head sharply. "Anyway, that is not the point. The point is that I noticed behavior that confirmed what you are saying. Harpies don't hunt at sea."

"They do for fish, but never out of sight of the shore, and never for large, airborne prey. Some prey might float, but harpies don't want to take that chance."

"So," Jordan's shoulders rose up to meet her ears, "what do you think he was doing this far out to sea?"

"I have been turning that over in my mind since the first time I heard him scream." Toth moved to sit in the second chair near the captain's desk, looking comical as his broad form perched uncomfortably on the narrow surface. He leaned toward Jordan and animated his words with his hands. "Rodania is shaped like a big crooked pie." He held his hands broadly apart, fingers splayed as his thumbs and forefingers illustrated the width of the pie. "Lower Rodania is eight hundred odd miles wide, and the protective shield arches like this," he moved a hand in a half-circle dome, to meet the other hand. "The shield is a marvel of magical-engineering, the only one of its kind. It was constructed by the Light-Elves." He glanced at Eohne and ratcheted his voice down a notch. "Their magic is widely considered to be superior to any other on Oriceran." He cocked his head, giving a small allowance, "In terms of white magic, anyway. No one can penetrate the shield who has not first been given permission to do so."

Jordan was nodding. "You have to give blood."

"Right, of course, you've been through it already." He waved a hand. "Even though you are Strix, and an acknowledged citizen of Rodania as a result of your species, you still had to give blood before you were allowed in."

"Yes."

Toth spread his hands again, making the original shape. "A harpy would have to first cross from the mainland to the edge of the shield, well out of sight of shore. Then skirt the shield," Toth moved a finger showing the long indirect path the harpy would have to take. "Making a journey of hundreds of miles out to sea to skirt Rodania's borders.

Then all the way out to Trevilsom—another long journey."

Understanding began to cross Jordan's face as she listened. "And still be strong enough by the time he reached us at the ship, to fight you the way he did."

Toth nodded. "Either that harpy was supercharged by some dark magic I don't understand, or--" His face grew long as a thought struck him.

"Or what?" Eohne asked from across the room.

The Strix glanced at the Elf, unaware that she had been listening. Eohne peered at her friends from her place on the edge of Allan's bed. A cornucopia of items were spread on the itchy wool fabric at Allan's elbow.

"A harpy fueled by dark magic and behaving the way that harpy did is extremely unlikely," Eohne went on. "I have a radar for dark magic, but I did not sense anything untoward, so 'or' what?"

"A portal?" Toth ventured, but doubt was already crossing his face.

Eohne looked down at her work. "That is even less likely," she muttered.

The Strix looked at each other unhappily. Toth leaned back, his shoulders dropping. He looked at Eohne. "You're the brilliant mind, here. Against all odds, the harpy was here. He was strong, not exhausted. You saw him with your own eyes. Can you explain it?"

Eohne shook her head and put a hand on Allan's chest. "I can't. Seems there is a lot I can't explain at the moment."

The three weary friends frowned at one another in a miserable commiseration of doubt. No one spoke for a long time after that.

CHAPTER SEVEN

Le Monarque made steady progress, even though Allan didn't. Captain Segolan generously slept in a hammock with his crew, allowing the guests to utilize his quarters. Even so, they were cramped and uncomfortable. Allan occupied the bed, which was large enough for two people, but Jordan with her wings could not fit, and so slept on the floor, cocooned in her own feathers. Jordan suggested Eohne curl up beside Allan, but the Elf sat up beside her charge all night instead. Toth lay in front of the door, wrapped in his wings, his head resting against the back of a dew claw, making him look like he had a long black nail protruding from his ear.

In the morning, all three of them were stiff, but no one looked more miserable than Eohne.

"Are you seasick?" Jordan asked the Elf as she rose and stretched her limbs and wings as much as she was able to in the small space.

The Elf gave a wan smile and shook her head, then

seemed to hesitate, "Not so much, anyway." Eohne had her hand resting on Allan's chest and was watching it rise and fall. "I tried three different processes of healing magic on him last night." Eohne looked up at her friend, miserable. "Nothing worked."

"Did you learn anything? See anything in his blood or hair or... anything?" Jordan didn't know how Eohne's magic worked, but she did know it was based on frequency, and often needed some organic matter from the body.

"Nothing," Eohne sighed. "The coma is deep and resolute."

Neither of the women heard Toth get up, so both of them jumped when he spoke from very close behind Jordan.

"What about your ancestor's memoirs? Can you remember nothing about what he said about this affect the Rakshaaks have on humans?"

"As far as I can remember, no human ever left Trevilsom alive——or if they did, they are not in Firohne's records. There may be other cases, but I am unaware of them." Eohne chewed her lip. She looked drawn, exhausted.

"You need to eat something," said Jordan, turning away. "It won't do my father any good to have you fainting from hunger."

Toth raised an eyebrow at Jordan's cold demeanor and opened his mouth to say something, but Eohne shot him a look accompanied by a small headshake. He closed his mouth again and shrugged. This was between them; he was just fine staying out of things.

The captain visited with food and invited them to come out on deck, as it was looking to be a fine day for sailing. Jordan and Toth followed him out. Eohne would not leave Allan's side. The two Strix stretched their legs and wings, ignoring the furtive glances from the sailors as they walked the deck.

After a half dozen turns around the ship, Toth and Jordan leaned their elbows on the railing and watched the waves drift by. The wind tugged at Jordan's hair and salt spray peppered their faces.

"It's not really her fault," Toth said, bumping Jordan's shoulder with his own as they watched the horizon. When she didn't respond, Toth looked at her. "She didn't throw Allan in prison. She had no way of knowing that he might be able to," he opened his palms, "follow those bugs back here."

Jordan didn't answer for a long time. Just when he thought she wouldn't, she gave a long, pent up breath. "I know that. I'm just worried."

"Course you are."

Jordan wiped the salt spray from her cheeks, and it seemed as though she was wiping away her own tears. "She *needs* to help him. I don't know who can, if she can't."

"She will." Toth laid a warm hand on her shoulder.

Jordan shot him a weak but grateful smile. "Really, it's my fault. If I hadn't fallen through," she glanced behind them to make sure they were not being overheard, "then he would never have had reason to follow me."

"If you hadn't, you would never have known what you really are." Toth nodded at the yellow arches of her wings.

"You belong here, Jordan. Maybe Allan does, too; we don't know yet."

Jordan searched the Nycht's face. "Why would he hide that from me all my life?"

"He's your father, I'm sure there is a good reason." But Toth's expression said he couldn't think of anything off the top of his head. "Have a little faith."

Jordan gave a humorless laugh. "I had faith in my mother, and she tried to have me killed." She looked out to sea again, and for just a moment, Toth caught a flash of despair so deep and strong a blade pierced his gut. Jordan gave a little shiver. Toth didn't know if it was the cold or the misery––probably both. He wrapped an arm around her, looping it under her wings. Toth spread the wing of his closest to Jordan to make a tent around her and she leaned in to the Nycht's warmth and bit her lip, fighting back tears.

As she stood there, feeling her weight bob up and down on the ship's deck, her misery evolved slowly into other emotions: first, anger, then a hardened resolve. It was as though the strength from the Nycht mercenary pressing against her was leeching into her bones. She set her jaw. Allan was alive. He was in a bad way but he had the most capable nursemaid Jordan knew at his side. Jaclyn was still a mystery, and she had staked Jordan with great offense. At the very least, Jordan would use any and every resource at her disposal to learn the truth. When Allan woke––and he would wake, she would not allow herself to think of any other outcome––he and Jordan would have the conversation they never got a chance to have back on Earth before this whole crazy journey began. She needed to know what her father knew about the locket, about Jaclyn, and about Oriceran.

Her emotions turned again, this time into a huge, swelling rush of gratitude for Toth, and for Eohne. She stole a glance at the Nycht's scarred face and cursed herself for being so selfish. No one had asked Eohne or Toth to help Allan, but if it weren't for them, Jordan wouldn't even have known her father was in trouble, let alone on Oriceran. She owed everything to them. The feeling ballooned in her chest, and she thought her heart would burst. A million grateful words rushed to her mind, but really, there was only one thing to say.

"Thank you." The wind picked the words up and ripped them from her lips.

Toth had heard her, but bent his ear toward her with a touch of a smile. "What was that?"

Jordan turned her face toward his, her lips a mere inch from his ear. "I said 'thank you'." She pressed her lips against his cheek, his stubble scratching her mouth in a pleasant way. She planted the kiss and then laid her palm on his hand where it rested on the railing.

Toth looked down at her, and their eyes held as though they were welded together. His wing pressed in tightly, cocooning them in warmth and privacy.

"You're welcome."

A soft jostling of Jordan's shoulder woke her in the dim light of early morning. The ship bobbed up and down in gentle swells. She blinked in the light of the candle illuminating Eohne's face as the Elf shook the Arpak awake. Jordan bit off a groan of pain as she lifted her head and her neck creaked. She'd fallen asleep on the captain's desk, and her hip and shoulder felt bruised, even with her wings cradling her body. A glance through the porthole displayed a pink and yellow sky, and soft light dusting the tops of the waves.

"What is it?" Jordan rubbed her eyes and sat up, blinking owlishly. The possibility that Eohne had found a way to wake her father then had her scrambling to her feet in an awkward flurry of limbs and feathers. "Is he awake?"

"No. Shhhh." The Elf pointed to the lump near the door where Toth was asleep under his wings. "I made some small way to help him, and I thought you'd want me to wake you."

Jordan nodded. "Yes, thanks." She followed the Elf to Allan's bedside and perched on a hip, her feathers folded back and away, splaying up against the inner walls of the ship.

"When I wasn't able to find a way to wake him right away, I became very concerned about dehydration and starvation."

Jordan nodded vigorously. This had already occurred to her, but she hadn't thought to mention it to the Elf. She'd assumed Eohne would have found a way to wake him by now. She would have brought up Allan's need for sustenance very soon, though.

"Watch." Eohne pulled the wool coverlet back from Allan's torso and lifted his shirt to reveal his bare skin. Allan's ribs were visible, his stomach a concave pocket between his ribs and his hip bones. Eohne held up a bowl containing a clear jelly. She took a spoon and dropped a dollop of the jelly onto Allan's stomach, then smoothed it into a thin layer with the back of the spoon. The jelly glittered momentarily like bioluminescent algae. Eohne set the bowl and spoon aside and picked up a cup of water. The blue glow faded slowly, and the jelly was gone, as though it had evaporated. Eohne poured the cup of water onto Allan's belly. Jordan expected the water to drip over the sides of Allan's body and soak the bed, but it disappeared the moment it touched Allan's skin.

"He's absorbed it!" Jordan looked up at the Elf, encouraged. "That's something then, isn't it?"

Eohne set the cup aside. "We can keep him hydrated while I figure out what's wrong with him. We can do the same with food, as long as it's been liquefied. When we get to Rodania, we'll have access to fresh fruits and vegetables. The only food they have on this ship is meat, cheese, and bread." The Elf looked down at Allan's still form and frowned. "Any one of which might just as soon kill him as help him, in his present state."

Jordan felt buoyed by the progress. "I'll start doing some exercises with him. I dated a guy once who was a physio. They do it for people in a coma, to keep some mobility."

Eohne took Jordan's hand and nodded. "Good idea. If we can just keep him healthy…"

"My sister has an incredible garden." Toth's voice made the women turn. His head was poking up from the arches of his wings, where they criss-crossed over his body. "She lives on Lower Rodania. I can ask her to make juices for him."

"That would be so kind." Jordan sent the Nycht a smile.

"I remembered you said most of your family lives on Rodania. Will you visit them before going back to The Conca?" The idea of Toth going back to The Conca was not a friendly one. Jordan had been trying not to think about it.

Toth nodded. "They'll be surprised to see me." Toth's wings folded behind him as he stood and stretched. "Speaking of Rodania, would you like me to arrange for a place to stay? I'm sure one of my sisters would love to have you."

Jordan hesitated. "Sol will be expecting me back at his place. But his apartment isn't very big, and now there will be me, my dad, and Eohne, at least until my dad wakes up..." she trailed off, uncertain. "Not to mention Blue."

The Elf and the Nycht watched Jordan ponder.

"Sounds like a houseful," Toth began. "If you want, we can take Allan to my sister's first-" But his own brow creased with uncertainty and Jordan didn't miss it. It would be a lot to ask of someone who didn't even know Jordan.

"Let's take him to Sol's first, if you don't mind. I already said I would bring my father to meet him once we'd rescued him." She looked at Allan, putting a hand over his brow. Eohne pulled Allan's shirt down and replaced the coverlet. "He doesn't know that my dad is like this."

"There are also Rodanian hospitals." Toth approached and leaned against one of the ship's posts. "There is one on Upper Rodania, two on Middle, and about five on Lower. He's not a Rodanian citizen," Toth added with some doubt, "but you are." He shrugged. "I don't know what they would do for him, but we could always ask."

"I don't think any Strix hospital will be able to help

him." Eohne's voice was full of cynicism. "No offence, but Strix suck at magical ailments."

Toth nodded. "I know. You're right."

"Whatever is wrong with Allan, it was caused by the toxic magic that leaches from the Rakshaaks." Eohne placed a protective hand over Allan's limp one. "I am the best one to help him."

"Or perhaps the Light Elves-" Jordan bit off the suggestion at the look Eohne shot her.

A shout from above brought the conversation to an end. A peek from the window showed land on the horizon. Eohne, Toth and Jordan left the captain's quarters and stepped out on deck.

The three-tiered mass of Rodania appeared on the horizon. Captain Segolan came to stand with them as the ship churned ever forward through the water.

"We'll use the easternmost port," the captain told them. He looked at Eohne. "Do you need to be registered at the border?" The young man pulled a small ledger from a breast pocket and opened it to make a note.

Eohne shook her head. "I was registered only a few days ago as I was going the other way to scout Trevilsom. Allan does, though. He's never been to Rodania, as far as we know."

"He is your father, I understand?" Captain Segolan looked at Jordan. "But he has no wings?" He was obviously confused by this, as anyone would be.

Jordan only nodded. "He is my father."

"So you got the Strix gene from your mother's side then." Captain Segolan made a note in the small ledger.

Jordan's lips parted, but no words came. Was there a

point in telling the ship's captain that her mother didn't have any wings either? Before she could decide what to say, the captain made his note and put the ledger away. Jordan let it go.

"Beautiful, isn't it?" The captain braced his hands on the railing and took a deep lungful of the salty sea air. "I remember the first time I was registered. Poof!" He made a little exploding motion with his fingers. "It appeared out of nowhere, looking like that--" he gestured at the sky where Middle Rodania slowly rotated like a planet through the solar system. He squinted, a line appearing between his brows. "Sort of like that. I don't remember quite so much pollution."

Toth, who had been watching the sky behind the ship, perhaps for more errant harpies, snapped his head around. "Pollution? Middle Rodania is as fresh and clean as sliced lemon." The Nycht shaded his eyes with a hand.

"No, he's right." Eohne's dark eyes were leveled on the north side of Middle Rodania. "Look over there."

A thick, gray mist blanketed part of Middle Rodania, like someone had smudged a dirty thumb across a painting.

Toth frowned. "Something's wrong there."

The party watched as the ship brought them ever nearer, and Rodania came into focus.

"It's smoke," ventured Jordan. "There sure is a lot of it."

"There must have been a fire, no?" Captain Segolan didn't wait for an answer. "Excuse me, I'm needed on deck. We'll be pulling up to border control in an hour and a half, I'd say. "You should ready your man for transport. Have you got someone meeting you? Bringing a stretcher or something?"

"I'll carry him," said Toth without hesitation. Jordan shot him a look so full of sappy gratitude that Eohne hid a smile behind her hand.

The captain nodded and the ledger was back, a note made. "What about you, Miss Eohne?"

"I'll be taking the public transport," said Eohne.

"No you won't!" Jordan said, affronted. She looked at the captain. "I'll be taking her."

He raised an eyebrow. "Are you sure?"

"Yes, and you can write that in your little book there." Jordan tapped on the page.

Eohne and Toth shared an amused look.

"It's alright, Jordan--"

This time the Elf clammed up when the Arpak shot her a look. "I can carry you, Eohne. And if it's hard for me, all the better. I need to get stronger; I need to start training, the sooner the better."

"Very well." The captain made his note and left them alone.

"Training?"

"Toth is going to teach me how to fight." Jordan crossed her arms. "I need to be able defend myself. This is a bloody dangerous place, and the two of you aren't always going to be around to rescue me."

Toth blinked down at Jordan. "You were serious about that?"

Jordan had asked Toth to train her when they were facing Ashley on that terrifying rainy night in the port of Maticaw. Apparently he didn't think she'd meant it.

Jordan dropped her arms in surprise. "Of course!" She

paused. "Oh." She blushed and put her hands to her cheeks. "I'm so dumb. I'm sorry."

"It's alright." Toth's own pale complexion had gone a little pink.

Eohne looked from one Strix to the other. "I missed something. What just happened?"

"I made a big assumption." Jordan blushed furiously. "I asked Toth to train me, but he has to go home, back to The Conca."

"Don't worry about it, Jordan," Toth murmured, his words barely audible. He looked miserable.

"I can ask Sol. I'm so sorry. I didn't think." Jordan put a hand over her brow.

Toth looked even more miserable at these words. Finally, he just turned away. "I'll check on Allan, rig up a way to make him comfortable." The Nycht disappeared below deck.

Jordan turned back to Eohne and put her forehead on the Elf's shoulder with a long agonized groan. "I'm such a numb-nut."

"A what?"

"An idiot." Jordan raised her head and looked at her friend. "I'm so vacant sometimes. Not to mention selfish. I don't suppose you have magic for that?"

Eohne grinned, her small white teeth glinting in the morning sun. " 'Fraid not. But I'm told time and maturity are usually a cure."

Jordan blew a lock of hair away from her face. "I hate that he has to leave."

"For what it's worth," Eohne squeezed her friend's arm, "I suspect he hates it, too."

"Do you think so?"

"Sure. Did you see how defensive he got when Captain Segolan called Middle Rodania polluted? You can take the Nycht out of Rodania--"

"But you can't take Rodania out of the Nycht," Jordan finished.

CHAPTER EIGHT

Le Monarque slowed as the ship drew nearer to the circular border control. It looked identical to the one Sol and Jordan had registered Jordan through on her first visit to Rodania. There was nothing to moor to, so Captain Segolan had the crew lower the anchor while they registered Allan.

A border officer came out of the small floating dome to greet them. She was a petite Nycht with tawny brown wings and matching hair pulled up into a huge bun on the top of her head. Her mouth was bracketed by lines of stress, and her face had a waxy pallor which didn't look healthy. Like most of the other Nychts Jordan had seen on Rodania, dark circles ringed her eyes from constantly battling her nocturnal nature.

Jordan smiled at the girl as the sailors lowered a plank connecting the ship with the border control station, but the Nycht didn't smile back. She only crossed the plank with a stiff stride and a limp. A sailor reached up to help her take the steps down onto the deck.

"How many for registration?" Her tone was all business.

Jordan stepped forward. "Just one, but he's ill. He's in the captain's cabin."

"Ill?" the Nycht snapped. "Ill with what?" Her gaze fell on Toth with this statement, and her brown eyes widened momentarily, then narrowed, like she might recognize him. Her dewclaws curled inward as her eyes raked him, then snapped back to Jordan.

Jordan hesitated, not sure what to say. Should she even mention that Allan had been on Trevilsom? What if border control didn't allow him through?

Eohne stepped forward. "He isn't contagious, if that's what you're worried about."

"We'll see about that." She pulled a syringe attached to a canister out of the bag strapped across her chest. It was the same tool Pabs had used on Jordan and Blue when they'd registered. "Show me this ill person."

Captain Segolan made his way through the sailors who'd gathered around. "Kheko," he said, with a smile. "How are you?"

"Captain Segolan." The Nycht's stiff expression seemed to relax a fraction. "How's business? Haven't seen much of you lately."

"Been busy on the Operyn line. You've lost weight." The captain's kindly gaze swept the short Nycht with concern. "They working you too hard?"

"It's been a nightmare lately," Kheko admitted. "Big trouble brewing."

Toth seemed to come alive. "Does it have anything to do with the smoke clouding part of Middle?"

Kheko's sharp gaze nailed the mercenary, and fire seemed to flare in her eyes. "Damn right it does." She pointed to the ring of pollution shrouding the spires of a Rodanian town. "That mess is from our second harpy attack in as many days."

Toth's mouth sat ajar as he gaped at the Nycht in blatant shock. The pink drained out of his cheeks. "That's..." he shook his head, "not possible." His voice broke on the last word.

"Yeah, that's what the Light Elves told us, but tell that to the harpies. They found a way." Kheko rubbed a hand over her brow. "It gives me a headache just thinking about it. You can imagine the fix Rodania is in right now--it's like civil war up there.

Toth seemed lost for words as he stared at Kheko. Finally, he absorbed what she had said, and his expression hardened. His icy gaze swung to Jordan and Eohne. "That explains where our harpy came from. He didn't have to go around Rodania; he went straight through it."

Kheko's dark blond brows shot up. "You had a harpy attack?" She paled. "Over water?!"

The sailors clustered about, nodding and murmuring their own responses to this question.

"How did you--" Kheko was completely disarmed by this. "What did you do?"

One of the sailors took the opportunity to jump in. He gestured toward Toth with an expression akin to worship. "This one faced him solo. I've never seen anything like it in all my livelong days."

Kheko's gaze pinned Toth with a solid stare. "I knew it," she breathed. Her entire countenance melted. The Nycht transformed before their very eyes from a border control guard to a starstruck teen. "You're a rebel."

Toth looked as though someone had dropped ants down his vest. He took a step back, uncomfortable with all eyes on him.

"Are you *him*?" Kheko's eyes were shining with adoration.

"*'Him'*?" Toth crossed his arms over his chest. "I should say not. I'm not anyone you would have heard of, certainly not any *him*." He echoed the way she'd said the last word, with awe.

Kheko shook her head. "You are. You're him. You're the rebel king."

Toth almost laughed, but still seemed too uncomfortable for levity to fully emerge. "You've got me mixed up with someone else."

"Toth." Kheko breathed his name like she was whispering a prayer. "All the Nychts know about you."

"What?" Toth replied with something akin to horror. "*How?*"

"I have a cousin who gets to hear what the letters say firsthand."

"What letters?"

The sailors, Jordan, and Eohne, as well as Captain Segolan, were all watching this with interest, their heads passing back and forth between the two Nychts like it was a tennis match.

"There's a rebel who writes letters to her mother. Some of the contents are published in a small memo that gets passed from hand to hand." Kheko seemed bemused at Toth's agonized amazement. "You think a bunch of Nychts can just leave Rodania to start their own colony? You think they can fight harpies in The Conca, and the rest of us wouldn't want to know about it?" She made a shrug that said 'this should be obvious'. "It's my favorite day of the month."

"There are *monthly* updates?" Toth looked like he was feeling seasick again; a sheen of sweat had formed on his brow.

Kheko nodded. "You're a hero." She softly added, "To the Nychts, anyway."

"But we failed." These words came out on a thunderstruck breath.

Surprise at these words blossomed in Jordan's chest, and she made a mental note to ask Toth about this when there weren't so many people around.

"You didn't." Kheko stepped up to Toth and put a hand on his forearm bracer. "You've given Nychts options. I have thought about joining you so many times." Kheko hesitated.

Toth looked down at the tiny Nycht. His words were so quiet, like he was afraid he might offend her with the subtext of what he said next. "It is a hard life, Kheko. It's not a decision that should be made lightly."

Kheko nodded. "I know. I never really took it seriously, but now that this has happened..." She gestured to the smoke-wreathed section of Middle Rodania. "I don't know what's going to happen here." Her chin quivered. "Everything is uncertain. Life in The Conca might look better than life here for the first time since you left. The Council is fighting with the Light Elves, saying they are to blame. The Light Elves deny that their magic has failed, and so far,

King Konig is a no-show." She shook herself, and her professional face was back. "But we are wasting time. Let's take a look at this fellow in your cabin, and see if we can't get you on your way." She gave Toth a brilliant smile, and it transformed her into a heart-stopping beauty. Toth looked momentarily stunned, and watched her follow Captain Segolan.

Jordan wanted nothing more than to pull Toth aside and ask if he was okay, but Kheko had already disappeared into the captain's quarters, and she rushed to join her. A question had been brewing in her mind at the sight of the syringe. She made her way to Allan's bedside, where Kheko was already withdrawing blood from Allan's arm. The little vacuum sucked up its sample, and Kheko rolled down Allan's shirtsleeve.

"I was wondering," Jordan began, but Kheko turned away abruptly, ignoring her. Jordan followed the border guard back out onto the deck and through the crowd of sailors. The men were still standing around like they had nothing better to do——maybe they didn't until the ship got underway again.

"Excuse me. Kheko?" Jordan thought perhaps the Nycht hadn't heard her the first time.

"Mmmm?" Kheko made a distracted noise and didn't spare a glance for Jordan.

"The machine you put the blood into, will it give you a diagnosis?"

Kheko turned and bared her teeth at Jordan abruptly. Jordan took a surprised step back at the anger in Kheko's face. The Nycht snapped, "This is border control, not an infirmary."

Jordan blinked, brought up short by the venom in Kheko's tone. The Nycht pushed her way to the gangplank and crossed over the water to the dome, disappearing inside.

"Don't take it personally." Toth was at Jordan's elbow. "She doesn't know you're not like the others."

"What if her machine reports some clue about what's wrong with him?" Jordan brightened with an idea. "Could you ask her? You're like a rockstar to her. She'd do anything for you."

Toth choked out a half-laugh. "I doubt that."

Jordan shot him a cynical look.

"I'll try," he amended.

Several moments later, Kheko emerged and crossed halfway over the water, stopping in the middle of the gangplank. "You can pass in a few minutes."

"Did you learn anything about his condition?" Toth asked, leaning his elbows on the railing.

Kheko hesitated. "I'm not really supposed to say." She pressed her lips together then added, "I can tell you that he's not contagious. Whatever he has is no threat to Rodanian citizens. But…" she paused again.

"What is it?"

Kheko crossed the rest of the way and leaned toward Toth. Jordan strained to hear what she was saying, but she didn't want to set the Nycht off by reminding her of the presence of an Arpak. Kheko whispered into Toth's ear, and Toth stared at her in response.

Kheko slapped the railing and gave Captain Segolan a nod. "You're free to pass. Good luck with your Operyn posting."

The captain waved, and the sailors withdrew the planking once Kheko had passed back to the dome safely. The anchor was drawn up, and the ship's sails were loosed to catch the breeze and carry them to the nearest port at Lower Rodania.

Jordan was at Toth's side in a flash. "What did she say?"

Toth turned a concerned gaze on her.

"Tell me." Jordan's heart felt cold at his expression. "Even if it's bad news."

"She said he's in a state the machine registered as 'pre-death'."

"No." Jordan shook her head fiercely. "She's wrong."

Eohne, who had been observing all of this quietly, put a hand on Jordan's shoulder. "I'm not going to let him die. I can help him; I'm almost sure of it. All I need is time. Now that we know how to keep him from dehydrating and starving to death-—"

"How much time, though?" Jordan turned to the Elf. "What do you need? Is there anything back in your lab that could help?"

"I don't know yet," Eohne's expression turned thoughtful. Her hair lifted in the wind as the ship picked up speed. "I just need time."

Jordan crossed her arms and turned her face to the sun, closing her eyes. She let out a long breath and gathered herself. She'd never felt so helpless, so on the edge of a precipice without any clear course forward.

She opened her eyes and looked at Eohne. "Sol's uncle Juer is the king's doctor. Perhaps we can ask if he's seen this before? He has a huge library, tons of references, and he's as old as the hills. It's worth a try, right?"

Eohne nodded, squeezing her friend's arm. "It's worth a try."

Sol's apartment was empty when they arrived. Toth deposited Allan on the bed, and Eohne went about watering him, checking his vitals, setting out her strange tools, and scribbling formulas on paper.

"Blue is not here," said Toth, emerging from the bedroom.

"He's probably out hunting," Jordan replied. "He hunts all his own food."

The sound of wings fluttering just beyond the apartment drew Toth and Jordan to the terrace. Jordan rushed ahead of the Nycht, expecting and hoping for Sol. She drew up short when it was someone she didn't recognize.

A male Arpak with short black hair, glossy black feathers, and skin the color of cinnamon was holding steady just beyond the terrace. He wore two satchels criss-crossing his body, the same way Sol did. He had several knives strapped to his hips and one thigh. He surveyed them with dark eyes, homing in on Toth.

"Are you Toth? Of the Charra-Rae Nycht rebels?" The Arpak's upper lip curled with a touch of sneer.

A look of surprise crossed Toth's face. "I am. Who are you?"

The Arpak retrieved a letter from inside a satchel. He swooped closer to the balcony but did not land. "I'm Modi, a courier for the Council. I have a delivery for you."

Toth stepped to the edge of the stone terrace and took the letter. "Who would be sending me letters here?"

"I'm just a courier." With a flat-mouthed nod, Modi flew away.

"News travels fast." Jordan came to stand beside the Nycht. "Who is it from?"

"I don't know." Toth tore the letter open and read, his gray eyes darting back and forth. His brows raised and he looked at Jordan, bemused. "It is from a Council member. A man named Balroc."

"The government? How did they find out you were here so fast?"

Toth frowned. "Maybe Kheko? I suppose, if they were watching for me, the shield could be wired to send them a notice when I cross the border."

"What does he want?"

"To meet with me." Toth held up the letter and read aloud, "At my earliest convenience."

"Do you have any reason not to go?" Jordan wondered if the Nycht was in some kind of trouble with the Rodanian government. After all, he was a rebel; the most well-known rebel, if Kheko's reaction to him was any indication. "Is there…" she paused, finding it difficult to imagine some force Toth couldn't face down. "Danger?"

"Not that I know of. I haven't been back to Rodania in a decade. What the rebels did offended them, but it wasn't illegal." Toth stood in silence for a long time. Jordan watched him think. Just before she was about to ask him what he was going to do, he said, "The sooner I meet with him, the sooner I can get back to The Conca." He turned his eyes to her, and Jordan nearly stepped back at the way they seemed shuttered against her. "I'll say goodbye, then."

Jordan's pulse skittered like a deer crossing ice. She wasn't ready to say goodbye. "Why don't you stay the night? Just one night. Be refreshed when you leave for The Conca. It's such a long journey."

Toth tucked the letter into a pocket. "There is no room for me here. Should my meeting go overtime, I can stay with one of my siblings."

Jordan felt as though she was standing on uncertain ground. She had no right to ask the Nycht for more than what he'd already so generously given. "Toth," she began, "I don't know how to thank you. Without you--" Her voice tightened, and she found she couldn't continue for fear of embarrassing herself.

Toth lifted one shoulder in a small, tight shrug. He amended his plans. "I will come say goodbye before I go."

Jordan let out a breath and nodded, it was more than she had been prepared to ask for. She reached out and squeezed his upper arm. "Whatever that is," she nodded at the letter, "if there is anything I can do to help you, please ask. I'm forever in your debt, and…" she pinned him with a weighted look, and he knew she was sincere, "I am on your side."

Toth's face seemed to relax, and he pulled Jordan in for a hug. Then with a rush of wind, he was gone.

The following hour found Jordan sitting at Allan's bedside, holding his hand and murmuring to him quietly. He couldn't die. There was so much left unresolved for the Kacy family. *How will he react when I tell him about Jaclyn? How much does he know already?*

"Jordan?" Sol's voice bellowed from outside. Jordan had been leaning back against her right wing as it braced against the ground, propping her up. She scrambled up and rushed outside, her heart staggering with excitement. She felt like a sports car that had just gone from zero to sixty in under two seconds flat.

With a gust of wind, a flurry of dust and feathers, and a *thud*, Sol landed on the terrace.

"Sol!" Until Jordan saw him, his wild brown hair with the tiny braids, the lively bright blue of his eyes, she didn't realize just how much she had been missing him.

She leapt into his arms, which he stretched wide to catch her. The two Arpaks collided chest to chest and fell backward off the terrace together. Both his tawny wings and her bright yellow ones took to beating at the air, working to keep them aloft. Jordan buried her face in Sol's neck as his arms wrapped tightly around her ribs, seeming to circle her torso many times over with his warmth.

"Jordan," he said into her hair, and his voice was little more than a croak. "I've been going out of my mind."

"I'm so happy to see--" Jordan pulled back and gave an enormous sneeze. "Why are you so filthy? And you smell like smoke." She sniffed and sneezed again, turning her face away from him.

Sol laughed and steered them back to the balcony. "I've been helping clean up the mess on Middle Rodania. Blue returned with your letter only yesterday. Thank God, I had been thinking the worst. I was about to launch a search party of one when he showed up."

"Where is he?"

Sol shrugged. "Who knows? It was like he checked in to let me know he was here, and then left before I woke up this morning. Probably out hunting. And your father?"

"He is here."

Sol let out a breath. "Thank heavens. Where?" His eyes darted about, apprehensive. His eyes fell on the bedroom door, then the water closet. "Is he alright? Trevilsom is a wicked place."

"He's in your bed."

Sol's brows drew together and he searched her face. "I can imagine he's tired and hungry."

"He's in a coma."

"Oh." Sol's face grew somber, and his shoulders sagged. "I'm so sorry."

Eohne emerged from the bedroom, tools of her trade clutched in her delicate fingers. "Hello, again. It seems we have invaded your home."

Sol smiled at the Elf. "Jordan wrote that you came to help her; very generous of you. You are more than welcome here. I would be offended if you went anywhere else." Sol searched for evidence of the Nycht. "And Toth?"

"He was asked to a meeting with one of the Council members."

"Really?" Sol's surprise at this was genuine, but Jordan got the sense that Sol was not as shocked as they were about how quickly the government was aware of Toth's presence.

"Any idea what they want?" Jordan searched the Arpak's face.

Sol's brows pinched together. "It will have to do with the harpy attack, I'm almost certain."

"They don't think he had anything to do with that?" A cold feeling crept over Jordan. She hoped that Toth wasn't flying into a bad situation.

Sol shrugged. "I don't know." His face was troubled. "There are things we need to talk about." He crossed to his sink to wash his hands and splash water on his dirty face.

There was a loud roar from somewhere beyond the apartment, and Sol and Jordan locked eyes, Sol's eyelashes dripping.

"That's one of them," he said grimly.

There was another roar, this one closer. The sound was intimidating, but jubilant rather than threatening.

"Was that…" Jordan began.

Sol nodded.

She darted for the terrace in time to see a blue dragon the size of a Great Dane skitter across the tiles, his wings hitting the stones on either side of the open archway with a *crack* before closing up.

"Blue!" Jordan cried. Happiness and disbelief blossomed in her chest. "You're huge!" The dragon put his head down and bumped Jordan's abdomen with his forehead. A long, deep rattle rumbled in his chest, ending with a high-pitched whistle. Jordan bent and kissed Blue on either side of his face. "You're so handsome. I missed you, look at you!"

Blue's scales had changed from the bright cerulean shade they had been into a deeper color, more like the sky before a storm. The yellow blaze under his chin and down his throat to his belly had mellowed from a bright canary to a buttery yellow. The elegant horns on his head had thickened at the base, and his black eyes had changed. Where before there had been no distinction between the pupil and the iris, now threads of color sprayed out from the pupil--a vertical slash--making an orange corona.

Jordan gaped at Sol. "How could he have changed so much in only a matter of days?"

Sol crossed his arms. "Because the gypsy lied to us. He can't be a Predoian Miniature. Some species grow exceptionally fast; clearly, he is one of them. We need to find out what he actually is, and soon. We have no idea when he'll stop growing. The only reason he hasn't been kicked out of Rodania for good is because everyone's been so distracted by the harpy attacks, but it's only a matter of time."

Jordan stroked Blue's scales and he hooked a claw behind her calf, sitting on his haunches. He closed his eyes to her ministrations. "How do we find out his species?"

"Juer's library in Crypsis would be the best place to start, if we want to keep things incognito."

"What about the Nychts at the border? They took his blood. Couldn't they tell what he is?"

"I wondered that, too. I don't know how the magic works exactly. I was afraid to go talk to Pabs, in case they realized their mistake and kicked him out."

Jordan looked to Eohne next. "Do you have a way of telling us what Blue is?"

Eohne shook her head. "I have never developed any magic for working with dragons. There has never been a need in Charra-Rae. I can't just look at his blood and tell you what he is——I would have to have something to reference back to."

"There is a lab in Rodania that could identify him, but I don't want to alert them to his existence." Sol shrugged. "Looks like we'll have to do this the old fashioned way: books. He might be done growing, he might not; but if he gets much bigger than he is now…" Sol shook his head. "It won't be good."

CHAPTER NINE

Toth landed on a terrace just outside a towering residence, south of the king's palace. Five tall obsidian pillars, insanely elaborate and expensive, glittered in the sun. He folded his wings away as a young Arpak female appeared from between the pillars.

She was dressed in a plain white robe that was cinched at the waist with glittering red rocks. She wore her long dark hair tied up high on her head and a thin gold band across her forehead. She had long, slender arms and hands. Her light blue wings were small, the primary feathers barely reaching her knees; they were the kind of wings that were considered beautiful in proportion, but not great for flying. Arpaks who had abnormally small wings were often mistaken for angels in paintings. This was exactly the kind of elegantly proportioned Arpak that artists loved to capture on canvas.

She's probably never known a day of hard work in her whole life.

She didn't introduce herself, only said, "He's expecting

you." The beautiful Arpak invited Toth, with a fluid arm gesture, to pass through the pillars. "May I bring you a drink, or something to eat?"

"No, thank you." Toth entered the residence with the young Arpak trailing behind. Expensive looking furniture decorated the spacious parlour. Cathedral ceilings gave the space an airy, hollow feeling, and small birds flew about the buttresses and sat in the high stained glass windows.

"Through there." The young woman pointed to an archway leading to a second, more private terrace.

Toth passed through the archway and onto a balcony, where a short, broad Arpak stood with his hands behind his back, facing the city below. He wore a vest of black velvet embroidered with gold thread, and pants made of a soft woven fabric. He had rings on his fingers worth more than anything Toth owned, or ever would own, in his lifetime.

Toth saw that the girl had come by her wings honestly; this man, too, had small, light blue wings. They were relaxed, and lay apart––a position typical of someone who didn't fly much. On Rodania, this draped carriage of one's wings was a sign of wealth.

Toth thought it just looked lazy.

The Arpak turned and presented Toth with a wide broad face. His expression was serious but not unfriendly. He looked young and sincere. "Thank you for coming, Toth." Balroc held out a hand. "I always liked the human custom of a handshake."

Toth gave his hand, and it was shaken heartily.

"You must be used to it by now, working alongside humans so closely."

Toth didn't bother to correct him. The humans of The Conca shook hands with each other; not with the Nychts who protected them, unless a deal was being made.

"As you'll know from my letter, my name is Balroc. Please, have a seat." He gestured to the stools positioned in front of a fountain in the middle of the balcony. Two silver cups had been set out on the small table.

"I'd rather stand, if it's all the same to you." Toth put his hands behind his back, a gesture that uncovered the heart and told of some small level of trust.

Balroc nodded. "I'll get right to the point. I am one of the Council of Ten."

"I know."

"Good. Now please help me understand more about who *you* are."

"With respect, where is this going?"

Balroc put out a hand. "I have a proposition for you. I hope you'll be patient enough to hear me out? I promise it is to your benefit."

I doubt that. "I'm not aware of any proposition an Arpak could make that would benefit a Nycht."

"Bear with me. I am going to have a seat, even if you won't." Balroc picked up one of the silver cups, filled it at the fountain, and settled himself on a stool. "Word of what you have done for the humans of The Conca reached Rodania a long time ago. It is a shame you and your," he tilted his head, "*associates* have abandoned your birthplace and taken your considerable talents elsewhere."

"You mean me and my rebels?"

"You may be called that in some circles, but I would

never assign that name to you. I can't say I would have done differently, were I in your place."

Toth narrowed his eyes. He did not fully trust sympathetic rapport from an Arpak, especially one on the Council. "Your *circle* drove us to leave. Your *circle* calls us traitors and turncoats and worse, yet refuses to recognize the gross discrimination you foment which brought about our defection." Pink spots appeared on Toth's cheeks, and he wrestled to keep his tone from becoming accusatory.

"We are not all the same," said Balroc quietly. "You have supporters you don't know about; I am one of them. I was only fifteen when you and your fellow Nychts left your posts on Rodania for good, and I have made every effort to follow your activities. I have always believed that a fully Arpak government makes for a shortsightedness that keeps me up at night. Rodania, she is my motherland, but she has several defects, which I am working to remedy. It takes time to change attitudes, even longer to change policy, but there is an opportunity coming that will not surface again in our lifetime. An opportunity to change things for Nychts and get the equality you deserve."

"What opportunity would that be?" Toth worked to hide his interest. If Balroc was speaking truthfully, he was one of the few Nycht sympathizers Toth had come across, and they needed every one they could get, if things were ever to change.

"Rodania is under attack, and not just from harpies. The Elven magic that protects us has been breached, and I do not believe it was simply an error in magical engineering." Balroc lowered his voice. "I have reason to believe it is sabotage." He put a hand out. "And before you jump to conclusions, no, I do not believe *you* have anything to do with that sabotage."

Toth cocked an eyebrow, but what he really wanted to do was gape. Sabotage was serious, a crime worthy of Trevilsom.

"Even if you are right, how is it my problem?"

"Come now." Balroc gave a sly smile. "Whether you like it or not, the harpies are partially your problem. Most of your family still lives here; your sister even works at the palace. A nurse, I believe?"

Toth frowned. It was unsettling that Balroc knew this. "You've been watching me and my family?"

"As I said, I've been interested in you since you left—— you and your brother, Caje. Your own people haven't made it difficult to keep track of your activities, what with their underground publication." Balroc took a sip of his water, but his eyes never left Toth's.

Toth kept his mouth shut, but irritation sizzled through him. Thanks to Kheko, he knew what Balroc was talking about, but only just. It made him wonder what else was going on behind his back. Toth's brows knit together, and he looked away, working to get a hold of himself.

"Let me explain further. Rodania has been arrogant." Balroc forged on before Toth's expression could get any darker. "King Konig has not been himself for years. He became neglectful over a decade ago, and since then has only gotten worse. He and most of the Council believe the Elven magic is all that is needed to protect us. They've been lulled into a false sense of security by the hubris of the Light Elves. I have been fighting this attitude since I joined the Council a year ago, and now it's too late. I have never been so unhappy to be proven right." Balroc took a steadying breath. His brow had begun to shine with sweat; he wiped a hand across his forehead. "We need a military, and we need one now," he concluded.

Toth's face softened, and the confusion cleared away like breaking clouds. "I should have known. You want Caje and I to fight for Rodania." He began to chuckle. "Now that you're in trouble, you need the Nychts of The Conca to return, even though you drove them away."

"Not just fight, but train and lead a mixed force of Strix. Take the best of both and channel them against this harpy onslaught."

"I've heard enough." Toth turned away.

Balroc leapt to his feet. "No, you haven't. Don't be a fool and leave before you really understand what is at stake here." His words may have been harsh, but it was the near pleading tone that gave Toth pause. Just like that, the tables had turned. Toth felt the shift of power as Balroc's desperation threaded his words.

Interesting.

"What exactly do you think is at stake?"

"The future of Nychts. You can change everything for your people, for all of Strix society. This chance only comes once every hundred years. If you miss it, you'll be condemning your people to the same oppressed existence they've had to bear since the beginning."

"What are you talking about?" Toth growled.

"There are those on the Council who would wish to see me exiled for telling you what I am about to tell you," Balroc's voice tremored slightly. "Believe it or not, I am at far greater risk right now for speaking with you than you are for speaking with me. Pay attention. I fully expect you to do your own research and verify that I am not lying to you." He took a step closer, holding the Nycht's icy gray eyes with his own blue ones. "Every hundred years the Council holds a private vote."

"What vote?" Toth's forearms prickled under his bracers at the look on Balroc's face.

"Whether to give Nychts a place at the table, or not."

The air seemed to go still. Toth's lips parted to call Balroc a liar, but the Arpak continued.

"They don't publicize it because, up until recently, none of the Arpaks on the Council would ever have supported such a change." Balroc put a hand on his chest. "What you don't realize, what none of your people realize, is that you are closer than ever to your goal. I have been fighting for Nychts since the day I joined the Council, and I have made many enemies because of it."

"Why would you care whether Nychts earn a place of power or not? What's in it for you?"

"I love Rodania. I believe that equality is better for our nation. I have seen many talented Nychts under-utilized and mishandled. Their situation not only hurts them, but it also hurts us. Those on the Council who would continue to hold your people down are doing so out of fear."

Toth's mind was spinning. *Is everything this Arpak is saying for real?* He seemed to share Toth's ideology. Looking at Balroc's face and hearing the passion in his words, it was very difficult to think that he was lying. But Toth had grown up not trusting Arpaks; he needed to verify this story for himself.

"When is this vote?"

"Roughly a year from now. The date is yet to be confirmed."

"You've been petitioning other Arpaks on the Council to vote for us?"

Balroc nodded. "It has been my sole focus these last six months."

"And where does the poll stand now?"

"I have three on the Council who are for you, and one who is undecided."

"That's less than half."

"Yes it is, but it's a huge shift forward from where it was, and I don't yet know where King Konig stands on it. His doctor won't let anyone near him. King Konig's vote counts as two. Now do you see why you need to help Rodania?"

Toth did see.

He turned away from the councilman, thinking. His eyes skimmed the rooftops and terraces of Upper Rodania. He had loved this city once, too, before he'd grown up and realized what corruption lay beneath its shining exterior. If what Balroc was saying was true, he and his Nychts had a chance to prove themselves invaluable to Rodania. The opportunity lay in exhibiting their worth to King Konig and earning his two votes. It was a chance to change the future for all the Nychts here, a massive step towards equality.

It was a bitter pill to swallow that the Nychts had to work so hard and risk so much to fight for something they should be granted as rightful citizens of Strix society. If Toth and his rebels took up the fight against the harpies, there could be deaths.

"I am not saying I'll return to Rodania." Toth turned back to the eager face of Balroc. "But, what are you proposing exactly?"

Balroc's face lit with hope. "I have the means to furnish you with training islands, weapons, and the authority to pull together an army. Your word would be sovereign when it came to military matters and the defense of our city, second only to King Konig himself."

"The Council supports this?" Toth staggered mentally at all Balroc was offering.

"They support your return to forge a military; they haven't thought far enough ahead to tie it to the vote."

Toth considered the monumental meaning behind his proposal. "It seems as though the Council is expecting more harpies to attack."

Balroc gave a sharp nod. "They are. In return for your service, you would be furnished with an excellent salary and a residence on Upper Rodania."

"I wouldn't want to live here."

"On Middle then," Balroc amended. "You must understand…more than half of the Council members would like to keep Nychts down forever. You are a soldier and a mercenary, I am a politician; I am telling you that this is your best chance to change all of that. If you turn it down, there will be no relief for the Nychts of Rodania for another hundred years." Balroc scanned Toth's face intently. "You do not need to answer now, but I need to know where you stand in the next three days. Things are moving quickly, and panic is rising. The people need to see that the Council is making strides to protect them, even if King Konig seems unable or unwilling to act."

These were treasonous words.

It hit Toth swift and hard that Balroc seemed to be purposefully giving him something to use against the councilman if he so wished. "You should choose your words more carefully."

"I chose my words very carefully, believe me." Balroc was unblinking and unafraid. "You are not the only one taking risks here. I need you to trust me if we are to work together, and the only way I can see to do that is to put a club in your hand to show you that I know you will not beat me with it."

This was either incredibly foolhardy, or incredibly brave. Toth looked down at the man with a new perspective. His wide face and sky blue eyes seemed guileless and trusting.

"I'll return in three days with an answer," said Toth.

Balroc let out a breath and nodded. "I shall eagerly await it."

Toth wasted no time winging his way to Sol's apartment. Eohne was kneeling on the terrace in the sunlight, a collection of instruments and tools laid out on the tiles in front of her.

"How is he?" Toth asked as he folded his wings away. He stepped around Eohne's work, careful not to bump any of her things with his boots.

"The same." Eohne's face was pale, and dark shadows ringed her eyes. She looked as tired as any Nycht in Rodania. She ran a hand through her hair, which she'd released from its ties for the first time in days. "Jordan told me about your letter. What did the councilman want?"

"He had a proposition." Toth scratched his chin where the shadow of a beard was beginning to thicken. "I was wondering if I might use your messenger bugs to contact my brother?"

"Of course, I'll go get them." Eohne rose and disappeared inside.

Sol appeared from inside the apartment, passing Eohne with a smile. He gave Toth a polite nod. "Toth." He held out his hand for the Nycht to shake, figuring the gesture might be meaningful to a Nycht who spent a lot of time with humans. "Good to see you again."

"Is it?" Toth looked down on the smaller Arpak.

"Of course. Jordan and Eohne told me everything you've done for them." A touch of color dotted Sol's cheeks. Toth was a hero, and he was grateful, but he wasn't about to fall down and fawn at the mercenary's feet. "Thank you."

Toth let Sol's hand go. "I didn't do it for you." Though his words were hard, he spoke simply, and not unkindly. Toth didn't like the way Sol assumed gratitude on behalf of Jordan; it was too close to suggesting the two were an item for Toth's taste.

Sol almost snapped that he knew that, but instead turned the conversation in a more productive direction. As a government employee, he was nothing if not diplomatic. "I heard you met with a councilman. No bad news, I hope?"

Toth eyed the courier, chewing his cheek thoughtfully. "Do you know anything about a vote the Council holds every one hundred years?"

Sol's brows drew together. "A vote? About what?"

"Whether or not to allow Nychts a place in government."

The Arpak's brows shot skyward. "I've never heard of such a vote. Is it real?"

"Balroc says it is." Toth's eyes locked with Sol's. "You can see why it would be a best-kept secret, if it is true."

Sol nodded in agreement. "I certainly can. I have a few choice words for some of our Council members in private, but I would have only good things to say about Balroc."

"Do you know him?"

"Not well. He's only been on the Council for six months or so. I have delivered messages for him, and he seems a good sort."

Eohne appeared with the bottle of bugs, and Sol's eyes dropped dubiously to the cluster of round glass balls. "Still using those things?"

"Only for intra-Oriceran messages." Eohne blew out a breath. "No universe hopping for these guys; at least, not until I can make a few tweaks."

"Still, seems like you have no way of verifying they're safe to use until something goes wrong." Sol frowned at the bugs.

"You're just afraid I'll put you out of a job one day," replied Eohne, elbowing Sol in the ribs as she passed.

"There's that, too," he allowed with a half-smile.

Eohne took Toth through the routine with the donisi pill, and injected the bugs with Toth's vocal vibrations. Toth made a simple request of his brother, which left both Sol and Eohne bemused. The bugs zipped off in the direction of The Conca, disappearing from sight at a blinding speed.

"Thanks," Toth said to Eohne. He turned to face the vista, wings opening.

"Where are you going?"

"I'll be back later," Toth called over his shoulder as he leapt into the air.

Eohne and Sol looked at one another. "Can Caje get here that fast?"

Sol shrugged. "He'd have to be a champion flyer, that's for certain."

CHAPTER TEN

Toth winged his way down to Lower Rodania. It was strange, being in his homeland again. Things had not changed since he was a young Nycht, fighting to stay awake during school hours. It had taken until his twenties to be able to function normally in daylight. It would never feel entirely normal.

The fields and towns of Lower Rodania sped by as he approached the place of his birth. Mavado was a small agricultural town nestled among a patchwork of colorful crops. Toth landed in a large yard of thick, green grass. Small jovial insects leapt up and bounced off his legs and chest as he walked to the stone house where he had begun his life. He used to spend hours playing with the spring-loaded bugs, catching them and setting them against his friends bugs to see which could leap highest. Life had been simple once.

He approached the familiar arched door and used the wooden knocker. Stepping back, he waited. Soft thuds could be heard inside.

An olive-skinned Nycht woman with dark brown eyes opened the door. For a moment, she only stared. She gasped when she realized he wasn't a figment of her imagination. "Toth!" Her eyes misted over, and she threw her arms around him, squeezing him so tight he nearly lost his breath. He squeezed her back. "You're here! Are you real? What are you doing back?" She gave another gasp and pulled back, her dark eyes lit. "It's the harpies, isn't it?"

Toth smiled at his sister. She'd always been sharp as a tack. "Hello, Mareya. Did I wake you? I'm sorry."

"Don't be daft," Mareya scolded, inviting him inside. She rubbed the wet tears away from her eyes. "If I heard my older brother had come back to Rodania for the first time in ten years and he hadn't woken me up, I would have sent someone to skin you alive. You are lucky I am not at work today."

"If you had been, I would have come to the palace to find you. You still work there?"

Mareya nodded and closed the door. "Come in, come in. Are you hungry? Thirsty?"

"I wouldn't say no to one of your krutch cakes, if you have any." Toth smiled again at his younger sister, his heart full of her. "You look well. I'm happy to see you."

She flapped a hand at him. "I will never get rid of these bags under my eyes." She laughed in good humor then put her hands on his shoulders. "Let me look at you." She scanned her brother's face. "The past decade has given you many new scars." Her thumb traced a thick line of scar tissue on his neck just above his armor. She shook her head, her face sad. "I worry for you every day. Come. Eat." Mareya crossed the living area, where a semicircle of steps led into a depression, in which sat a wood-burning stove. It was used only in winter, and even then rarely, as temperatures in Rodania were mild. "I'll wake Shad."

"No, let him sleep. I remember how hard it was, school on Arpak hours. Don't disturb him."

"Absolutely not. He never gets to see his famous rebel uncle. He would never forgive me if I didn't wake him."

Toth's mouth quirked. "Don't you mean 'infamous'?"

"Not remotely!" Mareya rifled through a cabinet and retrieved a plate and cutlery. "You are idolized by the young Nychts here. Shad couldn't be prouder of you."

"He is, what? Sixteen?"

She nodded. "This year."

"And his Arpak friends? That little one with the black feathers––what was his name? Is he still around?"

Mareya gave a sad smile. "Benn and Shad don't play together so much anymore. A lot can change in ten years."

"Is that because of me?"

"No, of course not." Mareya dropped her eyes to the dish of krutch cakes. She set one on a plate and slid it toward Toth. "Go sit down. I'll wake Shad after we've had a chance to catch up. But first, I'll bring your coffee.

Toth let out an involuntary groan. "I haven't had coffee in…I forget how long. The humans of The Conca don't drink it. They have their own vile drink called measil." He wrinkled his nose. "Tastes like dirt. I'll never understand why they like it."

"You have no coffee in The Conca?" Mareya looked appropriately horrified. "I'll send some to you. I am finally allowed to use the palace couriers," she muttered. "Only took twenty-eight years of service."

"Kind of you," said Toth. "But that would still be outrageously expensive, and you know it." He picked up a krutch cake and bit into it, ignoring the fork on the plate. The pastry, filled with fresh pinzo berries, crumbled in his mouth. He gave a groan of pleasure and looked at Mareya through one eye, closing the other in a funny face he hadn't made in a long time.

Mareya sat down to watch her brother enjoy the cake. She rested her chin in her hands. "I don't suppose it would do any good to ask you if you'll come home?"

Toth swallowed and grew serious. "You know I can't live here with things as they are. I had no intentions of coming home at all, but there have been some strange circumstances. A strange circumstance brings me to you today." Toth put down the cake. "Do you know Councilman Balroc?"

"Not well," replied Mareya, "but working at the palace means I cross paths with all the Council members at some point or another. Balroc is among the best of them. Why?"

"I met with him less than an hour ago."

Mareya's eyes widened. "Met with him?"

Toth nodded. "He sent a courier for me only moments after I arrived in Rodania."

"What did he want? Am I allowed to ask?" Mareya put up a hand. "I don't want to know something I shouldn't; it makes things so complicated. There are already too many secrets flying around the palace."

"He wants me to start a military force."

Mareya's hand flew to her mouth, and she stared at her older brother. "Because of the harpies? I knew it! I knew you were here because of them."

"I wasn't, actually. I was here for a friend. But the timing does make it look that way. I didn't realize there had been attacks until our ship docked at the border."

"But you'd never agree to it, would you? Making an army?"

"Normally, no. But I need to know if something he said is true. You're the only person I can think of to ask." Toth took his sister's hand. "He said that the Council of Ten holds a vote every one hundred years. A vote about whether or not to allow Nychts a place on the Council." Toth could see the light of understanding sweep across Mareya's face. "So it's true? There is such a vote?"

"It is true," Mareya confirmed, but her eyes were sad. "But it will never pass."

"How do you know?"

"There will never be enough support for it. The Arpaks have no reason to change things. They are stronger than they have ever been. They've got us all living life as though we're Arpaks, too."

"Balroc says there could be enough support. He has three votes for and one undecided."

"That's only four total, including Balroc, out of twelve votes..." she looked doubtful.

"Mareya," Toth squeezed his sister's hand. "Do you know which way the King would vote?"

Mareya sighed and gave a smile. "King Konig has always been for equality. For all his faults, he has a good heart. The problem is that..." She hesitated and pinched her lips.

"What, Mareya?"

"The king has not been himself for quite some time. He is unwell." She spoke slowly, enunciating and lacing her words with subtext. "And the vote is still a whole year away."

"You think he may not live that long?"

Mareya gave a small shrug of her shoulders, her mouth downturned.

"So what of his successor? Prince Diruk? You practically raised him."

"You'd never know it," Mareya sneered. "He has as much prejudice as the queen did."

Toth's face fell. The queen had been a tyrant and a bigot. If the young prince had taken after his mother, there was no good future for Nychts on Rodania. Toth's expression hardened. "We cannot allow things to stay the way they are for another one hundred years." He met his sister's soft brown eyes. "And I can't bear to think of harpies putting my family's lives in danger."

"Are you saying you're going to do it? Create a Rodanian military?"

"I can't do it without Caje's help, but if we can save Rodania, we can compel the rest of the Council to vote in our favor."

"And you would be here," Mareya added, her eyes shining. "You would be home, with your family."

"Yes," said Toth. "But I would only stay if we were successful. I cannot work for a government who holds no respect for us."

Mareya nodded. "I know. You never did have any tolerance for inequality. When do you have to give an answer?"

"Three days."

"And you will see Caje before then?"

"He had better come," Toth growled. "I need him."

"What about the humans you are sworn to protect?"

"It wasn't a vow, just a contract. We would dissolve it."

"They won't like that."

"No, but everything changes. They'll go back to living the way they did before us." *In constant fear of harpy attacks,* he added to himself silently. He took another bite of krutch cake and chewed thoughtfully.

"So it must be true, then," mused Mareya, pulling him from his thoughts.

"What's that?"

"The Elf magic has been broken. The protection that they said was unbreakable has betrayed us. The Council will be having words with the Light Elves over this, if they haven't already. I hope it doesn't escalate."

"Balroc insinuated that it was not the magic that was at fault."

Mareya looked puzzled. "Then what else--"

She paused and breathed out a long, "Ohhhhh." The two Nychts shared a look of understanding.

"Sabotage?"

Toth nodded. "If he's right, King Konig and the Council have more problems than harpies on their hands."

CHAPTER ELEVEN

Toth turned at the sound of flapping wings and watched his brother descend to the glade in the woods they'd played in as kids. The early morning light of dawn illuminated the knee-deep burbling stream as it wound through the trees. Small islands dotted the water, wreathed with bright green spearmint plants. They had often taken water from the spring-fed stream back to their family because it tasted like mint.

"Your message nearly gave me a heart attack," said Caje as he landed and walked to his brother. His face was pink and damp from exertion, but he otherwise looked well. He tucked his huge wings away. He'd flown all night and most of the day before, with only a brief rest in Maticaw, the halfway point. Caje was not the fastest flier, but he was strong and tireless.

"Sorry about that. Weird Elven magic, it was the fastest way to get a hold of you."

"Eohne's magic?"

Toth nodded. "And thank goodness for it." Toth settled

himself on a rock near the stream and waved his brother over.

"What's so important that you had me rushing out without any time to prepare, leaving Chayla in charge?"

"She must love that," Toth said with a half-smile.

"Woman's a tyrant," Caje grunted as he sat beside his brother. "Whatever is going on, I hope it won't take long, or we'll be going back to clean up corpses——and not the harpy kind."

"There's a chance we may not have to go back."

The big Nycht turned in surprise. "What are you talking about?"

Toth explained to Caje what had transpired between he and Balroc two days before. His brother listened silently, but when it came to telling him about the vote, the Nycht frowned and shook his head.

"Corrupt to the core," he muttered. "How do you know he was telling you the truth?"

"I asked Mareya. She confirmed it."

Caje made a sound in the back of his throat. "She would know. She probably sees things that would make our teeth crack in anger."

"Yes."

"So, you trust this Arpak? This Balroc?"

"Oddly, I think I do." Toth was as surprised by this as Caje was. "Either way, this has been the only opportunity I have ever seen to really change things."

"And maybe to come home," added Caje quietly.

The brothers shared a look. They hid it well from their people, never wanting to be seen complaining about anything, but life in The Conca was uncomfortable, primitive, and isolated. They'd left to make a statement that not all Nychts were satisfied being treated as second-class citizens, and that Nycht power would be missed.

At the time, they'd been hoping for the story of their defection to be a catalyst for changes in policy; instead they'd become heroes to the Nycht citizens of Rodania, and turncoats to the Arpaks. No laws were broken. It wasn't illegal to leave Rodania, but when two Nychts round up sixty of the strongest and most capable, and leave the city in the light of day, walking off their jobs and, in some cases, leaving family behind, it sent a prickly message.

The Rodanian government had chafed, but in the end, it was a gamble that failed. Now it was a decision they couldn't reverse without appearing weak, so they'd stayed away. Life in The Conca was accepted; babies had been born there, and the rebel group had flourished. But for Toth and Caje, whose family was still in Rodania, it had never really been home. Rodania was a city custom-built for its winged citizens; there was nowhere else on Oriceran like it, not for Strix.

"I can't do it without you," said Toth. "If you say no, then I'll say no."

"I'd give us less than five percent chance of success."

"Against the harpies? Or with the vote?"

"Harpies," Caje scoffed, "we could exterminate those abominations in a matter of weeks, if we had the resources." His look darkened. "I'm talking about the Council. A more crooked batch of Arpaks I never saw."

"We don't know that any more," argued Toth. "We've been gone for a decade. Half the Council are Arpaks we don't know. Balroc said three would vote for us and one is undecided. That's nearly half." He blinked and shook his head. "Wait, why am I the one defending them? You're the one who goes on about change only being a matter of time."

Caje was staring off into the bubbling water. "Every one hundred years," he muttered. He broke the stare and pierced his brother with a look. "If we lose, we go back to The Conca?"

"If the humans will take us back."

"They'll take us. They're too scared not to."

"You'll have to talk to them." Toth was referring to their group of Nychts, who knew nothing of the potential life change hurtling their way.

Caje nodded. "If Chayla agrees, the rest of them will too. And to be honest, I wouldn't want to fight a slew of harpies without her anyway."

"So, you're saying yes?"

"Yes, with conditions," Caje held up a meaty finger. "We do it our way. And no conscription is the first condition. I don't want any soldiers who don't want to be there."

Toth nodded, "Agreed." The two brothers bent their heads together and began to make their list of conditions.

Early the following morning, Toth winged his way back to Balroc's residence on Upper Rodania. The sky was gray and overcast, with a small, golden glow making every effort to break through. There was an unusual nip to the air, and Toth tucked his hands under his arms as he flew to keep them warm. In the breast pocket of his armor was the list of needs and the conditions of their acceptance.

He landed on the terrace with silent feet. His wings closed and warmed the muscles of his back. He blew out a breath and saw it hang in the air before his face.

"Hello? Miss?" He peered between the marble columns, looking for the girl who greeted him, but there was no one in sight. He called out a second time and padded silently between the columns to the inner rooms. His ears perked at the sound of voices emanating from a room in the bowels of the house.

He froze.

"You did not secure my permission before pursuing this foolishness, Balroc." The voice was deep, resonant, and unfamiliar. Whoever it was, they were authoritative and deeply unhappy.

"I don't need your permission," answered Balroc patiently. "I have secured permission from the Council, as well as your father."

The other voice gave a sarcastic snort. "My father is in no shape to give his permission for anything; he is incompetent, pathetic."

Toth took a silent step back. The voice had to belong to the prince.

This time, Balroc's words were filmed with ice. "I understand that he is still lucid and capable of rational thought. Your father is not well, but at least he puts his own ambition second to what is good for Rodania."

"Watch your words, Councilman."

There was a silence. Toth thought about calling out

again to alert the Arpaks to his presence. He took another step back, unsure of what to do.

"A Nycht army cannot be trusted," the prince spoke again.

Toth froze.

"Least of all those fools from The Conca," the voice continued. "Your lunacy will put Rodania at even greater risk. They are as good as traitors to the crown."

"They committed no act of treason," Balroc replied. There was the sound of something––a cup or goblet–– being set down on a table. "They made a political statement, one you cannot possibly blame them for. And their absence was keenly felt by the businessmen of Rodania, even if the citizens couldn't see it. Now…" Balroc's voice took on additional strength. "Their absence affects everyone."

"We don't need them," growled the prince. "I'll agree with your motion to start an army, but an Arpak army will be more than suitable."

Balroc began to laugh and then made an effort to cut it off. "And who would we call to the sword, my prince? The sons of our soft aristocracy? Our philosophers? Our lawyers and doctors?"

"Our Couriers are more fierce than any Nycht could be. They've been trained to deal with aerial threats like these harpy monsters."

"Oh yes, all twenty-five of them. And if they're fighting, all communication halts, which means trade halts."

"They could have handled that last attack if they'd all been here, prepared and ready to go."

"And what happens when we are attacked by a larger

horde? We don't know how many harpies there are, or how fast they are multiplying."

There was silence in response to this.

Emboldened, Balroc's voice continued. "You know it is only a matter of time. The Elves cannot fix the security breach overnight; they've admitted they don't know the source of the problem yet. The harpies *know* we are vulnerable now. You said it yourself, they like the flavor of Strix flesh. Rodania is a buffet for them. Ninfa's team has reported the species of dragon the harpies share blood with."

Toth cocked his head. The name Ninfa was familiar. She was also a member of the Council, and must have been for some time, if he could recall her.

"*Tchielis vulgaris*, so what?"

There were footsteps and the sound of pages being flipped. Balroc spoke as though reading aloud from some source. "The Northern species *T.vulgaris* is defined not only by their size, ferocity, and appetite but also by the phenomenon designated by human scientist Marcus Sherrer, as a 'superconsciousness', a group-thinking mentality driven by a pack alpha. Packs have been recorded as small as a pair, but have also been witnessed as large as a dozen. The telepathic nature of these creatures makes them efficient group hunters. They currently tyrannize the Northern territories." The book was closed. "Can you not see, my Prince, that we need our Nychts back most desperately?"

"And what have you promised them in exchange for their service?"

"Wages, lodging. It's only fair to care for those who are willing to lay down their lives for our nation."

"They'll be wanting more than that soon enough, the cretinous brutes."

"Perhaps its time to consider––"

"Never!" The prince cut off the councilman mid-speech.

Toth found himself in a great internal wrestling match. Unable to move, he took only shallow breaths. More light was being shed on the state of things, and he was loath to reveal himself.

"Nychts have their uses, even I can admit that. Their labor powers the great economy of Rodania. But, Balroc," the prince's voice softened, "they are not equipped to do more than this. The poor creatures are nocturnal; we have already weakened them by forcing them to adapt to our rhythms."

"On this, we agree, my Prince. How powerful would they become if we allowed them to do what is in their nature to do? Imagine a Rodania that never sleeps. A Council of Arpaks to rule the day, and a Council of Nychts to rule the night."

"This is lunacy," the prince barked.

"Or even better," Balroc forged onward, "a Council in which both are represented equally so that, through cooperation, we can make our nation one of the most advanced on Oriceran. I believe that by empowering Nychts, we can empower Rodania to levels we've not seen before."

"We cannot achieve our goals by handing authority over to a bunch of dull-witted grunts."

"Actually, Ninfa's research has already proven that there is no inferiority in a Nycht's brain or physiology. It's true they have some physical advantages over us, but it is not true that we have any intellectual advantage over them."

"All the more reason not to empower them. The moment we give them equality, they will use it against us."

"Forgive me, but this is antiquated thinking."

"No," Prince Diruk barked. "It is too late for this, Councilman. Maybe at one time we had an opportunity to repair the damage, but we have kept them in their place for far too long. There is too much resentment, too much bitterness. Do not make this mistake. I forbid it."

"You cannot. The Council has already given their permission, as has your father."

"My father will be dead soon," the prince seethed. "Do not make an enemy of me, Councilman."

"I have spoken to Juer; there is hope for the King. He is ill, but he is not an old man. Juer has deployed every resource accessible to him to find a cure." Balroc's voice was soft in the way a pelt of some predatory animal might be soft, cloaking secret teeth.

Toth's heart warmed to the councilman. As he listened to this political banter, his will galvanized.

This pigheaded young prince is in line for the throne? Under his rule, the Nychts will have no hope of ever freeing themselves of Arpak oppression. Prince Diruk's fears revealed enough about his nature to chill Toth's blood. He had even admitted that what they were doing to the Nychts was wrong, but had no intention of ever righting it.

"We want the same thing," Balroc went on. "To protect Rodania, to strengthen her position, and to set her up for future growth."

"Our goals might be the same, but our methods differ

greatly. When I am king, I will ensure that my Council is in all matters aligned with me. Better yet, I will work to bring back the autocracy that made us great nearly a millennium ago. Too many leaders means dissension. It makes Rodania weak."

Balroc did not answer this, and Toth wondered what kind of nonverbal communication has passed between the councilman and the prince.

"When the harpy threat is put down, you'll return the Nycht captains to their place. Do not make the mistake of trusting them." Footsteps echoed down a hall.

Toth stood his ground. He had been eavesdropping, but he hadn't come here intending to do so. He wouldn't hide like he was guilty. The Nycht mercenary crossed his arms and waited.

Prince Diruk strode into the hall of columns. He was tall and statuesque, and his feathers glinted as though dusted with gold powder. His skin was pale and freckled, not unlike Caje's, and hair so blonde it was nearly white caught the firelight thrown by the torches that crackled from the pillars. Dark blue eyes fell on Toth and he did not look away. The two Strix were matched in height and breadth, but Toth had all the presence of a killer, while Diruk embodied the arrogance of the entitled.

Prince Diruk's stride hitched momentarily, the only change that gave away his surprise. He walked up to Toth and stopped in front of him. The Strix stood eye to eye.

"So you're the Nycht traitor who has come licking power from Balroc's boots."

Toth held the prince's gaze. "And you're the tyrant next-in-line. I daresay Rodania needs protection more from you than any harpy threat."

"You *snake*," the prince seethed, stepping so close to Toth the Nycht could smell the spices the Prince must roll in every morning. "You filthy Nycht opportunist. You stink worse than any harpy. Your kind is the scourge that makes Rodania weak." He raised a long finger and jammed it into Toth's breastbone. "When I am king, not only will there be no Nycht army, there will be no Nycht citizens."

"Surely our new captain deserves better treatment than threats and insults." Balroc's voice cut through the prince's stream of bile.

Neither the prince nor Toth looked away. Their eyes bored into one another's skull.

"Come now." The councilman approached and put a hand on the prince's arm. "We have a much more imminent threat to concern ourselves with."

The prince shook off Balroc's hand and stepped back. His face twisted with cruelty and disdain, and his mouth worked. For a moment, Toth thought the prince was going to spit on him.

Prince Diruk turned on his heel, striding from the room of columns. His large golden wings shivered and snapped open as he disappeared behind the marble. The sound of him winging away filled the silence.

"Well," Balroc exhaled, "that was an exciting start to my morning. Please," he gestured toward the hall. "I am eager to hear what you have to say. I hope you will not allow our young prince's words to daunt you."

"Please tell me there is a way Rodania can avoid being ruled by that despot?" Toth asked as he and Balroc walked down a hall lined with paintings. They entered a library, warm from a crackling fire, with tall ceilings and huge, crammed bookcases.

"Alas, he will sit on the throne; the queen had no other children. It is only a matter of time." Balroc poured water from a pitcher and handed Toth a glass before pouring one for himself. "Which is why our move must succeed, and sooner rather than later. If we cannot defeat the harpies before the vote, or if the King dies before the vote takes place…well," Balroc shrugged. "I don't know about you, but I'll be looking for a nice little villa in Maticaw or Operyn."

Toth frowned. Of his eleven siblings, nine of them still lived in Rodania. They had children; their lives were rooted here. They were subject to injustice, but they lived well. They had good food and, up until recently, safety too. If Prince Diruk had his way, his siblings and their children would become refugees.

"So, Toth." Balroc took a seat. "What requests do you have for me? Will you join me in this great ugly game? Are you ready to make a play for Rodania's future?"

Toth sat and faced his unexpected ally. He retrieved the parchment of needs from his breast pocket. "For Rodania's future."

And for my family, the Nycht added silently.

CHAPTER TWELVE

'COMBATANTS! NOW IS YOUR TIME!
   Rodania Needs Defenders & Protectors. Is that You? Are you sick of feeling vulnerable to attack? Would you like to make your family feel safe? Do you think it's time to bring back a Rodanian military? Join the famous mercenaries Toth & Caje Sazak in the battle for freedom from fear!'

Jordan snatched the flier from the lamppost down the street from Juer's library. She was on her way there to do dragon research. Her eyes bulged at the names 'Toth & Caje,' written in large, screaming capital letters.

"Sazak," she said to herself.

She hadn't seen the Nycht since several nights before, when he'd left for the mysterious meeting with a promise that he'd come say goodbye before he left Rodania. Sol told her he'd dropped by the apartment, but he'd been in a hurry and left without seeing her.

Jordan folded the page and crammed it in the small

pocket in the front of her jacket. She strode towards Juer's place, but her mind was on anything but dragon research.

Where is he now? If the poster is to be trusted, Caje is in town, as well. Have other Nychts come back from The Conca to defend their homeland? Where is Toth living? Was the poster Toth's idea?

She couldn't imagine Toth giving his permission to dub himself a 'famous mercenary'; he didn't even like it when other Nychts gave him accolades for his daring move.

Jordan made a decision. She'd spend an hour doing research and then go find Toth. The poster directed potential combatants to a training island on the northwest side of Middle Rodania. Jordan hazarded a guess that if Toth really was involved in this military movement, he'd be on that island, getting ready to train Strix fighters.

The poster made it clear that the fighting positions were voluntary, but didn't mention anything about remuneration. *Surely the government will have to offer Rodanian citizens some kind of pay, for them to spend time training and fighting.* It struck Jordan hot and hard that it didn't really matter if the positions were paid or not; if Toth really was leading some defensive team against harpy attacks, Jordan wanted in. She'd already begged Toth to train her. Apparently, now he'd be training not just her but whoever showed up in response to the poster.

What Jordan couldn't work out was why.

Why would Toth agree to abandon his position at The Conca so suddenly? How had he managed to dissolve his agreement with the humans of The Conca so quickly? He seemed eager to return to his role as Nycht defender, yet within a matter of days, he's changed his mind and decided to stay? It has to be Balroc's influence, whoever he is.

Jordan retrieved the key Sol had given her to Juer's library. He'd told her the doctor wouldn't be there but was happy to allow them access to the library as much as they liked. She wished Sol was there to help her search, but he'd been occupied with deliveries every day since the motley crew had arrived from Trevilsom.

She jiggled the big iron key in the lock and pushed through the gigantic wooden doors. The foyer yawned, dark and dusty before her. Beyond, she could just make out the semi-circular library space she and Sol had visited several weeks before. She secured the door behind her and crossed the marble floors, her footsteps echoing hollowly, making her feel cold and alone. She crossed the library's threshold, where the floor became wooden planking in the shape of a many-petaled flower. She craned her neck up at the books, scanning the massive selection. Her eyes dropped to the first floor where a series of small drawers lined the wall. Jordan made a beeline for the drawers marked with the letter 'D' in beautiful, flowing script. Beside the 'D' on the placard were several other foreign letters.

She opened the first drawer and was greeted with the stale smell of moldy paper and old leather. She sneezed and began to search the titles, walking through the cards with her fingertips.

Her mind kept drifting to the poster tucked in her pocket. *How did it happen?* She would have loved to have been a fly on the wall in the meeting between Balroc and

Toth. *What did the councilman say to convince him to stay? Did he threaten him somehow? Take away Toth's autonomy?*

The catalogue cards flew under Jordan's fingers, until she found a handful beginning with 'Dragon'. Jordan thought Juer could do with a new system for cataloguing his books; perhaps one invented by an Elf and activated through voice control. She made a note to mention it to Sol to pass on to Juer.

One of the things that amazed her the most about Oriceran was its strange blend of magical technology alongside an archaic way of life. Rodania had a magical barrier that (until recently) was believed to be impenetrable, and yet one had to spend ages with a nose shoved into a dusty old drawer like some stuffy academic, just to find a book. She shook her head and closed the drawer, a collection of cards in her hand.

She spied the gigantic wooden lever hidden in a recess between shelves, and reached for it before remembering what Sol had said about the updraft system––that it would send all of Juer's research flying. She withdrew her hand.

"Guess I'll do this the hard way," she mumbled. Eyeballing the number on the first card, she gave tight, powerful flaps to lift herself vertically along the cylinder of the library. Hovering was hard to do without jouncing and bobbing jerkily, but Jordan was getting the hang of it. Her eyes homed in on the numbering system, which was on the edges of the wooden shelves as well as the books themselves. This seemed foolhardy, unless Juer never planned to add or take away from his collection.

She snagged three of the books and let herself drift down to the landing on the first level, where she spread the books out on a table. She plopped on a stool and opened the first volume.

Her wings drooped. It was beautifully illustrated, but not written in English——though the title was simple and deceiving: *Dragon, Draconi, Dragosus,* followed by some scrawl that looked like upside down Greek. She shoved the book away and tried the next--*Draco ex Speciebus Oriceran*, which, if she wasn't mistaken, sounded an awful lot like Latin. A quick flip showed more Latin, but also a second column in an old form of English. There were a lot of *'ye's* and *'auld's* and *'fyre's*.

Jordan scanned the color drawings of various species, but her heart sank as she realized just how in over her head she was. The dragons all looked the same, yet different. This one had the same horns as Blue, but three forks in its tongue. That one had Blue's coloring, but the eyes were much more bulbous. After half an hour of this frustrating confusion, Jordan slammed the book shut and shoved it away from her, frowning.

The third book was no better.

She blew out a big sigh. *I can't do this alone. There has to be a better way.* She decided to talk to Sol about it more when she saw him next. Maybe he knew someone who could help, without giving away their predicament.

Jordan gathered up the books, returned them and the cards to their rightful place, and left the library, locking it up tight behind her. She took a running leap off the walkway and took to the air, catching the wind and sailing straight for the northwest corner of Rodania.

The training islands were not far off the coast of Middle Rodania. Three of them, circular and looking a lot like floating football fields, hovered in a staggered way, just like the large Rodanian islands. Jordan wondered what it had cost to have the Light Elves make these islands, or if there was an agreement as Rodania expanded to provide more territory as needed.

Two of the islands were vacant; nothing but circles of low vegetation, dirt, and dark square shapes. As she drew near, Jordan's eyes homed in on two square shapes—trunks, likely full of equipment.

The third island was crawling with Strix, mostly Nychts. Jordan spotted Toth's silver hair and made a beeline for him. She came in for a landing at a run. Toth's arms bulged as he carried a wooden box that looked very heavy for its size. His eyes lit up when he saw her.

"Jordan! I'm sorry, I haven't had a chance to find you." His eyes were apologetic. "How's your father? Any change?"

"The same thanks." Jordan took the folded poster from her vest and unfolded it, hanging it out for Toth to see. "As for not coming to find me, that's okay. I can see you've been a little busy."

Toth's eyes widened at the poster, then narrowed as he scanned the words. He glowered and set the trunk down, snatching the page out of her hand. " 'Famous Nycht mercenaries'?" Toth growled. "He's good at the propaganda, I'll give him that much."

"Balroc?" Jordan guessed.

Toth nodded and shoved the page back at her. "I left the publicizing up to him. Apparently my guideline was not specific enough."

"Which guideline?"

"Not to use my name, or Caje's."

"That's pretty specific."

"You'd think so." Toth shouted instructions at a pair of burly Nychts carrying more trunks across the scrubby grass of the island.

"He also used your last name," Jordan pointed out, following Toth as he delivered the small trunk to a low wooden table.

Toth grunted.

"I was thinking," she said as she folded up the poster, "just how little I really know about you, Toth. After everything we've been through together. I didn't even know your last name."

"I don't have a last name." His face grew dark, and he shot a wary eye at Jordan.

"It says 'Sazak' on the poster. Is that a mistake?"

"I am no longer associated with that name."

"But it used to be your last name?"

"Jordan, I don't have time for this."

"Yet another layer of mystery added. Oh, how little I really know the Nycht I'll be forever indebted to. Why don't you have a last name anymore?"

"You're not indebted to me, and it's a very long story."

"I'm sure it is." Jordan threw an arm over his shoulders. "I was wondering, Mister No-Last-Name, what could possibly have happened to you in the last several days to make you completely abandon your commitments to the people of The Conca, and take up the sword for Rodania. You hate Rodania."

"I don't hate Rodania, this place is my homeland. I just

hate the inequality here. I also hate harpies. And I apologize, but I don't have time to go over the intricacies of my decision-making process at the moment. I have a lot to do before training begins."

"Which is when?"

Jordan released Toth. It was apparent he was not in the mood for levity or prying. Once again, she found herself unsure of where she stood with him. Was she a friend or a pest? The man's emotions were impossible to read, sealed off in the steel trap inside him.

"Tomorrow."

"Where do I sign up?"

Toth didn't even blink. "There is no signing up, just show up ready to work."

"Anytime?"

"Whenever you've breakfasted. The earlier the better." He turned to a Nycht carrying an armload of wooden javelins with blunted tips. "Over there, by Chayla," he directed the fellow. The metal of the weapons gleamed in the sun, looking brand new.

"Need help setting up?"

Toth shot Jordan a blazing smile at this offer of assistance. "You're not too busy?"

"Last time I checked."

"Great. Follow me."

Jordan followed Toth through a crowd of working Strix, mostly Nychts, who were laboring together to set up the training space. Wooden dummies as well as stuffed straw targets were scattered about on the grass. Big, muscular Nychts pounded stakes into the ground where small red flags had been erected. There was the clang of metal on metal as Strix sparred playfully with each other.

"This is Chayla," Toth said, stopping in front of a fierce female Nycht seated on a low, flat stone. She was bent over a blade, which lay across her knee. The woman looked up with a glower and cast the Arpak a gleaming white snarl, revealing sharp eye teeth that looked a touch too long. She looked downright predatory.

"Chayla, this is Jordan."

Chayla's eyes raked Jordan from head to foot. Jordan thought she might actually be shrinking under this Nycht's gaze. She studied the Nycht as the Nycht studied her. Chayla had sharp high cheekbones, lean, square, muscular arms and thick, fleshy wings as black as night. Her dewclaws were long and thin and gleamed like obsidian, and her moss green eyes were large and calculating. Not everything about her was dark, though. She wore a pale leather vest with rough edges, stitched together unevenly with fat thread. Jordan wondered if the Nycht made her own clothes. A small silver hoop glistened from the woman's nose, and her dark brown hair was clipped short and stuck out in all directions. Chayla's nails were filed to points.

Everything about her screamed *'Don't mess with me'*.

"Chayla is filing the burrs off these blades. They've only recently been forged and won't be ready to use until they've been cleaned up." Toth picked up a sanding stone from a collection of them near Chayla's booted foot. "If you can give her a hand, it would be greatly appreciated."

Chayla stopped what she was doing and stared at Toth

with a look broaching horror. "*Greatly appreciated?*" Her voice was thick and strangely accented.

Toth ignored Chayla, gave Jordan a pat on the shoulder and strode away, leaving the two women to tackle a mountain of freshly forged blades of all shapes and sizes.

"So," Jordan sat down on the grass next to Chayla and picked up a rough blade from the pile, laying it across her lap the way Chayla had done. "How do you know Toth?" Jordan picked up a stone, dipped it in the bucket of water on the ground, and began to file away the metal burrs.

"Don't talk to me, Arpak," replied Chayla with a curl of her upper lip. She made *'Arpak'* sound like a dirty word. "Just get to work."

"Okay then," Jordan said under her breath. She pressed her lips together, bent over the blade, and did just that.

CHAPTER THIRTEEN

Days later, the training ground was a paradox of sounds as the sporadic clang and ring of steel on steel provided a counter rhythm to the gusty sound of wings flapping. Jordan knew why she was here—-to train with Toth, who had agreed to spend some one-on-one time with her—-but she couldn't help feeling like she was just a starry-eyed spectator.

All around and above her, Strix sparred and trained, spiralling, swooping, and generally looking stunning as they moved with mastery of all three dimensions. Jordan, with just enough experience from her days training in martial arts, appreciated how they could move with such grace, even as they lashed out with spear, sword, and limb.

She stifled a gasp as she watched Chayla spar with another Nycht. The woman snatched a spear thrown at her out of the air, just to spin into a dive going after her opponent.

Toth followed her gaze. "Impressed?"

The mercenary stood in front of her with a staff of

polished wood in each hand. The ends of each staff were capped with bulbs of stitched leather. Sparring rods.

Jordan blushed. She had been gawking.

"Maybe they will be there to save you." A ghost of a smile tugged at his mouth. "But just in case, let's see what we can teach you."

He tossed the staff to her, and without preamble they began.

It was simple footwork and body positioning at first. He wanted to see her move, judge her balance. Could she track an opponent and keep her footing sound? Could she advance or withdraw fluidly, move quickly, without sacrificing stability? Did she keep her eyes on her opponent, still maintaining peripheral awareness, or did she stare at her feet? Thanks to her martial arts training, she managed to keep her guard up and move to match Toth's footwork.

"Good," he nodded. "But what if we stop dancing?"

Without warning, he made a quick overhead chop with his staff.

Jordan brought her staff around in a wide grip, stopping the stroke cold.

Her eyes slid from the quivering staff, over her head to Toth's face, and she saw something that surprised her.

Fear? Impossible, Toth has gone head-to-head with monsters with a smile on his face. He isn't threatened by anything, least of all me.

Toth spun the staff away, and she shifted into a vigilant stance. Wordlessly, he came for her, this time springing lightly into a thrust with the padded end of the staff. She was on her guard, so her staff snapped out and deflected the strike smoothly.

Again, she saw it—that anxious widening of his features—and then she recognized it for what it was.

Not fear *of* her, fear *for* her. Toth did not want to hurt her, not even a training bruise.

"Toth," she said, lowering her guard.

"Eh," he grunted.

"You need to stop babying me."

A sheepish look crossed his face, then he nodded in agreement. "You're right, of course."

She raised her staff.

As Toth came at her again, this time with a side-stepping sweep at her legs, Jordan determined she wasn't going to let one of his words or blows be wasted. Her forward foot shot up and came back down as soon as the sweep passed. Her staff shot downward and warded off the return blow. As soon as Toth's staff withdrew, she was back to guard, rod up, eyes on her opponent.

For the rest of the day, her training followed this pattern. Toth would move and she would follow, until he sprang to the attack, and she would have to defend. Occasionally, he would give some critique or advice, but never would he congratulate her footing or deflection after a particularly punishing series of blows.

Little by little, he pressed her to attack back, to drive off his aggression with some of her own.

As the sun began to set, Toth had her defend herself from aerial attacks. He swooped and dove upon her, which was truly terrifying at first, though she got the hang of it after falling over a few times. As the sky turned to bruised shades of purple, he had her in the air herself, her wings beating in time with her laboring heart. It was a new level of exertion, but also of exhilaration. She really did love flying; even if she had to protect herself from getting battered as she did so.

As the night came on in earnest, Jordan's shoulders and legs burned. Her back ached, and her hands prickled with numbness. It was a good, honest kind of pain, but it was still pain, and she was glad the training session was over.

The next morning was agony, as was every morning after that for a very long time.

Just when Jordan thought she was developing some mastery with the staff, Toth threw her a curveball––or more accurately, a blunt mace.

Jordan's hand flashed up to catch the training weapon. She hefted it in her hand, feeling its weight. It was a shaft of rough wood, with leather wrapped around one end and a weighted cosh-head at the other. The simple weapon felt more ungainly in her hand than the staff, even though it was only a little over half the staff's length.

"I thought I was doing well with the staff." She eyed the bludgeon dubiously.

"You thought so?" Toth had a way of making Jordan feel like a little girl; like she wanted to crouch behind a wing and hide. "Let's see how you do with this." He produced his own mace with a flourish, putting the muscular control of his hands on display.

Jordan fought to keep a twinge of jealousy at bay. Toth moved the weapon like he had eyes in every finger, like the mace was an extension of his own body.

Toth began probing her defenses with lunging footwork and shallow swipes.

Over the next several weeks, a pattern emerged. Toth started with Jordan in the morning, but as the sun crested, he would send her to train with her fellow combatants, always someone different. It was an endless round-robin; mostly of humiliation.

Jordan would wake with a whole new batch of muscle cramps and soreness, and drag her carcass out to the training grounds. Toth would hand her a new weapon and take her through the paces.

She went through an assortment of bludgeons and blades, axes and pole-arms, shortswords and javelins. The young Arpak never imagined there were so many varieties of death-dealing. Some weapons were an exercise in pure frustration. Axes…Jordan learned a deep loathing for those vicious implements. Toth showed her that the axehead's downward edge––what the Nycht referred to as the *'beard'*––could hook and ensnare in an insidious variety of ways. She would have been impressed if he wasn't demonstrating all this on her.

She knew that Toth was just trying to test both her aptitude and her will, tempering her with sweat and frustration. She never quit and walked away, but on axe day, she came very close.

On a warm, cloudless day, Toth put two blunt spikes of metal in her hands, each a little more than a foot long. They were unfinished iron, pitted, with simple wooden hilts.

"Training daggers," Toth said simply, and then he was lunging after her, the paired knives darting and slashing.

To both Jordan's and Toth's amazement, she took to those ugly little blades like a fish to water. Responding with sharper reflexes and an ease that she had thus far displayed with no other weapon, Jordan weaved a menacing web of steel.

Soon, without prompting, she was on the offensive; her eyes finding perfect openings, measuring the moments right. The blunt tips and rounded edges of the training daggers crept closer and closer to Toth's skin.

How one thrust flowed into a deflection was what thrilled and drove her forward, even when her muscles screamed for oxygen. Every weapon thus far had seemed too slow to allow her to do much else besides shimmy between attack or defend.

Not so the daggers.

They danced in her hands. She was attacking and defending, moving fluidly without hesitation. Her eyes received information, and her brain processed, her body responded without conscious thought.

They stayed with the blades, and Toth did not have to explain why. He'd been exposing her to many different weapons to figure out what she had an aptitude for––the way parents put young kids in gymnastics, then soccer, then hockey, then chess. How does the kid know what they are drawn to unless they get to try a little of everything?

As they fell into a ground-based flurry of cut and countercut, Toth made a scissoring lunge, wings flapping for impetus. On instinct, she leapt, her wings pulling at the air in complementary strokes. She tucked her feet and rose clear over the oncoming blades. Then she drove her feet out, each leg entwining the Nycht's sinew-corded arms.

She brought her blades, flashing, to either side of his neck. Her wings beat, dragging them both off the ground. There was a thud of metal on grass as the wrenching force broke Toth's grip on his own blades.

Her heartbeat thudding in her ears, she and Toth hung suspended in the air. A grin crossed the mercenary's face. He thwacked her thigh with a palm in compliment.

She released him, and they began again.

Later, they took a short rest for water. After splashing his face and rubbing the cool liquid through his short, silver beard and over his spiky hair, Toth met her eyes. "Now *that*," he said with that same open grin, "that was doing well."

Jordan's heart thrilled at the praise, something not easily won from the Nycht and never before so plainly stated.

She had found her weapon: daggers. Gone were the days of needing to be rescued, of feeling vulnerable and reliant. Toth was teaching her to fight, but there was a whole host of emotional and mental benefits that came along with that.

Unlike most days, Toth continued to train her through the afternoon, rather than leaving her to try her new skills against her fellow combatants. Before the sun set that day, they were chasing each other through the air, much the same as any of the other natural-born Strix. Her stamina wasn't yet on par with those born with wings, but with the daggers in hand, she moved with a confidence and quickness that made her feel nearly equal.

The next day, a long table had been set up on one side of the island. Arrayed across it was a vast collection of blades; some the length of her forearm, others little more than a hand's breadth. Some were thin needles of steel, while others were crescent fangs of flared metal. Beyond the table was a series of targets, arranged in a wide semi-circle——similar to the ones she had seen the other warriors training with, only thinner and smaller.

"Your patience pays off now." Toth gestured to the various blades. "You are going to learn how to knife-fight, near and far."

"Far?"

"Knife-throwing is an excellent discipline, even against the longer reaching weapons, if one is skilled." Toth picked up a small blade with a triangular shape and short handle. "Where harpies are concerned, normal rules don't apply. A harpy, especially a female, is too large for you to engage up close unless absolutely necessary. And so..."

With a flick of his wrist, Toth sent the small knife zipping to embed its head in the nearest target. "You are going to need to learn how to not be so close."

They set to accomplishing this.

Jordan began to divide her days between practicing her throws on the small targets, and learning about the kinds of knives available. She learned which were best for strictly throwing, which were suitable for either throwing or fighting hand-to-hand, and which could never be thrown, but were to be worn at the hip in a sheath or strapped within easy reach.

She learned the difference between a dirk and a rondel, why the rondel was excellent for delivering a final thrust to the heart or skull, and why, in the frantic cut and thrust game, the dirk was superior. If one needed to remove bony parts—-arms, finger, vertebrae—-the khukuri was king. There was an entire world of vocabulary to learn, concerning quillons, tangs, fullers, crossguards, and so many other words.

Jordan also had to learn not to think too hard about what the emotional effects might be of delivering damage with any one of these weapons. Learning the theory through training was fun, but would she be able to cut and gouge and slash and throw when it came right down to it? She thought about the harpies who had chased her and Blue over the ocean toward Maticaw, herding them toward land where they could deliver killing blows and leave their carcasses to rot.

Yes, she thought she could do what was needed against one of those repugnant beasts.

She spent days learning new habits, unlearning bad habits, and relearning things which she somehow managed to forget along the way. She found satisfaction in a well-sunk blade. New instincts took root.

There were other times Toth seemed determined to drive her insane with his constant corrections, his insistence that she alter her grip just so. The way he did it so calmly, too, as though it were so easy to make these fractional changes in the midst of wrenching acrobatics. It was infuriating.

In those moments, just as she was about to lose her temper, she would have a breakthrough. Then, like cogs clicking in her brain, so many other things in her training slid into place.

Yet what she lived for, even on those most difficult days, was the time they spent training in the air. When they were not darting and banking above the training ground to the clamor of clashing steel, Jordan and Toth would sail around the islands, with Toth throwing out thin wooden discs the size of dinner plates. It was her job to sink a knife as close to the center of these as possible.

She missed a lot. In fact, she missed all the time.

Again, just when she was close to giving up, she threw and struck. The blade did not sink in, but it was a step in the right direction and gave her a renewed energy. She began to hit the target regularly. The blade would spin away, flashing in the morning sun, and the cycle would repeat.

Then, one magical day, the blade sank home. Then it began to sink home more often than not. Then every time. Then she began to focus on getting the blades closer to the center of the plates.

As her skill increased, Toth had her focus on combining her draw and throw into one smooth movement.

"This is perhaps the greatest tool of the knife-fighter," he said as he demonstrated the movements in slow-motion. "Putting a knife in your target before he even knows you are armed can end fights before they begin."

"Could I really drop a harpy with one knife? Throwing blades seem too small for that."

Toth returned the knife to a sheath on his shoulder, only to send it hurtling into a target in the blink of an eye. "With a larger female, it would have to be a good clean shot. Even a bolt from a winched crossbow is no guarantee. Instead, aim to cripple, blind, or hinder. The distraction can give you time to either get away, or find a better position. Move first. Mobility is your first priority.

Compromise your enemy's and utilize yours. That is the way to make sure you get home and they get dead."

Jordan had become accustomed to chilling words such as these. When Toth changed out the wooden discs for dummy harpies stuffed with straw, Jordan's skill accelerated. She could call shots and reliably sink the blade home, even when Toth made the target swing.

In spite of the sense of pride and accomplishment, burying knife after knife into those dummies and seeing their wooden bodies shudder put one scary fact into her head on a daily basis: one day, it wouldn't just be targets at the end of her blades.

CHAPTER FOURTEEN

"Ow," Jordan squeaked as she stretched out flat on her back. Early morning light filtered through the tall, narrow windows and across the bedroom floor. Sounds of someone moving around in the kitchen lifted her head. She winced as her neck muscles protested. Looking around the room, she saw only Allan's form on the bed. Sol's mattress was an empty tangle of sheets and quilts.

He had arranged for three mattresses to be delivered to his apartment for Eohne, himself, and Jordan. Eohne's mattress was on the far side of Allan's bed, invisible from where Jordan lay. Jordan's mattress was on the floor beside the bed, and Sol's was under the window. At night, the bedroom floor between the bed and the window was a tangle of blankets, limbs, and feathers.

"Eohne?" Jordan pushed herself up to sitting.

No answer.

So the Elf is already up. My life has gotten so weird, she mused as she made her way to standing. Weeks had passed since her training had begun, and, as she did every morning, she stretched side to side and took inventory of her bones and muscles.

Most of her body ached, but it was an ache she was getting used to. She was also getting stronger by the day. At first, she had disliked the hand-to-hand combat. It was intimidating, and she had no faith in her own abilities. But slowly, as she did more drills and faced off with different combatants, her confidence grew. She had reached a point where she didn't feel anxiety every morning at the thought of training, but excitement. *What new skill will I master today? What will I learn?* Jordan knew she'd never be the force that Toth, Sol, or Chayla were, but she was becoming skilled in her own way.

How will I fare against a harpy?

It was the unanswered question, and not something they could simulate very well. Jordan could meet many a fellow combatant in the air, but the truth was that no Strix was as big and terrifying as a harpy. The fear of such a confrontation had given Jordan nightmares. But as her confidence grew, she found herself almost eager to try her hand against one of the hideous creatures. Almost.

She stepped over piles of scattered armor and underthings and chided herself for not doing a better job of keeping the small room neat and tidy. She wasn't alone in this; both Sol and Eohne left odds and ends scattered about. The mess made the apartment seem even smaller. There just wasn't enough room for the four of them.

Jordan made her way to the water closet, saying good morning to Eohne, who was holding something over a burner with a pair of tongs. A thin stream of green smoke drifted up from the stove. The Elf grunted, but didn't look up. Jordan smiled. At one time, she would have asked Eohne to explain what she was doing, but every day she was doing something different, and bothering her just made the Elf grumpy.

The Elf and the Arpak had developed a sisterly relationship, and Eohne didn't hesitate to tell Jordan to go away when she was working.

Jordan stepped over an open trunk with jars of strange looking contents spilling out of it. She made sure to lift her wings so she didn't knock any of the glass over, and send something magical and valuable spilling across the floor.

She'd once shared an apartment with a roommate in her second year of college, after having lived on her own and realizing she was lonely. But they'd each had their own bedroom and a sprawling study and den to use as they wished. Jordan's current living situation was a more close-quartered and spartan setup than any she'd had in her young, privileged life. Her grandparents would have been horrified, but Jordan was pleasantly surprised by how well she tolerated it. It felt as though she, Eohne, Sol, and her unconscious father had formed some odd yet functional family unit.

What surprised her even more was how well Sol was taking to the situation. When they'd first met, she would never have thought the prickly Arpak would be so hospitable, but Sol had happily provided everything they needed. Fresh food was delivered every third day by a plump and cheerful Nycht lady, and whenever Eohne needed something for her formulas, Sol did his level best to get it for her.

The threesome had fallen into a routine. Sol was up at

the crack of dawn and out of the apartment for work. Sometimes he was away for days at a time. Jordan usually woke to sunlight streaming in the window and limped around the apartment, sorting out breakfast and getting ready for another day of training, while Eohne looked after Allan by keeping him nourished and his limbs moving. Jordan didn't know how the Elf did her kind of magic, but she was constantly scribbling strange glyphs in a ragged notebook and using the kitchen counter to do small-scale experiments.

Jordan had watched her one evening, staying quiet and sitting out of the way, trying to discern what the Elf was up to. But often, the Elf tuned in to some invisible, inner magic. Eohne might extract some juice from a seed, apply fire and a tiny pinch of a sparkling white powder to make some strange substance, then put a drop on her finger and close her eyes, sometimes for several minutes at a time. Jordan often grew bored of this and just left the Elf to her work.

As busy days passed, worry for Allan never abated. If Eohne hadn't emanated such calm during all of this experimentation, Jordan would have suffered from extreme anxiety and sleepless nights. But she trusted the Elf. Whether she was lulled into faith by the Elf's own calm demeanor, or the Elf secretly ministered Jordan with some magic to keep her from freaking out, the Arpak didn't question. Focusing on learning how to fight kept Jordan occupied and exhausted.

When Sol was home, he'd drill Jordan with questions. What was Toth teaching her? Which weapons was she learning? What kinds of drills were they doing? How were the other combatants doing? How many were there? Had they started to talk strategy yet?

"Why don't you stop by?" Jordan suggested one evening, as they were cleaning up from dinner. "You're so interested in what's going on with the army, and I'm too tired to tell you. When you have time, just come out to the training islands."

Sol considered this. "You don't think Toth would mind?"

"Why would he?"

Sol shrugged. "He's got his own way of doing things. I'm not part of the army."

"So?"

Sol finished drying a ceramic plate and slid it into place over the washbasin. He eyed Jordan. "Maybe I will."

"Good. For the life of me, I can't figure out why you haven't come by already. You ask me a million questions almost every night."

"I learned to fight at the Academy," Sol explained. "Couriers are one of the few classes of Strix who continued to train for combat even after the original army was dismantled centuries ago." He shrugged. "I worry that my style and Toth's might clash, or that I'll see him doing something I disagree with and won't be able to keep my mouth shut. I was trained to fight solo; he's training you to fight in teams."

"Why did they dismantle the army?"

"After so many peaceful centuries, it became clear that a military was an unnecessary expense. Nothing could get through the Light Elves' magic barriers, or so we thought. The government was paying all of these Nychts to train——

feeding them, arming them––and nothing ever happened."

"Only Nychts?"

"Soldiers are considered laborers, and Nychts are considered better fliers. Also, their night vision and sonar makes them a force in the dark."

"But, no Arpaks at all?" Jordan pulled the plug from the sink drain and wiped her hands on a towel.

Sol shook his head. "That's how it's always been."

"And what do you think of that?" Jordan narrowed her eyes at Sol. She'd never asked him point-blank about the inequality among Strix before. It was something she'd always wanted to broach with him, but if she was really honest, she was afraid she wouldn't like his answer.

"It's wrong." Sol said simply.

Jordan stared. "You think it's wrong?"

"I know it is." He took the last wet dish from the drying rack, swiping over it with his towel. "I know it's wrong only because I've been through the Academy. They crammed so much history and studies of other cultures down our throats in school that I began to see a pattern. Where there is inequality, there is bitterness, and where there is bitterness there is weakness." A line appeared between his brows. "Rodania is weak because of it."

"How come you never did anything about it?"

"Do what?" Sol put the dish away and faced Jordan, leaning against the tile countertop. His wings tightened, and his primary feathers sprayed out sideways across the floor. "I'm trained to deliver messages and negotiate if I must. I'm trained not to let anything stop me on the way to delivering these messages; not harpies, not foul weather, not assassins, not distance or harsh terrain or any language barrier. But I'm not a politician," he held his palms out in a gesture of helplessness. "What could I do about it?"

"You could run for Council. Could you not go into politics if you wanted to? You could affect real change as a councilmember."

"I don't have those kinds of skills."

"It sounds to me like you do," Jordan replied.

Sol frowned, and his eyes cast downward to the floor.

Jordan suddenly felt bad, like she had made Sol feel guilty for having chosen the wrong path.

"I'm sorry." She stepped close to Sol and looked into his eyes. "Don't listen to me." She put her hands on his arms, wanting to wipe the expression from his face. It looked too much like shame. There was no reason Sol should be ashamed of anything. He'd been so kind and generous to her and Allan and Eohne. She felt her own shame heat her cheeks and wished she'd never said anything.

Sol lifted his eyes. There was pain there, and it sliced into Jordan like a hot blade.

"You're right, Jordan. Maybe I chose the wrong path. Maybe I could have done something when I realized all those years ago in the Academy that something was wrong. Maybe I could have changed it."

Jordan shook her head and put her palms on Sol's cheeks. "No," she said fiercely. "I shouldn't have said anything. I'm sorry. You're doing just what you should be doing, and you love your work. Don't let my stupid words make you feel like less than what you are. You are meant to be a courier for King and country."

"Am I?" Sol looked troubled, but his face softened at her

touch. "I'm having all these thoughts now that I've never had before."

"Thoughts?" Jordan's hands dropped from his face to his shoulders.

"Yes. Like maybe there *is* something I can do, I just haven't figured it out yet."

His eyes dropped to her lips, and he blinked as though realizing just how close their faces were.

Jordan became conscious of Sol's shoulders under her palms, his warmth, his breath. She could see the tiny braids threaded through his hair, and the details of the stubble shrouding his jaw. Her face warmed, and she made to step back––but his hands closed around her waist. He pulled her closer, moving his weight away from the counter. His wings flexed outward, blocking Jordan's periphery.

All she could see was him.

She tilted her face up to his. When their lips touched, Jordan melted. Her arms slid around his neck, as his snaked around her lower back. Her own wings flexed outward, meeting his. Their primary feathers tangled as they kissed inside their own little cocoon. The air grew hot.

"Hey, Sol, I was hoping…"

Eohne's voice broke them apart. Jordan stepped back, snapping her wings shut. The Arpaks looked at the Elf, appearing for all the world like two kids caught stealing candy. A grin broke across her face and then disappeared, leaving behind dimples of suppressed mirth.

"I just-–um…forgot something in the bedroom." The Elf disappeared again.

Jordan and Sol had looked at each other sheepishly, but the moment was broken. They smiled shyly.

"Guess I should see what Eohne needs," Sol finally murmured.

Jordan had nodded and tucked an errant strand of hair behind her ear, squashing an intense desire to throttle the Elf.

That kiss had happened over a week ago now, and neither of the Arpaks had brought it up. They had hardly seen one another over the past several days, as Sol was kept busy running messages for Prince Diruk, and Jordan was focused on her training.

As for Blue, the reptile had continued to grow at an alarming rate, and Jordan had become accustomed to seeing him only every few days, as his need for larger prey took him abroad. At first, she worried that the dragon would make dinner of the livestock on Lower Rodania, but Blue was too smart for that.

In fact, Jordan suspected that Blue understood the risk, as he could no longer be classified as 'miniature'. He seemed to come home most nights under cover of darkness——the scales on his belly stretched over some meal he'd hunted down miles from Rodania, likely north of Maticaw.

Blue was too big to sleep in the bedroom with the rest of them, so he curled up on the terrace, his long tail dangling down the stone wall toward the canopy below. Sometimes Jordan would join him there and fall asleep against the rise and fall of his belly.

This is how life went, for a time.

CHAPTER FIFTEEN

When the signal came, it came too late. The sun hoisted itself into the highest position it would reach that day, sending its unforgiving glare down on Rodania. Jordan thought later that if the attack had come at dusk or during the night, there would have been even more casualties.

She was on the training grounds, her stomach empty and growling for food, going through her aerial drills. She recognized a broad-winged shape nearing the training island from the direction of Upper Rodania.

As Sol approached, Jordan drifted to the ground.

"You finally came." She sheathed her knives. "I was beginning to think you never would."

"I had a quick delivery this morning and have a few hours to myself." Sol landed beside her and watched the skies where Strix continued training. A frown marred the Arpak's handsome face. "Is this all of them?"

"More or less; there might be a few missing."

"So few," Sol's voice sounded heavy.

"I told you there were only about three hundred. You forgot?" Jordan turned to follow Sol's gaze where a pair of Nychts wrestled in the sky.

"No, it's just that seeing them really drives it home. Where's Toth?"

"There." She pointed to where the mercenary stood on a far island, coaching a cluster of Strix on tight-quarters combat.

"He's not spending so much time with you anymore?"

"I know the drills now. We rotate partners. This morning I had Chayla, but--" she shrugged. "She hates me, so…" Her eyes tracked to the dark-winged Nycht, where she was throwing short spears with her back to them.

"I'm sure she doesn't *hate* you." Sol's hands drifted to the hilts at his own hips, as though he wanted to join in. "What kind of signals has Toth set up?"

"Every combatant takes a turn as a scout. He's outlined converging flight-paths around Rodania, and everyone gets one of these," she held up a small round device with three holes in it, which hung around her neck. "It's silent, but sends a pulse out to warn of an impending attack. We practiced with it a couple times. It feels weird; your ears pop, and your bones vibrate." She eyed the device dubiously. "It's not pleasant. It's amazing how such a small thing can be so annoying."

Sol reached for it, when his eyes caught on a rapidly growing series of black wounds in an otherwise unmarred sky. His cheeks paled. "The system has a major flaw. Blow that thing," he snapped, then bellowed at the top of his lungs. "Harpies!"

Jordan whipped around, feeling the blood draining

from her skull. As she turned, someone blew the alarm, and her ears popped. An angry hive of hornets seemed to take up residence in the base of her spine, and she clenched her teeth against the sensation.

Combatants moved liked a collection of marbles, rolling down an incline, winging their way to a central beacon on the main training island––Toth.

"Jordan, go back to the apartment." Sol's words had a pleading tone. He'd drawn a blade.

"What?" She shot Sol a look of horror. "Why would I do that? This is what we've been training for. You want me to *hide*? Are you nuts?"

"You're not ready." Sol seemed on the edge of desperation. "Go, now. Please!"

"We talked about this," Jordan snapped. " 'You have as much right as anyone to defend your new home,'" she mimicked, throwing his own words back at him. They'd had the conversation weeks before, when Jordan asked him how he felt about her taking up the sword. She hadn't been asking for his permission, only his thoughts. "Was that a lie?"

"No." Sol swallowed, his eyes on the approaching cluster of harpies. "I meant it; it's just too soon."

"You don't even know what I'm capable of!"

Jordan bit the words off, her face flushing with red. *How dare he ask me to turn tail and run?* She took off and joined her fellow fighters.

Toth was shouting orders, and squadrons of Strix were winging their way into the sky, positioning themselves for battle.

Sol followed Jordan. The depth of his fear for her took him by surprise.

Toth was bellowing instructions that made no sense to Sol, so he hovered, blades drawn, and watched as Jordan winged off with a squadron. The sun glinted on her bright yellow wings as she went, and Sol felt a cold dread settle in his stomach, like he'd swallowed a stone. He caught Toth's eye, and the Nycht flashed him a surprised look of recognition.

Toth drew his own blades as the last squadron flew straight up to level off between Upper Rodania and the approaching horde.

"You're with me," Toth bellowed to Sol.

The familiar stink of carrion reached their noses. Sol darted to hover at the Nycht's right-hand and squinted his eyes against the sun. "The objective?"

"Keep them from reaching the city. Fight in a minimum of two." Toth tucked his chin down and braced himself against a gust of wind laced with the smell of harpy. "And don't die."

"Right," Sol said under his breath.

He forced worried thoughts of Jordan out of his mind and responded to Toth's sudden forward flight. Sol picked up speed, chose a target, and brought his weapon to bear. The harpies, several dozen strong and a mix of males and females, were suddenly there, filling the air with screeching cries, stinking bodies, and bellowing wings.

Only half a kilometer away, three harpies came shrieking toward Jordan and her fellow warriors. The world exploded into a chaos of deadly, winged missiles in a three-dimensional world. Jordan had no time for real terror, only action. Her thoughts numbed and became a quiet voice in the background. She knew the theory of aerial combat now. Any doubts that had haunted her nights evaporated as the battle struck.

She couldn't help screaming as she dodged a set of raking talons. She wished it sounded fierce, like the cry of a valkyrie, but even in her own ringing ears, it sounded like the shriek of a woman trying not to die.

She banked up from a dive, a throwing knife in her hand, but the harpy was sweeping wide, and a group of Strix and harpies locked in combat came into her field of fire. She didn't trust herself not to strike one of the Strix. She gripped the knife in her hand hard enough to make her fingers hurt, and gave a snarl of frustration.

The harpy she'd dodged took its time circling back, seeming to mock her by dragging out the wait. Somewhere amidst the sudden sensory overload and the wild exhilaration, she exercised the patience Toth was constantly on about. She'd wait and ambush the oncoming harpy with a series of thrown blades.

Her plan, or a facsimile thereof, might have worked, but she was hit from behind and sent tumbling downward. Pain laced through her wings, and a cry tore from her throat. Something clutched her wings as she fell, and Jordan tried frantically to beat them, craning her neck to lay eyes on the thing holding her.

A small male clutched her primary feathers with his

talons, mere centimeters from her skin. Together they fell, spiralling, unable to arrest their gathering momentum. The towers, terraces, and gardens of Middle Rodania pinwheeled into view. Her wings jerked painfully where the joints attached to her shoulders. With her throwing knife in hand, Jordan stabbed upward.

She thrust wildly with her blade, flailing desperately. Then steel met flesh, and the thing at her back shrieked and loosened his grip.

Some of her cheerful yellow feathers went spinning away.

Talons. Poison. The thoughts whispered through her brain and were gone again as Jordan broke free of the beast's grip. He hadn't punctured her, but it had been very close.

Her wings snapped wide to catch a cushioning of air. Warm, wet spatters on her face made her think rain was coming, until she swiped at her eyes with a gloved hand and saw blood darken her leather. She grimaced. *At least it's not mine.*

Jordan slowed her momentum as a jutting rooftop came up sharply. It rose too quickly to avoid, and she tucked in her wings to hit and roll. There was the cracking sound of tiles breaking, and a sliding sound as they fell from the roof, tumbling into the streets below. Jordan hoped there was no one in the streets below the falling tiles.

The battle was not supposed to have made it this far east; Toth's directive was to keep it west of the city. *So much for that.*

She caught herself in the air as she dropped off the edge

of the roof. She was aware of her bones hitting against something hard, and of having no pain––only the dull sensation of thuds. Shock, and then the world was turning. Her senses were not entirely convinced that she wasn't still spinning end over end. She twisted to find her harpy pursuer, and a cloud of stinking feathers across her face sent her tumbling a second time.

Why am I suddenly alone?

The thought flew apart like a shattered glass as the ground came up fast. She hit hard and rolled. Wind gusted from her chest, and she struggled for breath. For a heartbeat, her face pressed into grass, and she had an errant feeling of gratitude that it wasn't stone. She considered just staying there and lying very still.

A close cry broke through her ennui. She raised her gaze to see the devious little male that had ambushed her and separated her from her comrades. Likely not yet full-grown, the male stood at a little over five feet, but he may as well have been death itself as he came streaking down toward her.

So much had gone off-plan in the chaos of battle: she was alone, on land, without a moment to orient herself.

Down, down he came, until she could see the glitter in his eyes and the glint of sunlight off his outstretched talons. A little voice screamed at her to get up. Brain connected with muscle, and she rolled to the side, expecting talons to rake the earth beside her. There was the sound of a hard strike of flesh on flesh behind her, and she scrambled to her feet as a dark blur struck the harpy a second time.

Chayla.

Blood streaked down her sinewy arms. It seemed her eyes were more whites than pupils as she landed between Jordan and the male. Two hand-axes spun in her hands, spattering the ground with red.

A gash had appeared in the black feathers of the male's chest, but still he landed, still he came on. A low rattling hiss could be heard as the crimson eyes locked on the bloody Nycht and her blades.

Chayla gave what sounded like a strange low laugh and foreign words. Jordan scrambled to her feet beside the Nycht, her blades drawn. Chayla ignored her. So did the male. It seemed she had become invisible, inconsequential to both of them.

The harpy flared its wings and made a hopping charge. Chayla launched forward, the twin hand-axes spinning from her hands to meet him. She threw one hatchet, then the other. The force of the successive blows brought the harpy up short. Chayla met him to tear her blades free, and the dying harpy snapped at her face. Liquid-smooth and lightning fast, she dodged him, planted a foot on his chest, and back-flipped, taking to the air. The harpy hit the ground with a *thud*.

Jordan watched Chayla shoot upward, amazed and bewildered. She would never be capable of what she'd just seen.

In the next moment, Chayla came to bear on another target, drew some small blade from some invisible place, and sent the shining metal hurtling. A second harpy dropped at Jordan's feet. She leapt back as the beast fell and landed a mere foot from her boots with a leaf-shaped throwing blade buried in its eye.

She looked up, and Chayla was gone. She'd simply vanished, leaving Jordan alone again. Dark shapes blotted out the sun as the battle raged on overhead. The sound of something heavy striking the branches of a tree made Jordan whirl, but whoever––or whatever––had fallen was now out of sight, lost in the forest beyond.

A cry drew her eyes to a tumbling Arpak in an imitation of what Jordan's own descent must have looked like. A large, craggy female harpy floated lazily behind the combatant.

The Arpak, a lanky male, struck the ground in a roll, came to a stop, and lay still. *Unconscious or dead?* The harpy was still coming; her horns bent low, eyes locked on her quarry.

Jordan moved. Snatching Chayla's blade from the fallen harpy's eye, she faced the beast. She sent the first of several throwing blades hurtling through the air.

In the air far above Jordan and off to the west, Sol's spear flew into a harpy's back, passing through meat and between ribs to tear through the monster's chest. The harpy floundered, throwing back his scarlet head. He gave a wet, choking warble as he tumbled from the sky. Sol gave chase. He grasped the spear and yanked it free as the creature plummeted to the sea far, far below. The blue expanse swallowed the harpy, and Sol searched the skies for Jordan.

How did she simply vanish?

The battle had spread like a contagious disease, leagues of space growing between small groups of fighting creatures. Even with the distance, the sounds of talons on swords, beaks on spears, seemed to fill the skies.

Toth was hot on the tail of a female, his wings hammering the air, fighting for altitude. The windy currents swirled with the thick scent of blood and harpy stink. Sol nearly lost his balance as a pair of Nychts shot by in pursuit. Straining upward after Toth, they closed in on the large female.

With a cruel set of horns glistening atop her haggish head, she bore toward Upper Rodania, beating her way there like she knew it was where the King lived.

Not for the first time since the battle began was Sol shocked by the determined nature of the harpies. The Strix men cut a path through the tumultuous skies after her. Toth strained to come up on her right flank, while Sol aimed for her left. Both had short spears drawn of the same weight, same length, same deadly iron tip.

The female screamed and wheeled, banking toward Sol; her body rolling like a barrel, bringing talons slashing toward him. Sol tucked his feet and lurched upward, releasing the short spear with a powerful throw. He aimed for her gut, but struck too low. His steel plunged through feathers just above the claw of her leg. It caught there like a pin in a cushion.

The harpy pulled up short, sending Sol's spear wagging as she turned her horn-framed stare upon him with a terrible malevolence. He banked sharply to keep from drawing too close, and an overpowering smell of death washed over him.

Fortunately the harpy had forgotten about Toth.

Two blades appeared on either side of the harpy's

wattled throat——her head came off as the spurs scissored sharply. The Nycht rose into view as the beast was claimed by gravity, and he churned the air between them with steady wingbeats, a bloody shortsword in each fist.

The battle raged around the two warriors for a heartbeat as a measure of respect and camaraderie passed between them.

A monstrous and deep-throated croak shattered the stillness, and their heads turned to the source the sound. An immense female, her bulky body streaked with dirty grey speckles, sailed lazily amidst a covey of smaller ones. The matriarch looked old in the way a twisted tree was old. She was swollen with bitter strength and bent with authority. Lesser creatures took shelter in her wicked shadow.

"Let's cut the head off this snake." Toth powered toward the matriarch on his great wings, and Sol followed close behind.

They made good on the promise, and moments later, a croak of a different nature echoed over Rodania.

Collectively, the harpies began to bank and fly west.

CHAPTER SIXTEEN

Eohne was drawn from Allan's bedside by the sound of screeches and cries in the distance. She padded through the apartment to the terrace. The sounds of battle made the place seem even more empty and lonely. Her breath caught in her throat as the smell of harpies on the wind came to her.

The skies beyond Upper Rodania to the west swarmed with dark forms. Feathered bodies hurtled through the air with croaking screams and hissing shrieks. The wind was rancid, making Eohne's eyes water. She brushed a hand across her eyes to clear her vision. Small winged figures darted between the heavy-bodied shapes of harpies—— Rodania's warriors.

Several great horned hags, two or three times the size of their opponents, floundered in the air as they were stung by steely darts and missiles.

Eohne did not at first notice the smaller male that peeled away from a cluster. Once harried by defenders, now streaking through a free patch of sky, his flight was labored, one wing stiff.

It was such a clumsy path amidst all the darting and soaring that it finally drew Eohne's attention. Clumsy, but heading straight for her.

The creature was already beginning to pull its wings in for a dive when the Elf realized she was not imagining things.

She staggered backward, crying out in disbelief. The harpy hit the balcony with a shattering crash, and Eohne heard the stonework crack. She fought to keep her panic in check as she found herself suddenly and unbelievably beneath the lethal attention of the monstrous invader.

The harpy swung its head about drunkenly. He scrabbled in the tiles he'd broken on the balcony, talons gouging, and sending them flying into oblivion. The monster leveled his hateful, bleary eyes on the Elf and loosed a hiss.

Every hair on Eohne's body stood at attention. Instinct moved her hands to the spot above her shoulders where the hilts of her curved blades should have been, but she grasped only empty air.

The bedroom. Her blades were on the floor in the room where Allan lay.

She scrambled backwards, picking up the nearest thing––a stool––and hurtling it at the advancing creature. The harpy drew back as the furniture smacked it in the face. It squawked and swung its tail. Eohne dropped to the floor and rolled as the harpy's scything tail whistled over her. Clambering across the kitchen floor, she hid behind the central island as the harpy's beak snapped forward, viper-fast. Wood paneling erupted in a spray of splinters.

Eohne flinched away as the fragments of wood flew by. The rest of her body was already in motion. She sprang to her feet, faking left and then darting right, she put the snapping and hissing raptor off-balance, drawing it to lean on its bad wing. He recoiled with a croaking exhalation of pain while Eohne darted toward the bricked-in oven. She snatched the long-handled paddle that hung beside the cast iron door, and spun to face the harpy.

The Elf bellowed, hoping she sounded fierce and unaffected. Somewhere in a distant part of her academic mind, she recalled reading that predators became addled when prey acted threatening and unafraid.

She pressed off her back foot, twisting onto her toes to scythe the wooden paddle at the harpy's face. The jagged teeth of his horny beak snapped at the wood, but Eohne's perfect aim landed the paddle with a loud *crack* against the beast's skull. His head snapped hard to the side, and his feathered body gave a soggy crunch as it slammed into the kitchen island.

Some unseen projectile, a wing or a tail, took Eohne by surprise. She didn't realize she was falling until her body shuddered with the impact. For what seemed like minutes, things simply ceased to make sense. Her eyes saw, but her mind did not comprehend; her ears rang dimly.

Some far away voice screamed for her to get up. She had something long and strong in her hands: the paddle. It was as good a tool as any to get her back on her feet.

With a harsh gasp, she made to rise, leaning on the paddle. Then there was a rush of air, and what had once been one thing in her hands became many things——many sharp things that bit into her palms as she crashed back to the floor.

The sudden pain brought her back to her senses.

Not more than two strides from her was the harpy, one clawed wing lodged in the open cabinetry beneath the kitchen island, his other, injured limb raking feebly at the splintering wood. That explained why, despite her incapacitation, she was still alive. The creature seemed torn between snapping his beak at her and ripping away the cabinetry in an attempt to free himself.

This was the moment Eohne needed.

Scrambling on all fours, she made a lunging slide over the counter, past the trapped beast. She spilled over the bar and scrambled toward the bedroom. She nearly lost her footing as she careened off the fallen stool. There was the sound of splintering wood from the kitchen; it drove her forward like a snapping whip.

Gripping the doorframe to control her skid, Eohne took in the room and the recumbent form of Allan at a glance. On the floor on the far side of his bed was the harness containing her sheathed blades.

There was a triumphant shriek, and a sound like the entire kitchen coming apart. Not daring to look back, she dashed across the room and snatched the weapons up. The hilts felt so welcome against her palms, their weight a comfort. She turned back toward the bedroom door with a deadly internal calm. She was armed, and she was a lethal Elf of Charra-Rae.

The harpy's savage glare met her at the doorway.

Though a smaller male among its kind, the creature filled the doorway with its hunched form. It spared a baleful glance for Allan's form before it leveled its cruel eyes at the Elf.

First you, then him, he seemed to promise.

"You will not touch him." Eohne's voice was as cold and sharp as the steel in her hands.

The harpy lunged, and Eohne sprang, planting one foot on the springy bed just below Allan's feet.

In a masterful move, the Elf razored the harpy's neck in that single, fluid motion the Elves of Charra-Rae were known for. The monster's head fell to the bedroom floor.

The harpy's chest bristled with no less than three of Jordan's knives, and still it danced with her in the air over an unconscious Arpak's body.

Even after that ear-shaking croak, when all the other harpies had begun to pull away, her opponent had remained doggedly on the attack. Jordan then realized that there would be no reprieve, no quarter, no 'okay call it a game' when everybody goes home. At the end of this, one of them would win and the other would die.

Her efforts to put a knife in the harpy's heart had so far failed. Jordan was tiring, and her aim was suffering. She sank another badly-aimed blade just to buy herself more time. She needed this fight to be over. She took a breath as she wheeled in a wide loop. The harpy banked after her, oblivious to the blades in the thick feathers of her chest. *What is beneath those feathers? Dragon scales?*

Jordan heard Toth's voice in her mind. *Stop trying for the killshot. Cripple her.*

Genius and desperation working in concert. Jordan spun to face the harpy. Feeling the cast of the knife flow down her shoulder, through her arm, and off her fingertips, she sent the little wasp of steel zipping into the nook where the harpy's shoulder became its wing. Inaudibly, it stuck fast in the joint. The harpy's wing seized, and she dipped inexorably toward the ground. The beast raged and hissed, but she could not will her wing to beat around the metal lodged in her shoulder.

Jordan followed the harpy down, sinking another knife into the base of the creature's neck, hindering her ability to move that lethal head, like a wedge in a door. The harpy hit the ground with a hopping skid that morphed into a face-first *plop*. Feathers went flying.

Jordan would have whooped with relief had she not spied how close they had landed to the wounded Arpak, who was on the ground in an unconscious heap. He seemed dead, until Jordan got close enough to see his wings quiver.

The harpy, as spiteful as any member of her species, spied her original victim as well. In a clumsy, clawing rake of talons and stiff joints, she dragged herself toward the injured Arpak. Her movements were piteous, stupid.

"You've got to be kidding me," Jordan cried. "You're like a horror movie monster! Worse! Die already!"

Tucking her wings, Jordan plummeted on an interception course. The dirks that lived on her back came into each hand. Wind whistled through her hair as she sliced open a single, wide wound across the harpy's withers. Another poorly aimed strike. Exhaustion was stealing all of her hard-earned technique. She heard the harpy's beak snap shut as she landed between it and the wounded warrior.

Jordan took a fighting stance and met the harpy's baleful glare. *Surely she's nearly finished?* Pained and enraged, the harpy came on in a staggering charge, telegraphing her confusion in a crooked path.

The beast closed in, making to snap at Jordan, but the metal thorn in her neck made her recoil in sudden pain. Springing upward, her wings snapping out, Jordan brought the two dirks around in scything arcs. At last, the reeking female flopped forward at her feet, eyes dull. Jordan flapped there, panting for a moment, before drifting earthward, relieved.

It was over at last.

She stared at the beast she had killed all by herself, the earth darkening around the carcass as her blood leaked out. She shuddered.

"Eurgh. So gross."

She wiped her blades on the grass, breathing through her mouth. It didn't help. A wave of nausea grabbed her by the guts, sudden and fierce. She fell to her knees and lost whatever had been left in her stomach, which wasn't much.

When she was done, she looked up, her eyes raking the sky for harpies. They were all toward the west and growing smaller by the second. Smaller winged shapes——her fellow combatants——gave chase, but were losing ground.

Jordan made her way over to see what could be done for her fallen companion.

Eohne had just sent the harpy carcass and head over the edge of the terrace, when a sound made her freeze: a croaked murmur of incomprehensible words.

She whirled at the sound, eyes wide, heart going off like a gong. She dashed back to the bedroom, where there was still harpy blood on the floor. Ignoring this, her eyes locked on Allan. He looked the same as always. Still. Pale. Eyes closed. Steady breathing.

Was I hearing things? She cocked her head with a sharp bird-like movement.

There was another murmur. Allan's lips hardly moved, but there was no mistaking where the voice was coming from. The sound was cracked and broken, barely human and difficult to understand.

Eohne dropped to his side. "Allan?" Her heart felt lodged in her throat, and her breathing became shallow. Again, louder this time, "Allan?"

His lips moved, and this time the croaked words came out near enough to her ear that she could understand them.

"U.S. military Woodsman's Pal Machete Knife."

Eohne stared at the man in shock. She put a hand on his shoulder and jiggled him gently. "What? Allan, are you awake? Can you hear me?"

"Italian M31 Experimental Helmet." He took a shallow breath. "B three-forty-eight R US Army Air Corps Receiver."

Eohne slowly straightened. Horror crept up her back at the monotone sound of his voice. She shivered.

"Allan?"

"German K ninety-eight bayonet."

She stared at the human, utterly confused.

"Italian fascist insignia RSI Brigate Nere skull with Gladio nineteen-forty-four black brigades." Allan took a slow breath, his lips warmer and moving more easily now. His eyes were still closed, his cheeks the color of pastry. "World-War two U.S. army signal corps TE-five equipment case with original contents." His voice broke on the last word, and it spurred Eohne into action.

She scrambled for her jar of messenger bugs and took them into the kitchen, where she hurriedly prepared them to send a message to Jordan. The sounds of the harpy battle outside were growing distant, but she couldn't tell if it was because the fight was moving away from the apartment, or the harpies were being defeated.

Allan's voice droned on from the other room, filling the Elf with bewilderment.

"Fifteen by eighty World War Two Takatiho Japanese big eye."

Eohne's hands shook as she injected the bugs and swallowed the donisi pill.

Is this some kind of strange brain damage? What if the rest of Allan's living days are just a long stream of strange words, all seeming to be war related?

Eohne uttered her brief message asking Jordan to come as soon as she could, and gave the command to the bugs. They zoomed off and disappeared.

"World War I and Two military philatelic covers field post, Red Cross, Prisoner of War..."

On and on, the strange words came, making no sense and sending judders of horror up Eohne's spine.

CHAPTER SEVENTEEN

The injured Arpak opened his eyes, and Jordan breathed a sigh of relief. "Don't worry," she told him. "You'll be okay. Help is coming."

Jordan realized with no small amount of surprise that her harpy fight had been conducted in the open square not far from Juer's library. She hadn't registered her surroundings before, but now she recognized the street.

Locked up tight during the battle, the houses and shops around Jordan began to open. Rodania's citizens emerged, mumbling to each other in shock. The harpy carcass soon had a crowd ringing it. People held their noses at the smell and dared not go too near the body. A young female Arpak claiming to be a nurse appeared at Jordan's side and took over care of the injured male combatant.

Strix milled about the scene, shopkeepers cursing as they picked up fallen and broken merchandise. People talked in small crowds with raised and fearful voices.

"Jordan!" Sol skidded to a halt and swept her up in a fierce hug. "Have I ever told you how much I love your garish, fluorescent yellow feathers?" He said into her hair. "You're like a lighthouse in a dark and stormy sea."

"That was poetic." Jordan hugged him back. They were talking over one another, checking each other for damage, when a cry interrupted them.

"Hey!" barked an indignant voice, loud and bold. Faces turned and searched, necks craned. The crowd parted to reveal a young Nycht soldier, his face upturned and contorted with anger. The crowd followed his blazing gaze, and a collective gasp swept the street.

A tall Arpak with broad but stooped shoulders was visible on Juer's tower balcony. He was gazing down into the crowd below, his face impassive. His eyes were pupilless, a blank white glow. His face was lined and drawn, pale and miserable. A white beard lay on his chest, stark against the black velvet of his vest. Tight black sleeves of some shiny fabric encased long arms, which rested at his sides, his fingers just visible over the stone railing of the balcony. The Arpak's wings were tall and the color of the sky over Virginia on a very smoggy day, a sort of dim ochre. The long bones of the wings drooped sideways, like they were simply too heavy to keep upright, and had long since given up trying. The Arpak's head was topped by a plain black skullcap, almost like a burglar's knit hat. The whole effect —-the hat, the illuminated eyes, the Arpak's height, and drooping wings—-was disconcerting. He gave the impression of great power having been brought low by tragedy.

Jordan's skin rose with gooseflesh as she stared at this vision staring down at them, expressionless. It was difficult to say where he was looking, given that he had no pupils, but the angry Nycht soldier on the street was a likely bet.

"Who is that?" Jordan asked softly.

Before Sol could answer, the angry Nycht barked again.

"You could have prevented this," he yelled, baring his teeth. "What have *you* done?" The Nycht raised his sword in the air and pointed it at the Arpak on the balcony. "What have you done?" he screamed again. "Nothing! Do you care that your people are dying? Do you care that your city crumbles before your eyes, and the air is thick with the stench of harpy?"

The aging Arpak just looked down passively. His face did not move; he may as well have been a statue in a wax museum.

"It's King Konig," Sol murmured in her ear.

Jordan had put that together from the latest accusations hurled by the Nycht soldier. Her jaw went soft as she stared up at the Rodanian King. A whispered question from a nearby Arpak made its way to the couple's ears.

"What's he doing down here on Middle Rodania?"

Someone answered, "That's Juer's balcony. The doctor."

"You are a failure." The Nycht mercenary was not finished. "You are an embarrassment to the monarchs before you and to your people. A Nycht King would never abandon his people the way you have." The Nycht lowered his sword and spat on the cobblestones. "A Nycht King would have fought by our side, Arpak and Nycht alike; he would have trained with us and bled with us."

Juer appeared beside the King, alarm etched into his features. The much smaller Arpak, bent and wizened, put an arm around King Konig. The king started at the touch, blinked, and looked down at the elderly doctor, his white eyes blank and staring. Juer led King Konig away from the balcony's edge. As the two Arpaks passed out of view, the crowd booed, hissed, and grumbled.

When Juer reappeared a moment later without King Konig at his side, the crowd took a collective breath.

"Your king is a very sick man," Juer announced, his own voice dry and grating. "I suppose it is of no use to hide the facts any longer. King Konig is unwell, and I am doing all in my power to heal him. Speak to your representatives in the Council, make your grievances known there; for, here, I am sorry to say, your breath will be wasted." Juer disappeared, and there was the sound of doors being pulled shut and locked.

Sol and Jordan looked at one another as the crowd began to break up. "Did you know?" Jordan asked.

Sol shook his head. "I knew he wasn't well, but I didn't know the extent of it."

"Why do his eyes glow?"

"I have no idea." Sol chewed his cheek thoughtfully. "Come on. Let's go find Toth. He'll want to do a debrief, and it's not going to be pretty."

They took to the air only to be sent staggering back when a collection of marbles clustered in front of their faces and spelled the question, *'Jordan Kacy?'*

CHAPTER EIGHTEEN

When Jordan landed and saw the state of the terrace and the kitchen, her heart felt as though it was going to explode from her chest in fear. When she saw the smeared blood trail leading from the bedroom to the terrace, she screamed for the Elf.

Eohne came barrelling out of the bedroom to grip Jordan by the shoulders. "It's alright, it's alright!" She said, her fingers gripping Jordan's bones tightly. "It's harpy blood. We're okay. Come." She grabbed Jordan's hand and yanked her through to the bedroom, skidding on the blood. "Where's Sol? Is he okay?"

"Yes, he's okay. He went to the debriefing. Ow, Eohne," Jordan's neck creaked at the abuse. Her whole body was beginning to stiffen up.

"World War II Winston Churchill matchbox holder," said Allan.

Jordan froze.

"Dad," she whispered, eyes stretched wide.

"World War I eight-centimeter memorial death plaque," Allan replied.

"Dad?!" Jordan flew to his side, repeating the call three more times when he didn't respond.

"I tried to talk to him," said Eohne. "He just––"

"World War II British medical bags."

"Keeps on like that," she finished, perturbed. "Does it mean anything to you?"

"World War II metropolitan whistle, nineteen-thirty-nine to nineteen-forty-five."

Jordan held her breath, her mind racing, her eyes roaming the terrain of her father's face. The tiny hairs on the back of her neck stood at attention.

"He's listing inventory."

"He's doing what?" Eohne put a hand on Jordan's arm and squeezed, desperate to understand.

Jordan looked up at the Elf, her face alight with hope. "Allan loves history, particularly war history. He collects memorabilia from the two World Wars we had on Earth in the twentieth century. Keeps his finds in a room upstairs in our house. They're his favorite things."

"World War II child's evacuee tag," Allan's voice droned on in the background.

"He's amassed a huge collection by now." Jordan looked back at her father, not sure how she was supposed to feel. *Is it a good sign that he's at least speaking?* "He's listing his inventory," she stated again.

"Oh," Eohne blinked, not sure what to think of this.

"World War II Nazi German era block four original stamps," said Allan.

The Elf and the Arpak listened for several seconds.

Jordan looked up. "This is good, right? It's a sign of improvement?"

Eohne pulled a stool over to the bed and sat near Allan's head. "Well, the part of his brain that knows his own possessions is certainly intact. I can't believe how specific he is being." The Elf took Allan's hand, but she kept her eyes on Jordan, her lips parted.

"What? What are you thinking?"

"It's just an idea; it might not work." Eohne clasped Jordan's fingers with her other hand, squeezing. The three of them were now linked.

"Anything is worth a try. We already agreed on that." Jordan squeezed her friend's hand in return and tried to temper the excitement rising inside her. "What's your idea?"

"Could you get one or two of these artifacts, and bring them here? There might be something I can do with them, something that could help him."

Jordan straightened, her eyes widening. "With your magic?"

Eohne nodded. "There is something about these items that has brought Allan partially back. Maybe having something of his here, something from this collection, would help bring him the rest of the way."

"It's a great idea, Eohne. I'll find a way to do it." Jordan's mind was racing, and it raced all the way back to Sohne and the Elves of Charra-Rae. *Did Sohne know this, or something like this, would happen? Is this why she made me promise to go back to her when I needed my wings again?* Going back to Earth would mean Jordan would lose her wings; she'd be in the same predicament that Sol had been in when they first met.

"Sohne knew," murmured Eohne quietly, as though reading Jordan's mind. "She said she couldn't see Allan, but she knew that something would make you go home. This was it." Eohne looked at Jordan. "But don't use your locket. It's too dangerous."

"I don't have the locket anymore, but you sound just like Sol," Jordan said with a laugh.

"How does she sound like me?" Sol's voice made them turn as he strode into the room, his wings just closing up.

"You look like hell," Eohne said, giving Sol a hug. "And you smell worse than I do."

"Thanks. What happened here?" The Arpak gestured at the floor and toward the door, where much of his kitchen and terrace lay in ruins. He seemed remarkably calm, to his credit.

"Hurricane World War II collectible pocket watch and fob," said Allan.

"Whoa," Sol sped to Allan's side. "He's awake?"

Jordan shook her head. "Not quite. He's listing inventory from his collection of war memorabilia back home."

Sol listened as Allan listed off more items, the wreckage of his apartment forgotten for the time being.

"What do you make of it?" He crouched so he could look up at the women.

Eohne and Jordan filled Sol in on Eohne's suggestion. At first, Sol glowered at the idea of Jordan passing through a portal again; his concern eased when he was told that Jordan would go to Sohne and ask for her help.

"She knew something like this would happen." Sol

shook his head with wonder. "Your promise will be fulfilled."

"There might be a small glitch," Eohne said, holding up a finger. "Sohne made you promise to go back to her when you needed to regrow your wings, but you actually need to go see her before you even leave. You need to be preemptive."

Sol was nodding in agreement. "She can help you pass through a portal safely. Maybe she can even give you some magic that you can stash somewhere, so it'll be waiting for you right when you get back."

Eohne nodded. "She can do this."

"When do we leave?" Sol asked Jordan, standing straight, his knees popping.

"We?"

"You don't think I'm letting you portal-hop alone, do you?"

"What about your work?"

"I'll put in for leave," Sol said simply.

Jordan blinked at him. Sol had been serious about his job since the day they'd met. It had seemed like nothing would ever take priority above his role as courier. Now he was going to take time off? For her? Jordan's heart melted, and she didn't know what to say.

Jordan's shocked expression made Sol shift uncomfortably. "I love my father," he explained softly. "I would be frantic to help him, were I in your shoes. I'm not going to let you fly back to Charra-Rae on your own; The Conca is dangerous enough, but now, even Rodanian skies are not safe."

"That settles it, then. You should leave as soon as Sol

secures his leave." Eohne got up. "It's time to hydrate and feed him." She left the bedroom, and they could hear her rattling around in the kitchen, preparing the vegetables Toth had provided for Allan's nutrition.

Jordan and Sol fell silent, listening to Allan drone on with his inventory. It seemed as though he would never come to the end of it.

"He sure has a lot of stuff," Sol said, taking Jordan's hand and moving to the stool Eohne had vacated. "I wonder if he'll just start over when he gets to the end of it."

Jordan nodded. "Probably."

"British WWI Lewis Aircraft Gun Modified for WWII Home Guard with 97 Round Drum Magazine," Allan said in his monotone voice.

Sol blinked at Allan and laughed. "He has a machine gun? We could use about two dozen of those right now."

"How do you know what a machine gun is?" Jordan asked.

"Educated, remember?" Sol jabbed his thumbs at his own chest.

Jordan's lips parted. "Machine gun," she echoed. She grabbed Sol's forearm. "Sol, listen. That day you went to see the bureaucrat––"

"Belshar? Oh! I still have to check on him. There just hasn't been time. There's still some issue with the medicine that Juer needs…"

Jordan nodded. "Yes, him. I walked through the Crypsis market while I waited for you that day, and I met the most amazing Nycht. She's a brilliant engineer. She specializes in reverse engineering artifacts from Earth." Jordan's words were speeding up. The more she thought about her idea, the more she liked it. "We do have a machine gun; it doesn't work anymore, but Arth—-that's the Nycht's name—- could reverse engineer it."

"How long would that take?"

"I don't know, but isn't it better to get it in motion now? You heard that Nycht yelling at Konig; he's not doing enough, he doesn't even seem to care. We have to do something. I don't see why this wouldn't work. We just have to figure out a way to get it back here so Arth can take it apart. We already have to go back to Earth…why not bring it back with us, somehow?"

"I don't think it's that simple, Jordan. Don't get me wrong, I love the idea, but it sounds pretty tricky. The gun is heavy, no?"

"Yes, but," Jordan was thinking ahead, "maybe Sohne could help? We can ask her, along with the rest of what we need."

Sol was nodding. "Can't hurt to ask. Arth would need time to build it, to make molds. One gun might hardly be worth the trouble, but many guns…" Sol was talking it through more to himself now, the idea taking on life as he ran through some logistics in his brain. "What about the bullets?"

"Arth could build molds for those, too, using the dimensions of the magazine that holds them."

"How big is this gun? Could a single Strix operate it?"

"Not while flying, it's too big for that." Jordan began to pace. "It was made to shoot from a plane; it would probably need two people to operate it safely, one aiming and shooting and the other standing by with bullets. We could fasten them to the highest towers--"

"What about gunpowder?"

"Gunpowder," echoed Allan.

Jordan and Sol whirled to face Allan, their faces lit with expectation.

"Dad?" Jordan flew to the bedside and went to her knees. "Can you hear us, Dad?"

"Fifteen percent charcoal," was Allan's response. "Seventy-five percent saltpeter. Ten percent sulfur." Allan took a long, slow breath and continued listing inventory.

"Allan?" Jordan grabbed his forearm and squeezed, but her father only listed more artifacts.

"Must have been a coincidence," murmured Sol, putting a hand on Jordan's shoulder.

"I don't believe in coincidences," Jordan shook her head. "He heard us. He just gave us the recipe for gunpowder. It's like he knows we're here, and he's trying to communicate with us."

Eohne returned holding a glass of green liquid. She set the glass on the top of the headboard and peeled back the blankets covering Allan's stomach. She lifted his shirt, exposing his ribs and belly.

"Doesn't he make any waste?" Sol asked matter-of-factly.

Eohne shook her head. "The gel I use on him helps him to absorb everything, so there is no waste. Maybe if I overfed him there might be, but--" she shrugged as she coated Allan's skin with the gel. "He seems to use everything up. Thankfully."

Jordan poured the green juice slowly onto Allan's skin, and they all watched as it disappeared, vanishing into his internal organs. The feeding didn't interrupt Allan's listing of items; he went right on without stopping.

"Did I hear something about gunpowder?" Eohne asked.

Sol caught Eohne up while Jordan replaced Allan's shirt and the covers, setting his hands over top of the blankets.

It was decided that they would ask Sohne for some magic to help get the machine gun through the portal, along with the magic for Jordan's and Sol's wings, and safe portal-passage back and forth.

"This is going to cost a fortune," said Eohne. "You're asking a lot from her. I'm confident she can do it all, but she won't do it for nothing."

"I have money," Jordan and Sol said at the same time, then looked at one another.

"You have money?" Sol arched a single brow and canted his head skeptically. "Since when?"

"Since we'll be going back to Virginia. My father has a small gold stash, and I can buy more. I can also withdraw funds from our family accounts. It will take a bit of time, and it'll probably alert the police, but I may as well deal with it while I'm home." She looked at her dad and chewed her lip. "I wonder if I should send a letter to my dad's lawyers, letting them know we're alive. Our family has money and property."

"What would you say to them?"

"I don't know yet, but I'll think about it. If my dad is gone for long enough, seven years or something like that, they might declare death in absentia, in which case his estate would fall legally to me. But I'm likely to be declared dead eventually, too, and there are no more Kacys after me."

"What would happen to your father's estate then?"

"I don't know. It might go to the government."

It was strange to be thinking about the legalities of Earth. Jordan hadn't been living on Oriceran very long, but already she felt like her citizenship on Earth was a thing of the past. She had to think through what living a life on Oriceran would mean for their property in Virginia. She gazed at her father, wondering how he was going to react to all of this when he woke up.

"We need to build in some time for you to deal with these things when we get back to Virginia," agreed Sol, breaking through Jordan's thought-cloud. "And what if you're seen? You would be detained."

Jordan frowned. Sol was right. They needed to be very careful in executing this plan; it was more complicated than just a portal-hop.

The three of them lapsed into meditative silence.

At some point, Jordan looked down at herself. She was still bloodstained and reeking of harpy. She looked up at Eohne and then over at Sol, realizing they were both just as filthy——their hair mussed, their clothes spattered with blood. The apartment was a disaster and featured a long streak of harpy blood running from the foot of Allan's bed to the terrace.

"Sol?"

"Yeah?"

"I don't suppose you've got a mop around here somewhere?"

CHAPTER NINETEEN

Sol put in for his leave. A mere two days later, with Toth informed and permission given to pursue their far-fetched but optimistic plan, Blue, Jordan, and Sol left Rodania as the sun peeked over the horizon. With the sun and the wind at their backs, they flew high until they found thermals they could ride with little effort.

They landed for a break in Maticaw, where they ate the meal Jordan had made and then carried in one of Sol's old, worn satchels. He had picked up bread and cheese from the market on his way back from the courier's office, and Jordan had made sandwiches and sliced vegetables. Blue did his usual disappearing act before they even reached Maticaw, and tracked them down in a field above town. He came ambling across the grassy slope, his belly distended, and a very satisfied look in his reptilian eyes.

"I don't even want to know what you found to eat," said Jordan, throwing an arm over the dragon's withers as he curled up next to her. He was much longer than Jordan now. His tail wrapped around her hips as she sat in the grass with her wings stretched out behind her.

"Evidently a seabird." Sol plucked a stray feather from between Blue's lips.

"At least it wasn't someone's pet goat."

Blue lifted his head and gave Jordan a look.

"What?" Jordan brought her nose close to his snout. "Do you know the difference between wild game and livestock?" she teased him.

Blue's tongue snaked out and curled around Jordan's ear, and he pulled his tongue back in quickly, giving her a tug.

"I'll take that as a yes." She wiped the side of her head. "Oh." She sat up straighter.

"What?" Sol began to pack up the remnants of their lunch, and got to his feet.

"I just realized we'll have to leave Blue in Charra-Rae. He can't come to Virginia with us."

"I figured he would just head back to Rodania, the way he did before you went to Trevilsom. Right, Blue?"

Blue looked up as a bird with an exceptionally long neck winged by overhead, ignoring Sol.

"Why don't we see what Sohne says? Maybe she can make a portal straight into Rodania, so we won't have to fly all the way from Charra-Rae when we return." Jordan got to her feet. Blue flicked his tongue at her as if to complain that he'd only just sat down. "Come on, Blue. You know the way."

The threesome took to the air again, crossing over the lush forests and agricultural terrain that lay between Maticaw and The Conca. Jordan and Sol talked for a time, but soon fell silent and got to the business of speed. Their wings ate currents and spat miles out behind them. They passed over a district full of lakes—small and large, clear and muddy. Jordan thought she'd never get sick of observing the world from the heights she could reach by wing.

"It must have been somewhere around here that you came through the portal," Jordan guessed above the sound of the wind.

But Sol shook his head. "I was in a dreesha forest much further south of here when I hit that tree." Sol became quiet and meditative for a time before speaking again. "I've been meaning to tell you something."

Jordan flew closer to Sol so she could hear him better. Blue was flying far below them, skimming along the top of a crystalline lake. She could see his scales glinting in the sunlight. "What?"

"I've wanted to say that I'm sorry."

Jordan couldn't have been more surprised if Sol had dropped out of the sky. "Sorry? For what? Sol, you've done so much for me, you have nothing to be sorry for."

"I do." He gave Jordan a sheepish look. "The day you and I met, I was so hard on you. I blamed you for my tumble through the portal and my dislocated arm, for the loss of my wings and for making me late."

"I can understand why. I didn't mean to; I didn't know the locket had magic in it. But when stuff happens, we look for someone to blame. It's okay. I get it."

Sol smiled. "The truth of it is, you probably saved my life."

Jordan gaped. "How?"

"I was being pursued by two big harpies. They were gaining. I don't know what would have happened if I hadn't passed through that portal." He gave a shrug, making one wing dip. "I might not have survived. I don't mind taking on one of those beasts, but two?" He shook his head. "It might have been pretty ugly. I'm sorry I was such an ass to you."

Jordan recalled thinking that Sol was an arrogant jerk the day they had first tumbled through the portal.

"You made up for all that when you made me those ridiculous leaf shoes," she grinned. "I think I fell in love with you a little then."

Her face flushed as the words came out before she could reel them in. She hadn't really meant 'in love', it was just a figure of speech. She blinked. Or had she?

Sol seemed momentarily stunned, but before she could get a grasp on his expression, he averted his gaze to Blue, gliding along the west side of The Conca.

"It'll be dark soon," he said with a crack in his voice. He cleared his throat. "Let's spend the night here and make for Charra-Rae at first light."

He arrowed toward the thick forest below, and Jordan followed him, cursing herself silently.

"You have wings," Sohne said with surprise when Jordan and Sol were delivered to her by the pale gray Elf. "I have been expecting you, but I thought you'd be wingless," Sohne gestured to the high arches of bright yellow feathers at Jordan's back.

The Elf princess was seated in a fabric hammock that was hanging from one of the tall trees outside the hut where she'd healed Sol. Her red hair was piled high on top of her head, half falling down in russet ringlets. She was mesmerizing to look at. She'd been reading from a small leather volume when they'd arrived, which she'd closed and tucked away. Her hammock was perfectly positioned to catch the bright rays of the morning sun. A tall slender goblet sat on a table beside the hammock. Small white butterflies were attracted to whatever was in the goblet and fluttered around its rim, landing and taking off, landing and taking off.

"I haven't been home yet," Jordan explained, tucking her hands behind her back.

Sohne's eyes skimmed Jordan's frame––the new leather armor, the red vest, the multitude of throwing knives tucked in their own little sheaths. "You've taken well to Rodania, I see." Her sapphire eyes fell on Sol, then Blue, who was crouched behind Sol's legs with his chin near the ground. His eyes were locked on Sohne the way they locked onto prey––only his posture was submissive, not predatory.

"And who is this?" Sohne asked, rising from her hammock.

Her pale green robes drifted around her, never quite settling. Her tiny waist was cinched with a thick band of green leather, and her wrists were wrapped in matching green silk.

"This is Blue." Jordan beckoned to the dragon, and he crawled out from behind Sol's legs, keeping his belly low to the ground. His gaze didn't leave the Elf. "Strange, I've never seen him behave like this before."

Sohne bent and put her hand down to Blue, who crawled forward on his belly. His tongue flicked out at her, and then back. He stopped just beyond her reach, watching her. Sohne stepped forward, her hand descending to the dragon's head. Blue's head drew back from her touch, like a dog afraid he was about to be beaten. But as her pale fingers touched his nose, his eyes closed. Jordan couldn't tell if he was enjoying her touch, or tolerating it. The Elf princess murmured some words in her own tongue, and Blue visibly relaxed.

Sohne rose. "Let's walk. You can tell me why you're here, since you are clearly not in need of regrowing your wings."

Jordan and Sol followed Sohne down a path of blood-colored stones, through the trees and toward a body of sparkling water. Jordan's eyes were drawn to the gnash-witted workers in the canopy, forever harvesting the strange fuchsia-topped fungus.

She looked back over her shoulder and saw that Blue remained in the clearing outside Sohne's hut. His head was down, and his eyes were closed. Jordan frowned, wondering if the Elf had done something to put the dragon to sleep. Sohne's presence was like that of a big, beautiful snake; she was graceful and hypnotizing, but you were never quite sure if she was going to coil around you to hug you or kill you.

Jordan gave an involuntary shiver as they wandered to a small beach and walked along the shore of an emerald green lake. She couldn't find it in herself to fully trust

Sohne, but she trusted Eohne, and Eohne trusted Sohne; that was better than nothing.

Besides, who else can we turn to, to help with the monumental task we've set for ourselves?

Sol reached out and took Jordan's hand, giving it a reassuring squeeze as they followed behind the Elf princess, toward a curving wooden boardwalk. Stepping up on the walkway, they skirted the shores of the lake until they reached a tall gazebo constructed of vines.

"We're here because we are being proactive and pre-emptive," Jordan began. Sohne tilted her head to indicate she was listening. "We need your help with more than just growing back my wings; I am of course prepared to pay you for what we need."

"Go on." The Elf leaned her elbows on the railing of the gazebo and gazed into the green water, watching silver fish with her sapphire eyes as they flashed below.

"You foresaw correctly——I will lose my wings again. So will Sol, as he'll be coming with me back to Virginia. We need magic that we can use the moment we return, because we don't have a lot of time. My father is sick, and Rodania is under attack."

Sohne put her back to the fish and fixed Jordan with a gaze, listening, her red lips parted. "Under attack?"

Sol nodded. "Harpies. No one in Rodania thought it was possible."

"It shouldn't be," said Sohne. "Your city is protected by the magic of the Light Elves, correct?"

"Supposedly."

Their host frowned, her otherwise perfect brow marred with concern. "Continue."

"We have a brilliant Nycht who can reverse engineer anything. I need magic to help retrieve a big heavy gun from Earth, and bring it to Rodania so she can copy it."

"What is King Konig doing about these attacks?"

"Nothing. He has left everything to the Council and our new military leader, Toth," Sol explained, crossing his arms, "who is expecting us back with this weapon as soon as possible."

"This plan sounds riddled with trouble," Sohne replied. Her eyes dropped from Jordan's face to her neck. "Does your locket have enough magic left to get you there and back safely? This I doubt."

Jordan glanced at Sol. He gave her an encouraging smile. "I no longer have the locket. I won't go into what happened to it, but suffice it to say, we need your help getting to Earth and back. Ideally, we'll leave from here and return directly to Rodania, with the gun."

Sohne's face had taken on an expression Jordan was having a hard time placing. She gave the impression of calm, but there was an excitement coming off her, an anticipation, like a snake waiting for the right moment to strike.

"So, if I understand correctly, you need magic to get you to your place in Virginia, you need magic to get you back to Rodania directly, you need to bring this gun back with you, and you need to have magic to regrow your wings immediately upon your return?"

Jordan was nodding.

"That's not quite all," Sol shot Jordan a glance that said *'trust me'*. "Jordan needs to do a few things back on Earth that have to do with taking care of her father's estate.

People are looking for her and Allan, and there is a possibility that she might be detained if she's recognized."

"Hmmmm," Sohne made a sound of understanding back in her throat. "This is expensive magic you are asking for." She shot Jordan a look. "You need to present yourself as yourself, but without alerting these humans there is anything unusual about your reappearance, as though you had never left in the first place?"

"Exactly." Jordan threaded her fingers together. Her hands had gone cold. "Can you help us?"

"Each item alone would be no trouble, but when you need multiple formulas like this *and* you throw in portal travel, there is something called the cocktail effect," explained Sohne. She left the gazebo, and the Arpaks trailed after her. The threesome walked the boardwalk slowly in the direction they'd come.

"Cocktail effect?" Jordan echoed, "like mixing alcoholic beverages?"

"One magic formula on its own is fairly predictable and easy to control. It's pure, and therefore simple. Multiple magic formulas all used in close proximity to one another, either chronologically or within the same biological organism, become more unpredictable."

"The risk is higher," Sol concluded.

"Precisely. Lucky for you," Sohne gave them a smile that made her face seem doll-like, "I am the most powerful Elf this side of The Conca. You couldn't ask for anyone better to master these formulas for you."

Jordan and Sol shared a look of both relief and apprehension. It was great that she was so confident, but was the

Elf pumping up the value so she could charge them some exorbitant amount of gold?

"How much do you want for this magic?" Jordan asked as they followed Sohne up the blood-stone trail and through the forest.

The Elf didn't answer for so long that Jordan thought she hadn't heard her question. She was about to repeat herself when they reached the grove where Blue was still sleeping, and Sohne turned to face them.

"I don't want gold for this magic." She stood directly in front of Jordan and looked down at the Arpak, putting her hands on her upper arms. "I want the unbreakable promise. Nothing else will do."

"What promise?" Sol's tone was sharper than Jordan would have liked it to be.

"You won't know that until it's asked," replied Sohne with a shrug. "It's very simple, and not unlike what I asked from you last time. That wasn't so bad was it? You've already fulfilled it, and it required nothing from you other than what you needed to give anyway."

"I make a promise to you without knowing what it is? That's what you want?"

"Just Jordan? Not me?" Sol asked.

Sohne gave a slow, single nod. "Just Jordan." The excitement was still rolling off her, underneath her calm exterior. Jordan's eyes narrowed, and she stared at the Elf, trying to divine what she could possibly want from her. "See how generous I am?"

Sol made a sound like a laugh, but Sohne ignored him.

"What happens if she's unable to fulfill this promise?"

"That can't happen. It's part of the magic of the agreement. I won't be able to ask for anything you can't give, and you will not be able to deny it."

"What happens if I do deny it?"

"You die."

"No, Jordan." Sol finally couldn't take it anymore. "We'll find another way. Don't do this."

"There is no other way." Jordan's voice was soft and her eyes were locked on the Elf. Her left hand felt relaxed and warm, with a pleasant tingle threading through her fingers. She began to raise her hand.

"Jordan, don't." Jordan felt Sol's hand on her shoulder, his fingers pressing into her skin. "There's always another way."

She felt like she was falling into the Elf's sapphire eyes. Her left hand floated up, feeling so light, it was as if butterflies were lifting it for her. Her fingers extended. "I promise."

Sohne's slender hand grasped her own, and their palms pressed against one another.

Jordan gasped as a hot, invisible rope wrapped around her left forearm. Her eyes dropped to follow it; though she couldn't see anything, she still felt the pressure of the cord on her skin. It travelled, wrapping over and under her elbow, around her bicep, through her armpit, heating her skin as it went. The hot cord wrapped over her shoulder, under her collarbone, and into her heart. Her heart slowed and gave seven strong, hot pulses, and Jordan felt every quart of blood as it flowed through her valves and arteries.

Her eyes widened as she stared at the Elf. Those dark-crystal eyes seemed to see right through her. Then the moment was over, and Sohne let go of Jordan's hand.

Jordan's arm tingled and then relaxed, all sensation dissipating.

"What just happened?" Sol asked, shaking Jordan's shoulder.

"We made a deal." Sohne turned away. "Follow me, please." She disappeared into her hut, and the Arpaks followed.

Sohne plucked a sack from a cluster of them on the floor and opened it. The sack contained small purple grains, and Sohne scooped out a tablespoon's worth. Taking a square of paper from a nearby stack, she proceeded to roll what looked an awful lot like a cigarette. Jordan and Sol shared a bemused look and watched as the Elf held the rolled paper containing the purple grains to her lips. With a flick of her fingers, a small flame appeared in the air cupped in her palm. She lit the strange cigarette with the fire conjured from nothing and inhaled, her eyes closed.

"You want to return directly to Rodania when you're through with your tasks in Virginia, correct?"

"That's right."

"Where, exactly?"

"My apartment on Upper will do," suggested Sol with an agreeable nod from Jordan.

Sohne took a deep draft from the cigarette and said "Upper Rodania," on her exhale. A thick cloud of purple smoke gathered over the table and formed a hologram of Upper Rodania. "East?"

"Midwest, actually."

Sohne took another draft and exhaled the word, "Midwest." The hologram zoomed in on a section of towers. "Which one?"

Sol pointed to a tall, thick tower; his terrace was easily recognizable by the lack of furnishings, which Blue had burnt to a crisp. Even in the hologram, the terrace looked crumbling and broken.

"Amazing," murmured Jordan, watching the smoky purple hologram rotate and zoom in on Sol's property.

Sohne gave a smug smile and took another draft. She puffed out a perfect 'O' with her lips, which drifted and turned, eventually settling over Sol's tower home like a ring tossed in a carnival game.

"*Ekko*," said Sohne, and the smoke ring snapped inward around the tower. The hologram blurred, and the visuals of Upper Rodania disappeared.

"I have more to do," Sohne told them." I'll need a few hours to prepare what you need. Wait outside, if you like, or down by the lake. Pohle will bring you some food and drink. If you'd like to rest, she can show you to a guesthouse."

Jordan and Sol turned to leave.

"Ow!" Jordan turned as a pain like being stabbed with a small, hot poker blossomed on the arch of her left wing.

Sohne stood holding a bright yellow feather in her hands, an amused smile on her lips. "Sorry. I think it hurts more if I warn you." She held up the feather. "Thank you, I'll be needing this."

Jordan rubbed the sore spot with her hand and glared at the Elf. "Sadist," she muttered as she and Sol left the hut.

"That was mean." Sol put a hand on Jordan's wing.

"Tell me about it," Jordan grumbled. Her wings flapped and tightened in an effort to ease the sting.

The silent Elf with the gray skin materialized from the forest as though Sohne had rung a bell for her. She beckoned for them to follow her.

"Blue, come on." Jordan woke the dragon up, and he ambled after them.

"I wish you hadn't done that," said Sol under his breath as they followed Pohle through the woods. "You have no idea what she'll ask of you."

"She asked for a promise before, and that turned out to cost me nothing. My father's life is at stake, and possibly hundreds of Rodanian citizens. It seems like a fair price to me."

Sol frowned. "You say that now, but I picked up on the strangest feeling from her, excited or something. Like she already knows what she wants."

"I'm sure she does, or she wouldn't have asked for a promise," replied Jordan as they walked through thick green ferns. She fell silent as an uneasiness passed through her; something clicked into place. The expression on Sohne's face that she had been trying to identify finally came to her.

It was greed.

CHAPTER TWENTY

Three hours later, Pohle came to retrieve Sol, Jordan, and Blue where they were resting on the beach. She materialized on the sand and stood there saying nothing until they realized her presence probably meant Sohne was ready. They walked up to the hut, where Sohne was waiting in the clearing. She held a brown woven sack and pulled out individual items as she addressed them.

She held up Jordan's stolen feather. "I've infused this with enough magic to take you through to the tree in your back yard and deliver you straight to Sol's apartment when you're done." She handed it to Sol. "When Jordan touches the feather, the magic will be triggered. Be sure you're touching her when it happens. You must keep this feather until you're ready to return. If Jordan touches it at any time, it will transport you, whether you're ready or not. So be careful."

Sol agreed, and took the feather.

"This," Sohne held up a small sack, "is the magic you need to transport a map of the gun."

"A map? Not the gun itself?" Jordan was about to protest, but Sohne held up her hand.

"It works in two steps. Dump the contents onto the gun and give it time to coat the entire surface. Once that's done, touch a flame to it. The second step will take several hours, if not a full day. But once the fire has done its work, all that will remain will be a collection of thin magic panels. I've enclosed instructions in this sack on how to assemble those panels to trigger a projection of the gun. Unfortunately, the gun itself will never be the same."

"What do you mean?" Jordan asked. Allan had been so excited about it; if it was damaged or destroyed, he'd be upset.

"The fire will permanently change the chemical makeup of the gun. There is a price to this magic, as I've told you before." She moved on, retrieving an amber glass vial containing a liquid. "This is the magic that will allow you to appear to people who might know you without alarming them. Drink the contents before you venture out where you can be seen. The effects will last one full day. Try not to act surprised if the people you interact with behave in a strange way; it's just the magic doing its work."

"What kind of strange way?"

Sohne shrugged. "It's hard to say; Earthlings and magic are unpredictable. You may not notice anything unusual, or there may be side effects. I could venture to predict that if a person has a certain feeling about you, like if you had a bad encounter in the past, and there was emotional residue," Sohne dropped the vial back into the sack, "the magic might exacerbate these emotions. Or," she handed the sack to Jordan, "they could make the person want to converse with you in song."

"You neglected to warn us of these side effects before we made the deal with you." Sol glared at the Elf.

"Would you have made a different decision?" Sohne shot the annoyed Arpak a mild look. "I told you I can do it, and I can. You'll make it through. But no magic is without some consequence."

Jordan let out a breath. "It's fine," she said to Sol, "I'll deal with whatever happens as best I can." She looked to Sohne. "Anything else?"

"That's it," said the Elf. "You can go anytime."

"And the promise?" Sol took the sack from Jordan and slung it over his body.

"You'll know when it comes due."

"Cryptic as ever," Sol muttered.

Jordan crouched in front of Blue, taking his reptilian face in her hands. "Sol and I have to go where you can't follow, buddy. Meet us in Rodania, okay?" Blue gave an unhappy whistle in the back of his throat.

Sohne watched the interaction with interest. "Has this animal imprinted on you?"

Jordan nodded and stood. "Yes, it happened in Maticaw. We were told he was a Predoian Miniature--"

Sohne laughed and shook her head. "Obviously not."

"Do you know what he is?"

"No, but I can guarantee you he's no miniature. You know that your portal passage risks breaking the bond between you, right? You should brace yourself for that."

Jordan paled. "Excuse me?"

Sohne's expression was a hair's breadth from an eyeroll.

"What do you think? That a bond between the two of you can withstand inter-dimensional travel and just snap back into place when you return?" She shook her head. "That is incredibly naive. The bond may be magic-based; if it is, your leaving Oriceran will break it for sure. If it's just a regular bond between humanoid and animal, then it should be fine."

"How can we tell which it is?" Sol asked, clenching a fist.

Sohne gave an elegant shrug.

Jordan felt Sol's hand on her lower back as she struggled for words. Anger flooded through her.

"You *knew* I didn't know this was a risk. You knew I didn't grow up here, and don't know the laws of magic," Jordan accused. "Why did you wait until now to tell me?" She took a step forward, her teeth clenched. "You are one greedy, manipulative Elf. We never should have come to you!"

Sol put a restraining hand on her arm. "Jordan."

She turned away from the Elf, seething, trying to keep herself from spitting into her smug face. She breathed in through her nose and out through her mouth, placing her cool palms against her hot cheeks. She looked down at Blue, who was watching her pace, and her eyes misted up.

Sol's voice was quiet in her ear. "You don't have to. We can think of something else."

"The unbreakable promise cannot be broken, even if you decide not to use the magic," Sohne interjected firmly. "The deal has been made. You owe me."

Jordan deliberately turned her back on the Elf and faced Sol. "We need to do this; my father and Rodania need us." She crouched before Blue, feeling frayed and emotional, and took his face in her hands. "I have to go. I hope you understand. Fly to Rodania; go home. We'll meet you there in a few days."

Blue cocked his head and blinked.

Jordan kissed his scaly cheek and stood, taking a shaky breath.

It had worked before; he'd understood when she, Eohne, and Toth had gone to Trevilsom without him.

But you weren't leaving Oriceran, a voice whispered. *This is different.*

She shook her head and turned to Sol. "Let's go."

Sol held up her stolen feather. Jordan threw Sohne one last look of disgust and reached for it.

"One last thing."

Sohne's voice stayed Jordan's hand.

"What?" Jordan almost snarled the word.

"A message for Eohne." Sohne cocked her head. "She is looking in the wrong place. Remind her that our worst poisons are also our best medicines. It is simply a matter of dosage."

Jordan was unsure what to think of this piece of advice. It had to be about Allan; he was the only one in Eohne's life at the moment that was in need of medicine.

"She'll know what that means?" Sol asked, his voice hard.

Sohne nodded. "She'll know."

"Fine," Jordan snapped.

She grasped the feather between her fingertips. Charra-Rae dissolved, and the bone-grinding pressure of interdimensional travel began.

CHAPTER TWENTY-ONE

Jordan had forgotten how disorienting portal travel was. The humming of electricity in her ears and the buzzing inside her joints brought it all back like a kick in the teeth. The pressure on her body was so tight and unforgiving she could hardly breathe. The near unbearable pressure was rapidly replaced by the whispering of thousands of voices. They filled her head like a hive of bees. She had no sight, no taste—-only sound. She flailed, trying to grasp Sol, but had no body with which to find him; it was as though she was alone in an endless universe of vibration.

A flash of bright daylight and familiar birdsong greeted her as she tumbled onto the damp earth, bruising her ribs on the roots of the oak.

"Ooof!"

All the air whooshed out of her lungs and a hot breath went past her ear as Sol's heavy weight landed on her back, crushing her into the earth.

"Sorry, Jordan," Sol exhaled as he rolled off her. "Did I hurt you?"

She rolled onto her back, taking deep breaths and blinking up at the sky of the universe she was born in. "I'm fine," she wheezed.

"I'll never get used to that." Sol lay beside her panting. His arms flopped out, and his hand took hers. They rested a moment, letting the vertigo of the inter-dimensional travel pass.

Jordan got to her feet, head whirling. Her backyard was a green and blue blur. She reached out a hand for Sol and whacked him across the stomach.

"Sorry. I can't see very well. Were my eyes really this bad?" She blinked groggily at the fuzzy world and swayed unsteadily on her feet. "How did I ever survive?"

She caught the yellow blur of her feather transport as Sol tucked it into his clothing, ensuring she wouldn't accidentally touch it.

He took Jordan's hand and put an arm around her waist. "Watch your step, there are roots everywhere." He led Jordan across the treacherous terrain to where the lawn smoothed out. He kept her hand in his. "You lost your glasses when we went through the portal last time," he reminded her. "Have you got an extra pair in the house?"

"I have contacts in my bathroom upstairs. If you can help me get there, I'll be fine." Jordan felt so light and unencumbered now that she had no wings that her knees locked with every step. She paused. "I feel so weird."

"Give it a minute, it'll pass."

The two Arpaks made their way to the house only to find the back door locked. Jordan directed Sol to where a spare key was hidden under the deck, and they let themselves in. They headed up the grand staircase to Jordan's bedroom. Sol waited while she trundled blindly around the bathroom; putting in her contacts took her twice as long as it used to.

She breathed a sigh of relief as the world was once again made of crisp edges and clear detail. She blinked into the mirror as her vision cleared, and what she saw made her cringe. She looked tired, and droplets of moisture dampened her cheeks, as her red eyes wept from being probed. Her leather armor and Rodanian clothing and weaponry looked like a Halloween costume, yet she felt naked without her wings.

She left the bathroom, still blinking.

Sol was sitting on her bed. She couldn't help but stare at him. "I'd forgotten how different you look without your wings."

He smiled. "Yeah, you look weird to me now, too. I'm so used to you having those canary feathers behind you."

Jordan crossed to her closet and retrieved a pair of jeans, a t-shirt, and a hoodie. "May as well be comfortable while we're here. I can't go downtown dressed like a D&D character." She turned back to Sol, eyeing his size. "And neither can you. I'll raid my dad's closet." Jordan felt grimy from all the travel, and she peered at her grubby fingertips. "Why don't you take a shower in my dad's room, and I'll grab one here? We can meet in the war-room. It's up the next level, you can't miss it."

"Sounds like a plan. I'd love to clean up."

Jordan rummaged through her dad's walk-in closet for something that would fit Sol. She found a pair of light blue jeans with the tags still attached, a plain black t-shirt, a pair of briefs, and a pair of short socks.

Sol waited awkwardly outside the closet, eyeballing Allan's bedroom.

"Try these on." Jordan emerged from the closet with the set of clothes and a pair of white tennis shoes. "You and my dad are close to the same height; they might be a little snug, but they should do."

"What is this?" Sol held the boxer-briefs up with a look of dismay.

"Underwear. Earth guys seem to like them." Jordan laughed at the look on his face.

"Pass. They look a little restrictive." He put down the clothes and shoes and held the underwear out with both hands. "Humans really wear these?" He poked a finger through the y-front and shot Jordan a look of horror. "Is this for what I think it is?"

Jordan hid a smile behind her hand. Her face heated, and she turned for the door. "Come upstairs when you're done. Take your time."

Jordan showered and dressed, feeling a million times better. When she stepped out of her bathroom, she heard the shower in her father's room still running.

Sol must be enjoying the luxury.

She searched the house for her cell phone, which she couldn't find anywhere. "Police must have taken it," she muttered, rummaging through drawers and combing every likely place. She had wanted to try calling Maria one more time, and also set up an appointment with her family's banker. She settled for booting up the old Dell laptop in Allan's office. It would do nicely for searching and printing off anything helpful she could find about the Lewis gun.

Jordan's fingers trembled as they scrolled through her inbox, which was mostly full of useless newsletters. Her index finger hovered over an email from one of her old climbing buddies. It was titled 'Where Are You?!?!? The Joke Is OVER!"

Jordan's heart pounded, but her finger did not click the message open.

What if the police are watching my email? Ugh, of course they are. They have access to all of my accounts by this point. Even if I wanted to respond, what would I say? I'm going back to Oriceran, I'm not in Virginia to stay. So what good would it do to tell anyone I'm here?

It was an ethical dilemma of proportions Jordan did not feel equipped to handle at the moment.

I wish Dad were here; he would know what to do.

Jordan sat with her finger hovering over the mouse a moment longer. Finally, she closed up her email and opened a browser. She ran a search for anything related to the Lewis gun, anything that might help Arth to recreate it and get some copies operational in short order. She got her dad's printer spitting out documents, and left it to its business.

She went upstairs and pushed open the door to her dad's war room. Everything looked just the way they'd left it, yet everything seemed so different. This was where she'd last had a conversation with her father; last seen him lucid.

The gun sat in its crate, but someone had swept up the styrofoam peanuts. *It must have been Cal.* Jordan wondered how the groundskeeper was taking their disappearance, and entertained the idea of leaving him a note letting him know they were okay. She didn't like the idea of leaving Cal in misery, but notifying him was probably a bad idea; he might take it to the police. She supposed she could use the magic Sohne gave her, but it had a time limit, and the most important thing was getting the gold.

Footsteps on the stairs made Jordan peek out the door.

Sol stepped up onto the landing wearing the black t-shirt––it was a touch too small. It stretched across his chest and accentuated the muscles that were normally hidden under his smooth leather armor. The jeans hugged his thighs, and Jordan realized with an embarrassing rush of heat to her face how attractive Sol was without all of the usual accoutrements.

He came in, eyes bouncing around the room.

"Wow. Your dad's war room. He really does have a lot of stuff."

"This is the gun." She knelt beside the crate. "We have to take it out of the box for this to work."

They pulled the wooden sides away, and Jordan retrieved a garbage bag to hold all of the packing peanuts and styrofoam molds.

Cal would find the gun missing and be alarmed, but it couldn't be helped.

"They don't make these any more?" Sol scanned the folded sheet that had been tucked inside the box. "It's an antique?"

Jordan nodded. "The guns they make now make this thing look like a slingshot."

"Too bad he doesn't collect anything newer." Sol scanned the documents with interest.

"My dad can tell you all about it when he wakes up." Jordan retrieved the sack Sohne had given them that contained the magic they needed. "First step." Jordan untied the leather thong and opened the mouth of the sack. "No touchy," she warned and upturned the sack. Out fell a sparkly gray powder that looked like metal shavings. It landed on the gun's magazine and immediately began to spread across the surface of the gun, flashing and turning as it went. It crawled across the gun's edges, down into its cracks and crannies, leaving a thin film behind.

When the entire gun was coated inside and out, Jordan pulled out the lighter she'd snagged from a shelf in her bathroom. She lit it, and held the flame to one corner of the gun.

"Sorry, Dad," she muttered. "It's for a good cause."

The powder caught fire, and a small ring of flame began to sizzle and burn, slowly spreading across the lineament of the gun. It moved at a snail's pace.

"That's it; she said this part will take hours." Jordan looked up at Sol. "Ready to see Richmond, my friend?"

They took a vintage Plymouth from the garage. Jordan didn't want to take her own car or the Land Rover Allan was known for. They were both missing persons, and the vehicles could easily be recognized. The Plymouth was a car Allan had restored in the likeness of the one his grandfather, Declin, had driven. Whitewall tires, cherry-red finish, and chrome everywhere. Allan rarely drove the car; he kept it for nostalgic reasons. Even though it was a little on the flashy side, Jordan thought it was the best choice. She found a couple of her old hiking backpacks and one of her dad's ballcaps, and threw them into the backseat.

They made the drive without incident, and Jordan parked outside their family's bank. She took out the vial Sohne had given her, and eyed it dubiously before throwing it back in one gulp.

"Want me to wait here?" Sol asked, taking the empty vial.

Jordan shook her head and wiped her mouth. "Come in with me. I believe I could use the moral support." The muscles of her quads were quivering, making her feel like her knees were literally trembling with fear.

What if the magic doesn't work?

She blew out a breath, pushing the thought from her mind. They got out of the car and shut the doors.

Sol craned his neck up at the bank. "Imposing."

"Yes. I believe that's intentional."

The Arpaks-incognito took the steps up to the bank's revolving doors and went inside.

Twenty-two minutes later, they emerged carrying two backpacks full of cash.

"That was so weird," said Sol as they got into the Plymouth and pulled away.

"No kidding. Sohne did say they might converse in song, but that guy was painfully off-key."

"Could have been worse; at least he wasn't an ex of yours. I'd rather listen to tuneless singing than have to pull an old flame off of you."

"Ha ha." Jordan whacked him on the shoulder.

She drove the Plymouth to a seedier neighborhood,

known for its pawn shops, and parked. The Arpaks each grabbed a backpack and headed into the little shop in the corner of a back alley.

She had never purchased gold bullion before; just the idea made her nervous. She put on her father's ballcap and a pair of sunglasses, but the attempt at the disguise only made her more nervous. Her palms were sweating.

The little man behind the counter was a consummate professional. He didn't even blink at her request to buy all the gold she could get for the amount of cash she had in the backpacks.

"Are you okay?" Sol whispered to her as the man disappeared into the back after counting her money. "You seem tense."

"I feel like a criminal," she whispered.

"Why?"

"Normal people don't buy up truckloads of gold bullion--" she bit off her words as the man returned, and heaved a very heavy trunk onto the countertop.

"Here we are," he said amiably. "And you're wrong. Normal people do this every day. You'd be surprised at how many gold bars you'd find under mattresses and floorboards across America. Can't be too careful these days; what with martial law coming, and the devaluation of paper money. Whole thing's a farce, anyway."

"Right," Jordan replied, chewing her thumbnail.

The transaction went smoothly, and the kind man helped them pile the heavy gold into the backpacks. "You'll be taking this straight to storage, I hope?"

"Yes," Sol said, hefting both backpacks. "No detours."

"Glad to hear it," the man crinkled a smile. He peered at

Jordan through the specs on the end of his nose. "Anyone ever tell you that you look an awful lot like that pretty Kacy girl who went missing all those months ago? Different build, but a similar face."

Jordan laughed and pulled her ballcap down. She slid her aviators back on, though she hadn't yet left the shop.

"Oh, I get that all the time."

"At this rate, the gun will be ready around midnight," Jordan said, entering the parlor. She'd just checked on the magical processing of the weapon, and there was still a few hours to go.

Sol was standing with his back to her, facing a cluster of family photographs on the wall. He looked over his shoulder, his expression clouded. "This is Jaclyn?" He pointed to a small portrait.

"Yeah." Jordan looked around, hoping to direct him to one of the larger photos on the mantel, but they were gone. "There were more; my dad must have taken them down." She frowned. "I just wish I could talk to him, ask him how much he knows. Part of me thinks he must have known about Oriceran. My mom's disappearance was so complete, so traceless."

Sol crossed the room to Jordan and crouched in front of the fireplace, selecting some paper and kindling from the basket that Cal always kept full.

"What are you doing?"

"We have a little while to wait yet. I thought you might like a fire. You said this used to be your favorite thing——a fire in the parlor fireplace, no matter the temperature outside."

Jordan smiled and knelt beside him, grabbing the box of wooden matches.

Sol prepared the kindling and the logs, and Jordan lit the starter. They blew on the small flame, coaxing it into life.

"Maybe Eohne will have woken your father up by the time we return, and you'll be able to ask him everything." Sol sat back on his haunches and stared at the growing flame. "What do you think Jaclyn wants?"

Jordan blew out a long breath. "I have thought over the details of the day I saw her so often in my mind, looking for some clue."

"Walk me through it again."

For the second time, Jordan described her confrontation with Jaclyn and her henchman, Ashley. She went back in her mind, closed her eyes, and called the scene to life in great detail.

"She's got ambitions," Jordan concluded. "That's the one thing I'm certain of. She's running the trade office and wants to expand her territory. She's also messing with the trade of that medicine your uncle needs. But why she's doing this, why she's shown such disdain for my dad and for this family, and why she's interfering with the trade of critical goods?" Jordan shook her head. "It's beyond me."

The fire caught, and the wood ignited, sending heat out to warm their hands and faces. Jordan made tea, and they settled on the sofa to wait for the processing of the gun to finish. Sol sat beside her, his warmth radiating into her side.

"How did you feel about the battle?" Sol asked. "I wanted to keep an eye out for you, but you just disappeared."

"I got pulled down to Middle by a harpy." Jordan let her thoughts take over as she sipped her tea. "I'm still processing the whole thing; the chaos, the stink, the blood, the danger. It was a crazy experience." She glanced at him. "Chayla saved my life, you know."

"Did she?" Sol gave a crooked smile. "Guess she doesn't hate you as much as you thought."

"Maybe." Jordan might have once cared a great deal more that there was someone on her team that didn't like her. Now, it was nice to be liked, but it wasn't a necessity. She shrugged. "However she feels, I don't take it personally."

"That's wise. And how is it going with Toth?" Sol took a sip of the tea.

"We've figured out my strengths and weaknesses. Looks like I won't make an archer or a swordsman anytime soon, but I can throw knives pretty well."

"Really? Show me."

"What? Now?"

"Why not? You've got knives here, right?"

Jordan laughed. "Not throwing knives! Only steak knives. But I'll tell you what…" She got to her feet, set her tea on the coffee table, and crossed to the far corner behind the piano. Sol followed her, curious. She opened the doors covering a dartboard, and retrieved three red darts and three black ones. "Know how to shoot darts?"

Sol took the black ones she offered him. "We have a

similar game on Oriceran, but we use small, star-shaped knives."

"Like ninja stars?"

"Very like, yes." He braced his feet and took a practice throw, sending a dart into the outer ring of the bullseye.

"Not too shabby." Jordan pushed him out of the way and threw her own. The dart planted itself outside the game board. She frowned, and her shoulders slumped. "It's my wretched eyesight. It's absolutely awful here."

"Sure it is," Sol teased and elbowed her in the ribs. "Explain to me how you tally this game?"

She went over the rules and explained the point system, while she retrieved the darts. They tossed a coin to decide who would throw first; Jordan won.

She stood in front of the dartboard, bracing her feet for the first throw.

Sol's hands slipped over her hip bones. "Turn this way, just a little bit." His breath whispered past her ear, and goosebumps sprang out on her neck and arms. She waited for Sol to remove his hands, but he didn't. The heat of them soaked through her jeans and warmed her whole body.

"I can't throw while you're doing that."

His hands stayed. Jordan could hear the smile in his words as he stepped closer. "A true warrior can perform even while distracted."

She closed her eyes as a shiver went through her. "And how likely am I," she asked, her voice almost a squeak, "to be distracted by your touch while in the middle of a harpy battle?"

One of his hands slid across her belly, over the fabric of

her shirt. "Just throw. No more talking." His lips touched the back of her ear.

Jordan threw. The dart slapped flat against the wall below the board and clattered to the hardwood floor.

Sol chuckled, his belly flexing against her back.

Who is this? Jordan felt like her mind was going soggy. *He blushes when we touch by accident, and now he's nothing but confidence? Two can play this game.*

She took a breath. Her pulse was ramping up.

Sol's pinky finger grazed the skin of her belly. She narrowed her eyes at the board. She threw again, and the dart embedded itself three inches above the bullseye.

"Better." He spoke the word quietly, right next to her ear. The surprise in his voice gave Jordan a deep satisfaction. "Last one."

She exhaled and threw, and he planted a kiss on her neck, just below her ear.

Her final dart struck just beside the bullseye.

"Ha!"

She turned in his grasp, and he relaxed his hands. The disappointment on his face was comical.

"Your turn." She batted her eyes and gave him a smug smile. Her knees were trembling, and her palms had grown moist, but she wasn't about to betray just how much his touch had affected her.

She wanted to win.

Sol stepped in front of her and took a bracing stance, balancing the dart lightly in his fingers. He eyed the board.

Jordan stepped up behind him. She didn't touch him; just stood there, her body a mere inch from his.

Sol threw.

Bullseye. Right beside her own dart.

Jordan frowned.

Sol levied his second dart, a smile dusting his lips.

Jordan lifted the back of his t-shirt. Just before he threw, she traced a finger along the skin just above his waistband.

The dart buried itself in the outermost ring.

"What were you saying about experienced warriors again?" she asked innocently.

Sol growled, but the rumble wasn't entirely unhappy. He lifted his final dart.

As he prepared to throw, Jordan lifted the back of his shirt higher, exposing the skin just below his wingless shoulder blades. The musculature of his back was so beautiful, powerful from a lifetime of flying.

Was he this beautiful when I first met him?

As he threw, she pressed a soft kiss right in the center of his spine.

Sol groaned and turned. "You win."

He planted his lips on hers and picked her up, carrying her backward. Jordan returned Sol's passion with everything she had. She wrapped her arms and legs around him. They hit the piano, which had been left open, and the instrument rattled off a dissonant, tuneless clamor.

Neither of them noticed.

Sol redirected, taking her toward the fireplace without breaking their kiss. He paused in front of the fire and pulled back, his eyes dazed and half-closed.

"Jordan."

Their breathing came in ragged bursts. Her heart was

working overtime, sending blood cascading through her, turning her whole body into a live wire.

Her voice was rough. "Winner takes all."

They collapsed together on the carpet in front of the crackling fire.

CHAPTER TWENTY-TWO

Eohne had just finished watering Allan when Jordan and Sol exploded from nowhere, and landed in a heap on the floor of Sol's bedroom.

There was a loud, heavy *clank* as the two backpacks struck the floor, and a *snap* and an explosion of paper. The sheets fluttered about, settling on Allan's form on the bed and all over the floor.

Eohne straightened, an empty water glass in her hand, staring at the tangle of limbs.

Sol lay on his back, blinking up at Eohne, dazed. Jordan was on top of one of Sol's knees, and under the other. He winced as her weight pressed on his kneecap.

"Watch me old bones," he groaned.

"Sorry," Jordan mumbled, rolling off Sol's leg and collapsing on the floor on her back.

They'd put their Rodanian clothing and armor back on, and Jordan had taken out her contacts before they'd portaled home. She blinked at the details of the room and at her father's form, happy to have her amazing vision back.

"Has he stopped listing inventory?"

"It comes and goes," Eohne explained. "Almost like he's following a normal schedule of sleeping and waking, if waking was nothing more than a constant drone of words."

Jordan's hand went to the satchel where the thin magic plates––the final product of Sohne's magical transformation of the gun––were stacked. Each piece was individually wrapped in a towel, and she peeked in to inspect them, patting and feeling for broken pieces. She breathed a sigh of relief that they'd made the journey safely.

"Welcome home," Eohne said, her dark eyes scanning the mess of documents spread all over the room. Her dark eyes passed to the two bulging backpacks, and then to her Arpak friends. "You both look naked without your wings. Everything went ok?"

"Everything went great," Jordan said, stretching side to side to work the kinks out of her back.

Eohne didn't miss the way Jordan and Sol caught one another's eye. The color was high on their cheeks.

"Mmhmm. Is that all gold?" Eohne pointed to the lumpy forms of the two backpacks at Sol's feet.

Jordan nodded and coughed, one hand on her chest where the tightness was beginning to ease. "Do you think it'll be safe here?" Jordan asked Sol.

"For now, until we can set you up at a bank. No one knows it's here. I have a false back in the closet in the main room we can tuck it behind." Sol heaved the bags of gold over his shoulder and took them to the other room to hide them.

"I don't see the gun," Eohne observed. The Elf did not appear alarmed at this; she knew Sohne well. The princess had done something clever, she was sure.

"The gun is in here," Jordan patted the satchel under her arm. "Sort of. Sohne transformed it into panels, and included instructions--"

Understanding passed over Eohne's features. "A map. How clever," she murmured, "and portable." The Charra-Rae princess was Princess of the Elves for a reason. This was very difficult magic; even Eohne marvelled at Sohne's skill. This was not frequency magic, but something else entirely--something Eohne herself was not capable of doing.

Sol returned with two bottles in hand, each containing a small stinging insect. "We made it, but we're not done yet." Sol handed Jordan her purple wasp. "Ready for this part?"

She let out a long sigh and nodded, bracing herself for the pain that would bring back her wings.

"Where's Blue?" Jordan asked Eohne once the pain of the transformation had passed, and she and Sol were once again sporting their feathers.

It felt good to have the weight of her wings again. She felt whole, and much more like herself.

"I haven't seen him. Not since you left."

Jordan's heart gave a heavy squeeze of anxiety.

What if our bond was only magical? Will he not come back at all, ever? Will he even know me if I go looking for him? Where would he have gone, if not back here?

Jordan's thoughts were interrupted when a mild burning sensation wound its way around her left arm. She shook her hand, thinking at first it was just some side effect of the wasp sting or the transformation. Her eyes widened as dark marks appeared on her wrist. She yanked her sleeve up, watching as marks emerged all the way up her arm, and disappeared under her sleeve.

"Eohne?" Jordan raised her left arm so the Elf could see where a long tattoo of glyphs and symbols had appeared, wrapping itself around her limb. The marks began at the tip of her ring finger, passed over her palm, between her thumb and forefinger and spiralled all the way around her arm and past her elbow. The burning sensation ran all the way up to Jordan's heart; she supposed the marks did, as well. The glyphs were not a language she recognized.

The Elf frowned as she lifted Jordan's arm to the light, and her expression grew alarmed. "What have you done?"

"What do you mean?"

"You made the unbreakable promise?" Eohne's eyes bore into Jordan's. "Why did you do that?"

"I *had* to. It was all Sohne would take in payment. I didn't have a choice."

Eohne's red lips flattened into a line. "There is always a choice."

Jordan felt a seed of fear take root in her belly.

"Why? What do you think she's going to ask for? Last time, it all worked out; getting my wings the first time didn't cost me anything."

"That's how Sohne works," Eohne explained, letting go

of Jordan's arm. "She sees pieces of the future and knows more than she lets on. She may have even manipulated you by making the first promise pass so easily. Who knows what she has in mind? You'll have this tattoo until the promise is fulfilled. I don't know what she wants—-I don't have the sight like she does. But I can promise you it will be no small thing." Eohne met her friend's eyes. "You will not be able to deny her."

Jordan's arms and legs swept with gooseflesh as she looked down at the tattoo that had wrapped itself around her left arm from hand to elbow like a boa constrictor. "That's what she said, but nothing can be done about it now," she murmured. "It's finished."

"No," Eohne corrected her regretfully. "It's not finished. It'll be finished only when you have fulfilled your end of the bargain. She could come to collect a decade from now; the unbreakable promise does not expire."

"You're scaring me with this talk. At this point, I just need to hope for the best." Jordan averted her eyes from the tattoo. "By the way, Sohne had a message for you."

The Elf's expression went from unhappy to wary. "What is it?"

"She said that you're looking in the wrong place. She said to remind you that our worst poisons are also our best medicines, that it is simply a matter of dose. Does that mean anything to you?"

Eohne's face twitched as something clicked into place.

A slow smile spread across her face. "I'll be damned," she whispered. "That clever Elf, how does she do it?" Her eyes drifted wonderingly to Allan's form.

"What does it mean?"

A loud voice from outside the apartment boomed, "Solomon Donda. Show yourself."

Jordan thought the voice was oddly familiar.

Sol winced, and Jordan registered that he didn't look all that surprised at this summons.

The Arpaks and the Elf went to the terrace.

"Modi," Sol growled. It was the same Arpak courier who had summoned Toth to see Balroc.

The Arpak hovered in front of them, his glossy black wings flashing in the sun, his black curls blowing in the wind. On Modi's face was a look of Machiavellian satisfaction; whatever message he was about to deliver, he felt smug about it. He retrieved a small black envelope from one of his satchels.

Sol stood at the edge of the terrace and lifted his chin. He held out a hand to take the envelope.

Modi tossed the envelope to Sol with an uncaring flick. The envelope spun and caught a draft of air, but Sol snatched it with his fingertips, keeping his eyes on his colleague.

"You know what this means," Modi snarled. "Solomon Donda."

"He already said his full name once," Eohne whispered to Jordan. "Awfully formal."

"I know what it means." Sol lowered the envelope to his side and stepped back. He pried the gold signet from his finger and held it out to Modi, not daring to throw such a precious and significant piece of jewelry.

"What are you doing?" Jordan stepped forward with alarm.

Modi darted in, snatched the ring, and deposited it in a

small pocket in his vest. Then he spun away, spiralling around the tower and out of sight.

"Sol!" Jordan hooked his shoulder with a hand and turned him to face her. "Why did you give him your courier ring?"

"I've been released from my duty as a courier," Sol answered simply. "I'm okay with it."

He passed the gaping Arpak and the bemused Elf, wandered into his kitchen, and opened a drawer. There was a *thunk* as the drawer got stuck; the island was still crooked from the damage the harpy had wrought. Sol tossed the black envelope inside and slammed the drawer shut.

"What do you mean *'released'*?" Jordan sputtered. "You love your job! It was one of the first things I recognized about you. Your job as courier was paramount, priority above all else."

Sol's voice softened, and he held her eyes with his. "I have other priorities now."

Jordan swallowed, locked in his ice-blue gaze. "But…" Jordan stuttered. "Why did they dismiss…"

A look of understanding crossed her features.

"Ohhhh, Sol," she breathed, her shoulders slumped.

"What? What am I missing here?" Eohne was pulling on her overcoat and looping her satchel over her head as she asked this.

"There is no such thing as 'putting in for leave' with the King's Couriers, is there?" Jordan guessed. "You never went to secure permission; you *knew* it would cost you your job, and you did it anyway."

Sol didn't need to speak or even nod for her to know she was right.

Jordan closed her eyes and let out a long exhale. "I don't know whether to hug you or throttle you. Why did you do that?"

"I couldn't let you go alone. I just realized some things." Sol stepped closer to her, his eyes begging her to understand. "Don't be angry."

"But it's your livelihood!" she cried, "What are you going to do now?"

"I hear I'm not such a bad soldier, for an Arpak."

Sol's mouth quirked, remembering Toth's words after the harpy battle in which their losses had been so high. Jordan had gone ahead to the apartment, leaving Sol to attend the debriefing. Toth had pulled Sol aside and offered him a place in his squadron, should he want it. The Arpak had been both surprised and flattered.

"You don't want to be a soldier," Jordan argued now.

"Maybe not for the rest of my life, but I can do better for Rodania right now by protecting it." Sol's look darkened. "My trust in my government has eroded over these past few months. I used to think they were incorrupt, altruistic." He gave a bitter laugh. "I'm not sure about that anymore, and I don't want to be party to helping them continue along this path. My government is how Rodania ended up in this mess in the first place."

Sol's eyes fell on Eohne, who was standing at the edge of the terrace peering down. "Where are you going?" he asked.

"How does a non-winged body get down from here?"

"There are stairs, but I'll take you wherever you need to

go," Sol offered as he and Jordan went to the Elf. "Why? Where do you need to go?"

Eohne pointed a finger at the hole in the canopy directly below them, where she had thrown the harpy carcass. "Straight down there."

CHAPTER TWENTY-THREE

While Sol took Eohne where she wanted to go, Jordan winged her way directly to Arth's showroom. Eohne said she and Sol would be gone less than five minutes, and they agreed it was okay to leave Allan's sleeping form alone for such a short measure of time.

Pink tinged the sky as dusk settled in. Jordan couldn't wait to fall into bed that night. Exhaustion from the portal travel and the transformation that followed burned in every blood cell in a way unlike normal fatigue.

She wondered if all this magic was having some adverse affect on her and Sol's DNA, the way plane travel exposes travellers to radiation. She supposed she could ask Juer, but she wasn't sure she wanted to know the answer. Sohne had already told her that magic came at a price; if it was radiation, or any other toxicity, for that matter, there were enough similarities between Oriceran nutrition and Earth nutrition that a diet rich in leafy greens, veggies, and fruits should help stave off the damage to their DNA.

The small Middle Rodanian town of Crypsis came into

view. Jordan drifted into town on open wings, catching any draft she could to buoy her up with the least amount of energy output. Her flying techniques had changed so much since she'd started training with the Strix soldiers. When she'd first gotten her wings, she'd powered her way around, not paying any attention to technique. She burned through her energy quickly, was constantly hungry, and her shoulders and back ached most nights. She had finally learned how to fly efficiently using wind and air currents as allies to serve her, rather than as enemies to overcome.

She drifted to the street and closed up her wings as the soles of her boots made contact with the cobblestones. She walked toward Arth's shop without breaking momentum. An elderly female Arpak with small, dark green wings watched her graceful landing with an appreciative expression. The two Arpaks nodded to one another as they passed.

Jordan smiled. She really felt like she belonged here. One thought led to another as the street passed under her feet, and she found herself contemplating her and Sol's living situation. He'd been so generous to allow her, Allan, and Eohne to use his space the way they were, but it wasn't a great long-term solution. She made a note to bring it up with Sol when there was an opportune moment.

Arth's shop appeared at the end of the street. The display in front had been pulled inside for the evening, and Arth herself was locking the front door.

Jordan broke into a jog and called out to the Nycht as she approached. "Arth!"

The woman turned, and a smile of recognition broke over her features. "Well, hello!"

"Remember me?" she smiled down at the Nycht; Jordan had forgotten just how petite she was.

Arth's spray of dreadlocks had been cut off, and her hair had been cropped super short, making her look like a pixie. Her large, coal black eyes sparkled at Jordan, and her white teeth blazed from her face as she returned the smile.

"Of course I do! Hard to forget a bright yellow Arpak with a blue dragon for a pet. Where is your little friend?"

Jordan's shoulders slumped at the mention of Blue. "I'm not sure, to be honest. I'm hoping he'll be home by the time I get back."

Arth nodded. "I've heard they're adventurous and independent." She dropped a small brass key into her pocket. "My shop is closed for the night, but I'm happy to open up again, if it's quick. Do you know what you're looking for?"

"I don't know if it'll be quick, but I need to present an idea to you. If there was an opportunity for you to do something great for Rodania, would you want to do it?"

Arth's eyes narrowed. "Of course," she growled. "I have never seen Rodania in such a state. Everyone is battening down the hatches, complaining about the government, afraid for their lives and property." She shook her head and clucked her tongue. She brightened immediately though, and Jordan was reminded vaguely of a big, bouncy ball. "I saw you fighting those blasted birds," Arth told her. "You were so brave, you and the other soldiers. I am so proud of my brothers for what they are doing."

"Your brothers joined the Strix army?"

The Nycht nodded. "They are good men, both of them. They have no reason to save Rodania." She glowered. "It has not given them any reason to be loyal."

Words stalled on Jordan's tongue as a suspicion crept up.

"What are the names of your brothers?"

"Toth and Caje."

Jordan gave a laugh of amazement. "Are you kidding me?"

"No. Why? I mean, I guess you know them, too. You train under them, right?"

"Not just that." Jordan clasped Arth's hand. "Toth has saved my life at least twice, maybe more––and he saved my father's life, too. He is amazing!"

Arth chuckled. "Saving lives. That sounds like Toth, alright. He's the best." She snugged her black scarf up under her chin. "So, what can I do for you and Rodania on this fine evening?"

"Can we take a few minutes inside, and I can explain? Please?" Jordan gestured to the shop. "It's kind of an emergency, and I think you're going to want to talk through a few details."

"Sure. Okay." Arth dug out the keys she'd recently deposited in her pocket and reopened her shop door. "Come on in."

The shop was not the way Jordan remembered it. It smelled the same, of oil and metal and smoke, but all of the inventions she remembered––the clock, the radio, the gun––were gone, replaced by different ones. Now there was a long-necked electric lamp, a cherry red Vespa parked in the middle of the floor, an antique foot-operated sewing machine, complete with the Singer logo on the back of it, and many other things.

"You've been busy, Arth!"

Arth set down her bag. Her wings fluttered and tightened as though she was a touch on the chilly side. It was cool in the shop. "I turn over inventory quickly."

Jordan gaped at the perfect replicas, amazed at how like the real thing they looked. "You really are just what Rodania needs right now," She grinned at Arth. "Where do you do your work?"

"In the back room. Would you like to see?"

"Yes, please. And I think it best if I show you this idea away from the windows."

Arth led Jordan through an archway, to a room with tall ceilings, multiple tables, and tools Jordan couldn't even begin to recognize or comprehend. Among tools, piles of sheet metals, and jars of mysterious, sparkly shavings, there were books and scrolls haphazardly stacked and shoved into open wooden trunks and scattered over tables. Arth pulled shut a sliding door, dividing the shop from her workspace.

Jordan stopped in front of a long wooden table. "Can we use this? I have a sort of hologram to show you."

"A hologram? How intriguing." Arth cleared away the jars and books, making way for Jordan's presentation.

The Arpak went about setting up the metallic panels according to the instructions Sohne had included. Her hands were growing clammy as doubt crept at her edges, the way it always did when magic was involved.

What if the magic fails? What if Sol and I did something wrong when we did the first part of the spell?

She worked slowly and precisely, trying to keep these thoughts at bay. The panels stayed erect until Jordan had laid out every piece, even though there was no visible force keeping them up. She stepped back and took a breath. Arth hovered at her elbow, watching with as much attention as a child seeing the circus for the first time.

"But this is some kind of magic, no?" Arth breathed. "How do you know how to do magic?"

"I don't have a clue what I'm doing, trust me." Jordan pulled the jar of charcoal powder from her bag and unscrewed the cap. "I was instructed by an Elf, but I'm just crossing my fingers that this actually works the way it's supposed to." Jordan read the last instruction and cast her gaze about the shop. "Do you happen to have a hammer with a metal head? A small one?"

"Of course. I have dozens." Arth went to a tall wooden cupboard and swung the doors open. Inside were hundreds of tools, each sitting neatly in their own holder or cup on the shelves, or hanging on pegs inside the door. "Will this do?" Arth held up a short hammer with a small bronze head in the shape of a mushroom.

"Looks like it."

Arth handed the hammer to Jordan, who closed her eyes and uttered a silent prayer that the magic would work; otherwise, she'd destroyed her father's newest acquisition for nothing.

She tapped the panels, which were now all connected, and the workshop rang with the clear *ping* of a small bell. Jordan then tossed the charcoal into the space created by the membranes. A cloud of dust filled the box, but as the women watched, the particles began to vibrate, arranging themselves into lines. The map of the gun took perfect shape before their eyes, each nook and cranny and piece outlined with the vibrating charcoal dust.

"Well I'll be..." Arth's eyes grew wide as saucers. "It's a weapon!"

The charcoal lines solidified and began to glow with a beautiful violet color.

"This is a model of an antique gun from Earth," Jordan explained, her heart pounding with elation. *It worked!* "It's to scale, and it's just what Rodania needs to help fend off the harpy attacks. It was originally modified for aircraft, but we can mount them to the ramparts and towerheads around the city."

Arth's jaw dropped. Her face took on a soft purple, cast in the light of the weapon. "You want me to reverse engineer it?"

"Can you?"

"That depends. Can I touch it?"

Jordan nodded. "The Elf said you can dismantle it piece by piece if you need to, so you can see the exact shape of everything that is needed. Oh." She rummaged in her bag for the printouts. "I also have these for you." She handed Arth the sheaf of crumpled pages. "Sorry they're a little wrinkled. They've come a long way."

Arth snatched the sheets like a starving woman. She rifled through them, her face growing more and more excited. "Bronze. Wood. Aluminum." She chewed her lip, her brows drawing together, her eyes darting back and forth along the pages.

"It's not the most sophisticated weapon out there," Jordan said, apologetically. Arth's concerned expression made her feel the need to explain. "But it's all I had access to on short notice."

"Where did this come fr--"

Arth blinked and shook her head sharply once.

"Nevermind, it's better I don't know." She looked from the pages clutched in her hands to the glowing map of the gun and back again. "But this gun can be mounted to point upward?"

"That's what I understand, yes."

Jordan's heart gave an unexpected ache. *Dad would have loved to be a part of this.*

Rodania was in real danger, and that was terrifying, but the fact that Jordan was being proactive made her feel stronger, more in control, less afraid.

Now the gun was in Arth's hands.

She watched the Nycht make calculations in her head, biting her lip.

"Potassium chlorate," Arth mumbled. "Sulfur. Hmmm."

"Do you have the things you need?"

"I don't know yet." The engineer walked around the gun. "Making the molds is the easy part; it's the ammunition that may prove difficult. Especially in the quantity that…" She straightened. "How many of these guns do you think we need?"

"As many as you can manufacture, as fast as you can manufacture them. And there's no mount shown here—the gun didn't come with one—so you'll have to invent one."

Arth made a masculine sounding grunt. "I don't do factory output. I'm a one-of-a-kind girl." Her brow wrinkled.

Jordan held her breath. "But…? There's a 'but' in there, right?"

"I know some of the boys down at the metal shop on

the south side of Lower Rodania. They'll likely jump at the chance to make something other than speartips, daggers, and buckles. Question is, can they do it? You understand there is no one on Rodania who handles ammunition like the kind needed to outfit these guns?" Arth leveled Jordan with a look. "This is ambitious. We're going to need help; not just with convincing the metal boys to mobilize, but they'll need to be paid, and they'll need to be pulled off whatever they're working on now. I need…"

The Nycht and the Arpak looked at each other.

"Toth," they said simultaneously.

Arth nodded. "I'll go talk to him. Tonight. If anyone can swing the funding and handle the mobilization of this, it's my big brother."

CHAPTER TWENTY-FOUR

The sky was a black maw by the time Jordan returned to the tower apartment, but light was burning in the windows. She landed on the terrace as her jaw creaked with a yawn.

"Hello?" Jordan called as she took off her satchels and loosened her vest. The armor had taken some getting used to, and she definitely felt protected by it, but at the end of a long day, she wanted nothing more than to take it off and wear something light and airy.

"In here," Sol called, his voice sounding muffled.

Jordan listened. "Where?" She peered into the bedroom. Allan's form lay still and sleeping where he always was. Sol and Eohne weren't in the bedroom.

"In the closet."

Jordan wandered through the kitchen, bemused, seeing piles of fabric, boots, blankets, and wooden trunks scattered on the floor behind the small kitchen island. The door to the closet was open a crack. She pulled it open all the way.

Eohne was crammed in the back of the closet, wearing a strange looking set of goggles and fine leather gloves. Her thick dark hair had been pulled back and piled up on top of her head beneath a kerchief. A second linen kerchief was tied over her mouth, and a heavy butcher's apron covered her body. The overall effect was both frightening and funny; she looked like a mad surgeon, or perhaps a steampunk serial killer.

Many small vials were lined up in front of Eohne, filled with liquids in various shades of gray, and sporting hand marked labels. Each bottle, save the one Eohne was currently working with, was stoppered tightly with a cork.

The small space was illuminated by lanterns that were hanging on pegs and nails that had been haphazardly hammered into the walls. Sol hovered just inside the closet door with a kerchief over his mouth.

He turned to put an arm around Jordan.

"What are you guys doing?" she asked warily.

"Eohne is making medicine." Sol pulled his kerchief down.

Jordan watched the Elf. "Is it radioactive? Why are you wearing a hazmat suit?" She then looked back at Sol, who was holding a sheaf of small squares of paper and a pen in the hand that wasn't on her; his fingers were stained with black. "And how come you're *not* in a hazmat suit?"

"She only just let me in. I've been helping." Sol gestured to a hole in the closet door, which looked as though it had been gnawed by a rat.

"Where did you get all this stuff?"

"I went to visit Juer with a list from Eohne. He let us take what we needed from his stores."

"Nice guy, your uncle," said Eohne through the fabric over her mouth. She didn't take her eyes from what she was doing.

"It ain't pretty," Sol gave Jordan a heart-stopping grin and squeezed her, "but she's pretty sure it'll help your dad." Sol bent toward her and sniffed. "You smell like grease. I like it."

Jordan laughed, but her mind skipped over the humor and latched onto what Sol had said.

"It'll help my dad?" Jordan's heart began to run like a little rabbit in her chest.

Eohne pulled the linen away from her face and lifted her goggles. Her face was damp with sweat, and her hair curled in tendrils at her forehead. "The worst is over, but I'm not done yet." She lifted one of the small vials containing a clear liquid. She held up a second, also of clear liquid––crystalline in the lamplight––and poured one into the other. "I still need to cut the poison into another thousand parts." Eohne stretched her neck from side to side and pressed her shoulders down. "At least."

"Poison?"

"Sohne's message," Eohne began. "It was shortly after the harpy attack that your dad started to list his inventory. It was the harpy poison that woke him, I'm sure of it. It didn't even have to touch him, just be in the vicinity. Sohne's message was cryptic, but it made perfect sense to me. I need to make a mild medicine from the harpy's venom. There's probably an easier way to do this, but I don't want to take the time right now to invent it. I'd rather just do what works."

Jordan swallowed. "You think harpy venom will wake my dad up?"

She watched as Eohne continued cutting and pouring, cutting and pouring, each time taking a fresh vial from a trunk on the floor and setting the full one in the tight line of bottles on the closet shelves. These small vials already filled every shelf above Eohne's head.

"Even Juer thinks so," said Sol. "I thought it was weird at first, too, but he agreed with Eohne after hearing her story of the harpy attack, your dad's partial arousal, and Sohne's message that poison is also medicine."

"It's just a matter of dose," murmured Jordan.

"That's right," Eohne smiled. "Now, if you wouldn't mind helping Sol make about a thousand more of those labels, I'll keep working."

"Can you come out of the closet?" Jordan asked as she backed out of the small space. "It's stuffy and kind of smells like something died."

"That's the harpy venom. And I could, but I'm on a roll. I've got my rhythm. Labels, please. I have thirty here already, but I need more. You can start from 1 and go to 1000," the Elf instructed. "I'll know where I am."

Sol grinned at Jordan, his expression hopeful. "We got told."

He went to the kitchen counter where there was another stack of blank paper. Jordan and Sol made a thousand or more small squares and began to number them.

"So, what did Arth say? I wish I could have been there," Sol was bent over the paper, numbering and stacking, numbering and stacking. Jordan was numbering backward from one thousand, while Sol was numbering forward from one.

"She thinks she can do it, but she's going to talk to Toth about mobilizing a team."

"Makes sense. She can't do it all herself. Any idea how long before we have a prototype?"

"I don't know. Arth said she needs time with the plans."

The two Arpaks grew silent and thoughtful as they worked. Jordan yawned. Then Sol yawned. Minutes later, they heard Eohne yawn from the closet.

"Take a break, Eohne," suggested Jordan. "You must be stiff and sore from all that pouring."

"Just a few more," Eohne's voice drifted from the closet. "Another sixty-three, and I'll rest at a round number."

Jordan and Sol finished up the labels and set them where Eohne could reach them.

"I'm going to wash up," Jordan said, fighting back another yawn.

"Good idea." Sol went to Jordan's back and loosened all of her laces, opening up the back.

Jordan closed herself inside the water closet and sighed with pleasure as she wormed her way out of her armor, shedding it into piles on the floor like snakeskin.

The shower in Sol's house was a tall, wide box lined with textured rectangular tiles. Two thin chains hung from the ceiling, fastened to levers which, when pulled, allowed hot and cold water to mingle and cascade down in a waterfall. The wash area wasn't quite large enough to stretch her wings out fully, but she was able to open them and let the water pour over both sides.

Sol had explained that every residential tower had been

engineered to capture and store rainwater. Part of the Light Elves' magic included an eternal flame that heated some of that water, which was then distributed via gravity to all of the apartments beneath it. It was, like most things in Rodania, medieval with a magical twist.

Jordan's mind wandered to Blue as the hot water eased her tight muscles and washed the smell of leather, armor, sweat, grease, smoke, and oil off her body and feathers. Her heart grew heavy when she thought of her little reptilian companion.

Where is he? I wonder if it's better this way, she thought with a touch of bitterness. *He's free now; we won't have to endure him getting kicked out of Rodania, or make some agonizing decision about what to do.*

These thoughts only made Jordan feel mildly better. She missed Blue so badly she could taste it, but she loved him enough to want what was best for him. He was a wild creature; a beautiful predator who belonged in acres of wilderness, not cramped up in some apartment in rural Rodania.

Jordan closed up the waterfall and toweled off. She stepped out of the wash-space, but turned her back to it, leaving her wings inside. She shook her wings, and sprays of water splattered all over the inside of the tile room.

A full-length mirror had been fastened to the back of the bathroom door––which towered high above Jordan's head, the way all Rodanian doors did. She caught a glimpse of her reflection and paused. Her skin was pale from being completely covered in armor and protected from the sun, except for her face, which was tanned and dusted with freckles.

Her body, while it had always been fit from climbing and running, had changed dramatically since she'd begun to train as a Strix combatant. Ridges of muscle outlined her shoulders and arms, and shadowed crevices across the terrain of her stomach revealed the kind of musculature any Amazon warrior would have been proud of. Jordan's thighs had grown hard, but her legs remained slender and lean, as they were used now for balance and momentum more than running and climbing.

Jordan turned and flexed her wings open. The yellow feathers were fluffy and glossy from her shower, and the speckled brown secondary feathers reflected a reddish tint in the lamplight. Her eyes widened as she gazed at the musculature of her back through her wings. Her shoulders had broadened. Where her human scapulae ended was where the primary bones of her wings began. Ridges of muscle lined her spine, and her lats had acquired striations that had not been there before. Her hair had grown so long that it cascaded down her back and mingled with the soft downy feathers on either side of her spine.

"Everything okay?" Sol's voice on the other side of the door made her jump. "You didn't fall asleep in the waterfall and drown, did you?"

Jordan blushed, feeling as though he'd caught her in a moment of vanity. "Almost done!"

She pulled on her soft sleeping pants, which had once been Sol's, and a thin, long-sleeved undershirt, which she put her arms through before reaching behind and tugging on the laces to cinch it closed. The undershirt had also been Sol's. Between her armor, her sleeping garments, and the clothing Sol had given her way back in Nishpat, Jordan had a sparse wardrobe.

She yawned and moved through the rest of her routine before vacating the wash-closet.

She padded barefoot into the kitchen. Half of the lanterns had been extinguished, save for the ones inside the closet. Eohne could still be heard cutting and pouring, cutting and pouring. Sol winked as he passed Jordan on his way to the water-closet to prepare for bed.

"Come to bed, Eohne." Jordan leaned against the doorjamb of the closet and watched her friend work. "You need to rest, or you'll make a mistake."

"Just a little longer. You go ahead," Eohne replied without looking up from what she was doing. Eohne was now completely surrounded by small vials lined up like soldiers. Everything she now poured was crystal clear.

"Will there even be any harpy venom left by the time you're done?"

"No," Eohne said. "That's the point. All that will be left is the essence of it. Your father needs the lightest dose possible to start with, and if that doesn't work, we'll try a stronger one until we get a reaction."

The question, *'What if it doesn't work?'* was on the tip of Jordan's tongue, but she bit it back. There was no point in asking. Tomorrow, they would find out––or at least start finding out.

Instead, she asked, "Any idea how long it might take to work?"

"The right dose should work immediately. The question is…" Eohne looked up for the first time, her slender fingers grasping the vials and holding them up.

"What's the right dose?" the two women asked together.

They shared an exhausted smile.

"Go to bed, Jordan." Eohne went back to her work. "I won't be far behind you."

"Okay. Thanks, Eohne."

Jordan padded silently into the bedroom she now shared with the three most important people in her life. Sol had shoved their two mattresses together and arranged the blankets across the double bed. That suited Jordan just fine.

She crawled under the quilt and let her wings relax on the floor behind her. A short while later, Sol came to bed, clean and smelling of trees. His hands reached for her, wrapped around her torso, and pulled her to him. Then he planted a soft kiss on her forehead.

"I love you, Jordy," Sol whispered, his lips moving against the skin of her temple.

Jordan felt her bottom lip tremble at the nickname her father had always used for her. She'd never told Sol that was her pet name growing up, and she hadn't heard it since the last day she'd seen her father in Virginia.

"I love you too, Sol." Jordan tilted her head back and planted a kiss on his warm lips. His stubble grazed her mouth pleasantly.

She tucked her head beneath his chin and fell asleep to the quiet rhythmic sounds of Eohne cutting and pouring, cutting and pouring.

CHAPTER TWENTY-FIVE

The sound of multiple sets of feet and wings landing on the terrace jolted Jordan awake. She sat up, thinking she had to be dreaming. It felt as though she'd just fallen asleep, but the barest light of dawn filtered in through the window, dusting the sky with peach and yellow tones. She hadn't just 'gone to sleep'; she'd been in a comatose and dreamless stupor for hours.

Sol's warm hand pressed against her lower back as he sat up beside her, the quilt falling down around their waists. Sol's bare chest raised gooseflesh in the cool temperature of the early morning.

Jordan got to her feet and glanced at the floor on the far side of Allan's bed, where Eohne's mattress was. The Elf wasn't there, but the sheets were rumpled. Jordan wondered if they were rumpled because the Elf never bothered to make her bed, or if they were rumpled because she'd slept in them.

Hushed voices could be heard outside the bedroom. The Arpaks went to the door to peek out.

Eohne, Toth, and Arth were talking with their heads bent over something on the kitchen island. Arth caught a glimpse of Jordan peeking out of the bedroom door.

"Morning! Did we wake you?" Her face was lit and devoid of any real regret, if the Nychts had awakened them.

Sol, yawning, reached from behind Jordan and opened the door. "Who's there? It's an ungodly hour for a visit, and I'm no longer a messenger, so it can't be––"

He pulled up short.

"Oh! Toth." He crossed his arms over his chest in a self-conscious manner as he nodded to his new military leader.

"Well, hello there." A wide grin spread across Arth's face, and she came around her big brother to introduce herself. Her beetle-black eyes glittered as she unabashedly swept Sol's half-naked form with an appreciative gaze. "You're a lovely sight, first thing in the morning." She glanced at her brother. "You never told me how handsome he is."

"Handsome?" Toth looked genuinely clueless, as though he hadn't heard the word in a very long time and needed to access some deeply buried language files in his brain before comprehension emerged. His gaze swept to Sol, and he arched a brow, giving a non-committal grunt.

Sol's eyes narrowed. "What *did* he tell you about me?"

"Only that you're the strongest of all the Arpak combatants; almost as good as the weakest Nycht. That, and you used to be a courier, so with some training, you show real potential."

"Oh." Sol looked as though he didn't quite know what to think of this mixed review. "Jordan has spoken highly of your abilities, as well. I'll just…" he took a step back, cheeks reddening under her bold stare, "put some clothes on."

"Not for my sake, I hope."

Jordan approached the kitchen counter, her curiosity outranking the need to get dressed for their company. "I didn't know you were such a flirt, Arth," she teased.

"She came from the womb a flirt," Toth replied, looking down at his little sister with a kind of exasperated fondness.

Jordan took in the brother and sister pair, marvelling that they could be related. Toth was pale, with skin that took on only a light golden cast even after hours in the sun. His eyes were a bright, piercing gray, and his hair a shining silver. He was tall, broad, long-limbed, and powerful, with thickly-membraned wings and long, curving dewclaws. His face and arms were criss-crossed with scars, and his expression was always guarded and coolly detached.

Arth, on the other hand, was petite and delicate; the top of her head barely reached Toth's armpit. Her skin and wings were both a rich, chocolate brown, and her eyes glinted like black obsidian. Her expression was open and enthusiastic, almost guileless. Her wings were lean, on the short side, and her dewclaws were two glossy brown nubs that looked more like accessories than weapons or tools for climbing. Her hair was as dark as Toth's was light, and as curly as his was straight.

"Same mother, different father," Toth grunted in answer to Jordan's questing gaze.

"Oh." She blushed. She would do well to learn to hide some of her thoughts and feelings, the way Toth did. She shifted her assessing gaze to Eohne. "Did you sleep last night?'

"I did, but I got up early. I was just finishing the last batch when these two arrived. Just a few more cuts, and I'll be ready to give him his first dose."

"Who?" Arth sounded more like an owl in that moment than most owls did.

"My father. He was trapped in Trevilsom, and..." Jordan saw Toth's expression growing mildly impatient. "Well, I'll fill you in some other time."

Sol emerged from the bedroom in his armor, as Eohne disappeared into the closet to finish up her medicine-making.

Arth looked disappointed at Sol's having covered up.

"What brings you to our humble apartment so early this morning?"

Arth snapped out of her reverie, and the engineer was back. "It's this gun I'm working on."

Sol approached the table, looking down at the plans spread out on his kitchen counter. "Looks like you've drawn up a blueprint from the model?"

"Yes. It's part of my process. I have to take the build-out from scratch as though I'm the one who invented it, even when I'm reverse engineering. It's the only way I'll thoroughly understand what I'm doing."

"Makes sense," Jordan looked down at the neat blue lines of the sketches. "What can we help you with?"

Toth stepped in. "We've got metalworkers already building the first prototype, she just needs clarity on a few details."

Jordan and Sol looked at one another in surprise.

"Already?" Jordan's brows jumped. "I just gave you these plans last night!"

"Nychts are nocturnal," Toth reminded her.

"It wasn't hard to find laborers ready to trade a day shift for a night shift, even after they'd worked all day. I think they're hoping it'll become a permanent thing." Arth chuckled.

"It will if I get my way," Toth murmured.

"According to the specs you gave me," the small Nycht whipped out the tattered roll of papers Jordan had brought back with her from Virginia, and began to shuffle through them. "This gun is gas operated."

Eohne emerged from the closet with a small vial in her hand full of crystalline liquid. She winked at Jordan as she passed by the cluster of Strix bent over the plans and papers, and disappeared into the bedroom.

"As far as I can tell, the gas comes from here," Arth pointed to the barrel of the gun on the large drawing. "It drives a piston which hits a spring. The piston has a vertical post," she shifted to a bisected drawing of the gun showing a cutaway revealing where the piston lived, "which rides a helical cam track and rotates at the end of its path," she moved her finger along the drawing, "here, nearest to the breech."

Sol and Jordan looked at each other, lost.

"None of that made any sense to either of us," Sol said, then looked at Jordan. "Am I right?"

"Very. Layman's terms please."

"Those were the layman's terms," Arth said, putting her little fists on her narrow hips in exasperation. "Try to keep up. Look at the drawing, it's all here." She held her palms out. "The post also carries a fixed firing pin, which sticks out here," she pointed to another part of the drawing, "which fires the next round into the foremost part…" Arth trailed off at the vacant look on the Arpaks's faces. She sighed, and her shoulders drooped. "Is this really that complicated?"

Jordan nodded. "You're an engineer, Arth. You have a brain for mechanics; we don't."

Toth put a hand on his little sister's shoulder. "I tried to tell you." He shrugged. "It was worth a shot."

"But…this is dangerous work," Arth cried. "Yes, I can produce the parts based on this plan, but I need someone to sanity-check my work, otherwise the prototype could blow up in the face of the first person who fires it!"

"Are there any other engineers you could bring on to help?" Sol asked. "Someone from Lower Rodania who works with weaponry?"

"Swords and javelins are not in the same category," Arth jabbed her finger down on the drawing in front of them, "as this incredible weapon. This Lewis gun could single-handedly turn the tide of the harpy war––but I can't have the design and manufacture of such a volatile piece of equipment under my charge alone. That would be foolhardy."

"Did I hear someone say 'Lewis gun'?" A soft, hoarse voice asked.

Allan stood in the bedroom doorway, his arm over Eohne's shoulder, and her arm wrapped around his thin waist. His face was pale and drawn, and Jordan thought she'd never seen him look so old. But his eyes were bright, and color was already touching his cheeks as the Strix turned to stare.

"Dad!" Jordan cried.

"Wings!" Allan croaked, his eyes jumping about the room at the Strix and landing upon his daughter's bright yellow arches.

"You're awake!" She went to her father's side and looped her arms around him, being careful not to squeeze too hard.

She almost broke down in tears at the feeling of his ribs jutting into hers, and his soft, unused muscle squishing under the pressure of her arms. She pulled away and sniffed back tears, her vision blurring as her eyes misted up.

She gave Eohne a smile as a single tear tracked down her cheek, her heart threatening to burst with gratitude. "You did it," she said to the Elf.

Eohne nodded. "He responded immediately. When he heard you talking in the next room, I couldn't keep him down."

"Dad, you need to go back to bed. Please, lay down and rest." Allan's frame was trembling under the strain of his walk to the doorway; she could feel his muscles quivering under her hand.

"I will," Allan agreed, "I will. But…" He stared at his daughter, his eyes devouring the huge feathered additions to her back. "You have wings."

"I'll explain everything, Dad, I promise." Jordan pressed her father back toward the bed, her heart skipping with relief and happiness to see his face animated, to hear his voice.

Allan craned around her feathers to squint at the crew clustered around the kitchen island, who, in turn, were staring at the father-daughter reunion.

"How long have I been out? These are your friends?"

"Several months," said Eohne. "Come on. Back to bed. Yes, we're Jordan's friends. There's time to explain while you recover. I'll bring you some real food."

"What's going on?" Allan rasped, his eyes dropping to the papers on the counter. He shuffled forward, with Eohne reluctantly helping him. It was clear she'd rather be taking him the other direction.

"We're reverse engineering a Lewis gun for Rodania's defenses," said Arth. "You're Jordan's father?"

The pale freckled man nodded. "Allan. And you are?"

"I can explain it all later, Dad." Jordan thought that Allan was handling waking up amongst a crowd of Strix extremely well, and attributed it to shock. "Please go back to bed before you fall down."

"I will, I will. But, I'm dying of curiosity. My last memory is of being thrown from a small rowboat by a turnip. Where am I?"

"I'm Sol, and this is Toth," Sol introduced the Nycht. "Toth, with Jordan and Eohne––the one holding you up there," Sol nodded at the Elf, "rescued you from Trevilsom. You can't remember it because the island is toxic, and made you blackout."

Allan let out a long breath. "Trevilsom--" His gaze went soft and muzzy around the edges, and his hazel eyes drifted to Jordan. "I've been dreaming of you. I was waiting for you," he reached for Jordan's hand. "In my war room.

Counting my treasures until you arrived. Somehow, I knew you would."

Jordan and Eohne shared a glance over Allan's head.

Allan's eyes shifted to the kitchen counter, and he and Eohne shuffled forward. "These plans, they look just like my Lewis gun."

"That's because they are, Dad. Sol and I, we mapped the gun. We need it."

"Are you familiar with this weapon?" Arth asked, her expression hopeful.

"Very," he said with fondness. He gripped the edge of the counter. Jordan thought she was getting an excellent impression of how Allan would be in his old age, and her heart gave an aching squeeze in her chest.

He will get stronger.

"What drives the magazine?" The Nycht engineer eagerly leaned forward.

"This cam." Allan pointed at the drawing. "It sits on top of a bolt which operates a pawl mechanism by a lever."

"Dad, I have to insist that you lay down. You aren't strong enough for this."

Eohne put a hand on Jordan's arm, her dark eyes locked on Allan's face. His complexion was growing less pallid by the moment, blood was returning to his cheeks. His lips were turning pink, and the sallow pockets under his eyes seemed to be shrinking.

"The gun from my collection was rendered inert; that might be why you're confused by these plans. It was also a World War I weapon that was modified in World War II. It doesn't use a helical coiled recoil spring, but a spiral spring."

"Like a clock spring?"

"That's right." Allan touched another area on the plans. "It sits in this housing, just in front of the trigger. When the gun is fired, the bolt recoils and the cog turns, which tightens the spring. The gas pressure in the breech falls, the spring unwinds and turns the cog, which winds the rod forward for the next round."

Everyone but Arth looked confused by this commentary. Jordan didn't care that she couldn't understand a word Allan had just said; her heart swelled with pride. His brain was fully intact, even after months of being comatose.

The Nycht engineer was leaning forward and absorbing Allen's knowledge like a starving person inhales food. Jordan watched her father, amazed, while he and Arth discussed the gun.

"It should fire five or six hundred rounds per minute," Allan was saying. "What are you using to build them? Iron?"

"I have access to carburized bronze."

Allan showed his teeth in a grin. "Even better. It'll be harder to forge, but the finished product will never rust. And––" Allan coughed, and Jordan jumped.

"Dad, that's enough." Jordan put an arm around her father's thin shoulders. "I'm sorry, Arth. My father needs to go slow. He needs to eat and rest, build up his strength."

Arth nodded. "Of course." She nodded and gave Allan a smile. "Thank you. You've helped. If you don't mind, I might be back later to run a few things by you."

Jordan shot her a warning look, but Allan was enthusiastic.

"Please do; it'll give me a reason to get strong as quickly as I can."

"We'll get to work, then." Arth gathered up all of the plans and documents she'd laid out on the kitchen counter and beamed up at her big brother.

"Let's go talk to Desl."

CHAPTER TWENTY-SIX

Jordan found herself torn on a daily basis.

She wanted to remain at her father's side——feed him, help him walk laps around the apartment——but the desire to be out at the training islands with the other combatants pressed on her. The obligation and desire she felt to be with her fellow soldiers was unexpected in its fervency. Eohne repeatedly shooed her from the apartment with encouraging words that Allan would be well looked after.

The Elf was in fine spirits now that Allan had woken and was on the mend. Her shoulders recovered the strong set they'd had when Jordan first met her, and the line that had taken up residence between her brows since Trevilsom eased away with every passing day.

Jordan would fly home, exhausted after a solid day of training, and arrive to the sounds of laughter and conversation. As she got stronger day by day, so did Allan. Whatever Eohne was feeding him was filling him out in record time.

Weeks had passed, and there were murmurings among the combatants that the harpy threat had subsided, that the last attack had been enough to deter them. Toth warned them daily not to lower their guard. The Nycht leader seemed absent more often, leaving Caje in charge. When Jordan asked Caje where Toth was, the burly Nycht told her he was working on battle strategy with Balroc.

"How does he know there will be another battle?" Jordan asked over a lunch of steaming feroth stew, a treat provided to them by the king's own chef.

The combatants had no chairs at the training islands, so they broke in twos and threes and sat on rocks or sprawled on the ground to eat their lunch. In Toth's absence, Jordan found herself drawn to Caje, and sat at his elbow while they ate. There was something steadying about the overgrown Nycht, and Caje seemed to enjoy her company—or at least, he didn't openly despise her presence the way Chayla did. Even now, Chayla was glowering at Jordan from Caje's other side. Jordan ignored her.

"Because, the last attack was *organized*," Caje said, raising his brows on the last word to emphasize it.

"Organized?" Jordan drew a blank. She couldn't remember anything about the last attack that seemed organized. The whole affair had been messy and noisy and chaotic.

Caje set his spoon down.

"The Nychts of The Conca know more about harpies than anyone else on Oriceran. We've been fighting them for a decade. Harpies are a nasty business, but what you don't realize is that, prior to the rebel Nychts leaving Rodania, the beasts either didn't exist, or they lived so far north that we never came into contact with them." He waved a hand the size of a dinner plate. "Oh, there were other kinds of harpies––smaller, stranger beasts with the faces of human women––but they're from a different land, and don't even warrant a place here beyond a passing mention in Rodanian classrooms."

"Harpies are a new threat," added Chayla, her voice absent of the sneer to which Jordan had so become accustomed to. The Nycht woman gave Jordan a steady look in the eye. "It's not their talons or beaks that make them frightening."

"It's not?"

Caje shook his head. "It's the fact that their behavior is mystifying, and it's still changing. They're evolving. If I was King Konig, I would pull my head from my bunghole and hire a team of scientists and warriors to go straight to the caves of Golpa."

"Golpa." Jordan remembered this name. It was where Toth had said the harpies were from, the caves at the north end of The Conca.

"Someone needs to study them, understand them. How can we prepare for a battle with creatures we can't predict?" Caje leaned over and fixed Jordan with an unblinking stare. "Do you know what a harpy is?"

Jordan nodded. "They're a cross-breed––dragon and greater-vulture. Toth told me they're a species that shouldn't exist."

Caje nodded, his dewclaws tightening above his head. "We've since learned that the dragon species breed whose genes they have is *Tchielis vulgaris*. This particular breed of reptile is characterized by a kind of group telepathy."

"Whoa," Jordan exhaled as the harpy threat came into perspective. "That's what you mean by organized?"

"Yes." Caje shovelled a heaping spoonful of stew into his mouth and spoke around it. "Every subsequent harpy attack has been a little more deadly, a little more efficient. They're learning."

"What do you think they have against Rodania? Why attack us? We're several hours' journey across the water; surely there is easier prey closer to Golpa?"

"Not necessarily." Chayla shifted on her hip, pulling a pinned wing out from under her butt, and letting it relax behind her. Jordan was pleasantly surprised by how Chayla was engaging in conversation without lacing it with sarcasm. She almost mentioned it, but decided not to mess with a good thing.

"Once harpies have a taste of something they like," Chayla informed her, "they won't settle for lesser prey. They like horse, feroth, and human, but they like Strix even more. Rodania has been protected by a dome of Elvish magic for the last century or so. Now that the harpies have found a way through, Rodania is an undefended feast."

Jordan's stomach was full and warm, and she felt the inevitable post-lunch drowsiness creeping up on her. Her eyes combed the skies to the northwest, where Toth had trained all of the combatants to watch. The vast blue horizon was empty of clouds or any winged threat, as empty as it had been for over a month.

"How do you think they got through the barrier?" she asked.

"They didn't do it alone," Caje grunted, getting to his feet and lumbering across the grass for another helping of stew. Several large copper pots sat steaming on the ground in a haphazard circle.

Jordan got a chill as she watched the big Nycht scoop a helping the size of Jordan's head into his wooden bowl. "They didn't do it alone," she echoed thoughtfully.

"If you ask me, the Light Elves have grown tired of King Konig. They're not getting enough out of the deal, and," Chayla snapped her fingers, "they made a breach, and stepped back to let the harpies do their work. I heard the Elves are denying having anything to do with it; they're pointing fingers at the Rodanian government." Chayla snorted a laugh. "Ridiculous."

Jordan blinked at this horrifying theory. She knew nothing about the nature of the Light Elves' agreement with Rodania, only that Sol had told her the deal was ironclad. If there was ever a problem with the Elves, they would simply lower Rodania's islands into the sea, and the floating nation would become an island nation. Just your garden-variety cluster of islands with regular ports of trade.

"I hope you're wrong about that," Jordan replied.

"Me too," added Chayla. A look passed between she and Jordan before the Nycht got to her feet and walked away.

Jordan puzzled over that look for the next several hours, and settled on labeling it as uneasy respect. It was better than no respect at all.

That same evening, Jordan came home to an empty apartment.

"Dad? Eohne?" She poked her head into the bedroom, into the water closet, and into the closet that had turned into storage for Eohne. No one was home.

A warped glass cup sat on the island, and Jordan spotted something yellow trapped beneath it. She lifted the glass and snatched up the note.

'We've gone to the forges on Lower.'

The note was scrawled in her father's nearly illegible writing.

The sound of wings and boots on tile made Jordan look up. Sol closed up his wings and strode into the apartment. His face was dirty, and as he snapped his wings together, a cloud of dust drifted in the air.

"Hello there," he crossed the room and planted a kiss on Jordan's cheek. "How come we never get to train together?"

Jordan caught Sol's lips with hers. They'd had no time or energy or privacy these last few weeks, and she'd missed him.

"I think Toth reckons we'd just distract one another."

Sol nuzzled her neck. "He's right. We've already proven that." His voice was muffled and laced with comical resignation.

"Where are the forges on Lower Rodania?"

Sol pulled back. "Why?"

Jordan held up the note for Sol to read.

Sol's eyes passed over the words, pausing to discern the scrawl. "I guess your father is feeling better." Sol brushed a lock of Jordan's hair away from her face. "Concerned?"

"Not as long as he's with Eohne, no. It's just…I've hardly had any time to talk with him. At first, I was putting it off to give him a chance to get better. Suddenly, he's better," Jordan's shoulders hiked up, "and he's not here."

"Want to go? I can take you there."

"You're not too tired?"

"Of course not." Sol took the cup from the counter and filled it with water from the big brass tap. He handed it to Jordan. She smiled at his gallantry, took the cup, and drank. Then Sol filled a cup for himself and guzzled it. Water trickled from the corners of his mouth, and made tracks through his now thicker beard. He let out a satisfied '*ahhh*' and clopped the glass into the sink.

"Let's go."

Jordan grabbed Sol's hand, pulling him around to face her.

"Sol."

"Yeah?"

She put her palms on his cheeks, wanting just a moment to themselves. "Your beard has grown." She used the pads of her thumbs to wipe away some of the grime from his face, only managing to smear it. She guessed her own face was just as filthy.

"Don't like it?" Sol ran a hand over his beard, unsure.

"I love it. You seem happy under all that dirt and hair."

Sol's white teeth appeared, breaking through his beard like the sun breaks through clouds. "I am. I'll be happier when we know for sure that harpies will never get through the barrier again. And when we have five minutes to talk like civilized Strix." He took a sniff. "Strix that don't smell like sweat, leather, and metal."

"You don't miss your job?"

"Jordan," Sol put his arms around her waist. "I'm so glad to see that my battle-hardened love hasn't lost her nurturing touch. But don't worry about me. When this harpy disaster is over, I'll make our lives right again. You'll see." He planted a soft kiss on her mouth, sending her stomach spiralling. "Now do you want to go to the forges tonight or not?"

Jordan nodded.

As they flew over Middle Rodania and dropped over the edge for Lower, the two moons of Oriceran came out, and the stars danced alongside them. Jordan wondered if there would come a moment where the pure craziness of her life, all the events that had brought her and Allan to this moment, to this place, might hit her all at once. One thing had tumbled into the next, and there still seemed no rationale for much of it. Her life felt like one big puzzle; a half-sewn quilt, with giant patches of color missing.

The harpy threat was so big, so demanding of everyone's time, that Jordan came to feel that taking a bathroom break and a shower was pure luxury. Even her father had gotten swallowed up in the maw of preparing for battle. The worst of it was that she didn't understand how it started, why it had happened, or what was going to bring it to an end. This feeling that something even uglier than a harpy flock was at work behind the scenes pervaded every thought. Jordan had to shove it aside to make room for what was happening in the moment.

Again and again there was no time for rumination, no time to work things out. These were the thoughts that captured her mind as she followed Sol through the darkening sky over Lower Rodania.

CHAPTER TWENTY-SEVEN

Jordan realized as they swooped over Lower Rodania that it was her first time flying over the massive island. Below her, yellow lights illuminated the streets of long, low buildings, the parks, the squat stone towers. Strix could be seen throwing shadows as they moved about in the evening light--flying, walking, carrying things.

Sol led Jordan to the northwestern coast of Lower Rodania, where a long strip of beach snugged up to a row of semi-circular buildings. Each one was half-open and manned by at least three or more Strix, hard at work.

Lit forges sent light and waves of heat from great ovens nestled in the back walls of the stone buildings. The sounds of chatter, crackling fire, laughter, and metal banging on metal blocked out the sound of waves lapping up on the beach.

The Arpaks landed on a stone walkway that connected all the forges--too many to count at a glance. Putting their wings away, they noticed passing Nychts all headed in the same direction. With a bemused glance, Jordan and Sol fell into step with the crowd, and headed north along the coast.

"What's happening?" Sol asked a muscular, bare-chested Nycht glistening with sweat.

"Firing the prototype," the Nycht's voice was a deep rasp, and his face was alive with excitement. "If it works the way the little engineer says, production will be full-steam ahead."

Sol and Jordan shared a look. "That's why Eohne brought my father down here. He wouldn't want to miss this for the world."

The Arpaks took to the sky again and skimmed over the heads of the moving crowd, their eyes raking the scene below for a familiar face.

"There," Jordan pointed to the beach where torches flickered, and the slender wingless forms of her father and Eohne stood out among the arched silhouettes of Strix.

They landed on the beach.

"Dad!" Jordan called.

Allan turned, his face alight. He crossed the beach to his daughter, his feet kicking up sand. "You are simply brilliant." He kissed her cheek.

"I am?" Jordan blinked at the scene behind her father.

Arth, Toth, Caje, and Chayla were all there, and a perfect replica of her father's Lewis gun glittered from a crossbar erected on a platform. The whole construction had been erected on the beach, just beyond the lapping water. The gun's barrel was pointed out to sea.

"How come no one told us this was happening?"

"It's all been very last minute. Toth wants to get the guns operational as quickly as possible. As soon as one step is finished, boom, it's on to the next." Allan spoke quickly and with great energy.

"You've been working with Toth?"

"Of course! He's been consulting with me for the last several days."

"He has?"

"Sure, every mid-morning for the last four days, he's come to pick me up. Marvelous." Allan was oozing the excitement of a little kid on Christmas morning. "Balroc, Toth, myself, and Eohne——" he elbowed Jordan conspiratorially, "she's always there, won't let me go anywhere without her——meet to discuss strategies of aerial combat." Allan crossed his arms and rocked forward on his toes. "I knew all that study would one day come in handy. Bats and birds are a far cry from bi-planes and Republic bombers, but" he gave a jovial shrug, "who am I to complain?"

Jordan felt dizzy. She turned to Sol. "Did you know this was happening?"

"Hadn't a clue." Sol looked as mystified as Jordan felt.

"How come you didn't tell us in the evening when we got home?"

"Because," Allan spread his hands, looking as though the answer should be obvious. "You've had your hands full with training. I didn't want to distract you or make you worry."

"I wouldn't have worried." Jordan bit her lip.

Yes, she would have. If she had known her father was getting entangled in the harpy war, she would most definitely have worried.

She gazed at her father, observing how his eyes twinkled in the firelight. He was watching Arth make last-minute preparations with the gun.

How is it he can seem so happy? He hadn't once mentioned going home to Virginia; he hadn't even pushed Jordan to sit down and discuss their bizarre circumstance. Either there simply hadn't been time and it wasn't a priority, or he'd been avoiding it for some reason.

Jordan wondered if Eohne was slipping Allan some Elven tea to help him cope with the shock of Oriceran and a winged daughter.

"Ah, she's loading. I'd best go help." Allan planted a kiss on Jordan's cheek and left her and Sol standing there with their feet wedged in the sand, feeling a bit dazed.

"I guess the gun was a good idea." Sol slipped an arm around Jordan's waist.

A shout drew their attention to Arth, who was calling instructions to some invisible ear across the water.

Torches out in the ocean blazed to light.

"Oh my..." Jordan breathed.

A long, low island appeared off the coast. Nychts moved in the shadows, lighting torches. With every blazing light, the target became clearer until a mound of dirt on a platform appeared.

Tacked into the dirt wall was thick fabric decorated with life-sized, cartoonish paintings of harpies; they had been done in a hurry, and by someone with a sense of humor. The harpy drawings had bulging, googly eyes and tongues that flopped out. One of them was wearing a crude bra.

A swell of laughter drifted up from the crowd, and Jordan and Sol found themselves joining in. Somehow, even in the face of a deadly threat——and certain death for some——joviality could be found among the Strix.

The Nychts on the platform waved, and some of them even took a bow in response to the laughter and applause. They spread their wings and took to the dark skies, making their way back to the beach.

"They've never seen anything like this," Sol whispered in Jordan's ear. "Look at their faces."

Jordan scanned the crowd. Mostly Nychts, but some Arpaks, had come together to watch this ceremonial firing. They chewed their lips, shuffled restlessly, and rarely took their eyes from the small engineer behind the weapon.

Arth faced the crowd. She had round goggles on her head, and she pulled them down over her eyes as a signal.

It was time.

The crowd settled into a tense silence.

Arth turned to Allan, and there was a buzz of words between them. Allan stepped back, and Arth grasped the trigger of the Lewis prototype.

A loud CLACK-CLACK made everyone jump and gasp. The effect was so comical that Jordan burst out laughing. Her laugh was echoed with a titter of nervous chuckles. Silence descended again as Arth, who had jumped as well, swooped forward again, her hands on the trigger.

This time, the CLACK-CLACK didn't cease as Arth fired steadily for a full ten seconds. She swept the barrel from one side of the target to the other, and back again, tearing up the drawings with a hail of bullets. When she stopped, silence rang. The drawing of the harpy in the bra was the only one left hanging, and it was in tatters. As the crowd watched, the drawing flopped forward and peeled away from the sod wall, sliding into the water.

The Strix crowd exploded in a cheer. Howls and yips accompanied hands whacking sharply together. The demonstration had lasted mere moments, but it had been enough to inspire them.

Allan came jogging across the sand toward Sol and Jordan.

"It was over so fast!" Jordan said.

Allan nodded. "We can't waste bullets."

The crowd dispersed, and the atmosphere of celebration dissolved into one of determination and productivity.

"Or time," Sol observed. In moments, the beach was cleared, with everyone knowing exactly where they were headed and what they needed to do.

Jordan waved to Arth, hoping for a chat with the engineer, but she was deep in conversation with Toth, Caje, and a cluster of Nychts. Arth spared the Arpak a grin, but bent back to the conversation, her face intense.

"I have a message for the two of you from Toth," Allan said.

"What's that?"

"He says go to bed."

"Bossy-pants. What about you? It's late, aren't you coming home?"

"Caje and Toth will bring Eohne and me home in a little while. I want to discuss a few things with Arth before I crash for the night. We have to discuss where to mount the first of the guns: obviously on the northwest side, but where exactly will they be the most effective? I'm told the last attack had, what," Allan cocked his head, "Forty some-odd harpies?"

Sol nodded. "About that."

"Arth tells me that in a matter of three days, we can have twenty guns. Positioning will be critical, and ammunition stores, of course. Lots to do."

"That's great, Dad." Jordan's lips felt numb. Was this crazy Lewis gun strategy actually going to work then? Looking back, it seemed like such a wild idea, destined to fail. Too much could go wrong. But somehow, it appeared to be going right.

Allan gave Jordan a hug. He drew back and pinched her cheek. "Have a shower before you go to bed, Jordy. You smell like an old shoe."

Jordan watched her father cross the sand toward his cohorts. In moments, he was in the heart of the conversation and clearly loving every moment.

Jordan and Sol leaned into their training. Allan and Eohne worked with Arth and a team handpicked by Toth to learn how to man the Lewis guns. Communication broke down between groups as their ranks thinned, and it was all Caje could do to keep the Strix focused on hand-to-hand combat. A full two dozen of their number had been carved away to focus on guns, and the ones who were not chosen were disappointed and voraciously curious about the new weapons.

Sol and Chayla had been paired by Caje, while Jordan had joined a pair of Nychts who had come up from Lower

Rodania. A feeling of anxiety had begun to grow in Jordan's gut as the days flew by. She felt like a cog in a huge wheel, working in a mechanical system she couldn't see. She was learning how it felt to be a soldier--a single part of a larger body, all driving for the same purpose.

She grappled for faith and trust that Toth, Balroc, and her father knew what they were doing. But how could they? Like Caje had said, the harpies were unpredictable. What else could Rodania do? And all the while, King Konig remained silent. He was ill, that was clear, but Sol had told Jordan that according to Juer, the king was still capable of communication and rational thought, though he never addressed the accusations flung his way that day after the big attack. He'd sent food to the combatants, but made no appearance.

The celebratory feeling of the evening they'd fired the first-prototype dwindled as the days passed. Over the lunch hours, debate took place between the combatants. The harpies hadn't been seen for weeks, so what were they training for?

Strix who answered the call from Rodania were the ones who questioned the most, while the Nychts of The Conca argued that being ready to face any threat at any time was the point of an army.

This bickering was what Caje, Toth, and Arth flew into one day, each with scrolls tucked under their arms. Caje and Toth listened for a moment, to get the flavor of what was being said.

Caje's expression grew dark and he finally lost his patience.

"This is what soldiers do!" he bellowed to the crowd of

now silent warriors. Nychts from The Conca looked smug, while Strix from Rodania stood with their eyes downcast, ashamed. "You need to change your mindset," he barked. "We are not training for a fixed point in the future, a single event which needs to be faced and then forgotten. You think you can go back to your soft lives? Don't be foolish. An army is always ready. Forget the last thousand years of laziness and arrogance," yelled Caje, spittle flying from his reddened face. "Get it through your thick skulls. The Elven magic is broken." Caje bellowed instruction at the combatants, sending one group over to Toth, another group to Arth, and calling another to himself.

"All of you, get close." He unrolled the large parchment as the Strix clustered in around him. On the parchment was a drawing of three circles: a small one, a medium one, and a large one. They'd been labelled as Upper, Middle and Lower Rodania. A total of eighteen red 'X's had been painted at various positions on each island, concentrated on the northwest sides.

"Listen up, you maggots," barked Caje, still angry about the doubtful bickering. "Here's where the guns have been placed. We're manufacturing bullets like Rodanian lives depend on them, which they do. Every day, magazines––that's the metal thing shaped like a big cookie that holds the bullets––are getting sent up to the machine gun nests."

Jordan squeezed closer to Caje, flesh and feathers tight on all sides. She pushed an errant Nycht dewclaw out of her face and crouched over the map. Her stomach was jumping with hope. This was what they needed. The Strix army had been divided for too long, with one arm not knowing what the other was up to, and sowing seeds of doubt. It was finally time for the two arms to work together.

Already, Jordan felt more hope than she had five minutes before.

Beyond the group around Caje, clusters of combatants hid the forms of Toth and Arth, each delivering a similar message to their warriors.

"As you've heard, we've got a consultant from Earth working with us on how to marry this cutting-edge technology with our ancient hand-to-hand aerial combat."

Jordan's mouth quirked. The Lewis guns were hardly 'cutting-edge' technology, but it sure sounded good. A few eyes darted to Jordan and then back to the map; some of them knew that the consultant Caje was speaking of had some relationship to her. The looks were a little more awed than she was comfortable with, but there was nothing she could do about that.

"In the event of a harpy attack, the guns go first. No one," Caje raised his voice, "and I mean *no* one, is to take to the skies while these weapons are firing. They are our first-line of defense. Best-case scenario, we pick off the wretched hag-birds using only guns, or, they get a taste of our new toys and never come back. But we're not here to prepare for best-case scenario; we're here to prepare for the worst."

The battle strategy went on for another hour, and the atmosphere changed. It became hopeful, empowered, focused. They had a plan, and everyone was clear on which squadron they'd been assigned to, and how the guns played into the larger defense.

It was a shame it didn't work.

CHAPTER TWENTY-EIGHT

Jordan was snugged up against Sol's chest, cradled by the spoon shape his body made, when an unpleasant tingling sensation in her pelvis woke her. Her ears popped, and she felt Sol's body jerk awake. She held her breath, hoping that she'd only been dreaming.

Both Arpaks's bodies went tense and still, like sprung wires. The vibration in their bones repeated itself. They bolted to their feet in a flurry of blankets and feathers. Jordan's heart went from a sleepy crawl to an adrenalin-fueled sprint.

"What's happening?" Allan croaked from the far side of the bed.

The first tinges of a pink dawn laced the underside of cloud-filled sky.

Eohne, whom Allan had insisted should take the bed, was on her feet in a moment, her dark hair a tangled mass. "Harpies," she whispered, her face drawn in the dim light. She left the room like she was made of vapor, heading for the peg where her armor hung.

Sol and Jordan bolted about the room, all traces of dreams and cuddly sleepiness long-gone. They didn't speak, only yanked on armor, tightened laces, strapped on weapons. All the while, the ear-popping and pelvis-jarring warning looped on repeat, annoyingly, apocalyptically.

Jordan finished her preparations and turned to her father, finding his mattress empty and blankets scattered. "Dad?"

"I'm here, Jordy," his voice came from the kitchen, where he and Eohne were finishing their own preparations. A rifle lay across the kitchen island, and Jordan paled when she saw it.

"Where did you get that?"

"Arth gave it to me."

"Jordan," Sol called from the terrace. "Now!"

"You are not going to fight. You're not going anywhere," Jordan snapped, suddenly irrational with fear. She'd just gotten her father back; there was no way she was going to lose him again. It would kill her.

"Jordan," Sol barked from the terrace. The ear popping continued. Whoever was blowing the alarm didn't know when to quit. The buzzing in Jordan's hips felt like an angry hornets' nest, and was setting her teeth on edge.

"This apartment is not safe, we already know that," Eohne said with an irritating calm. "I'll be with him. I won't leave his side."

With a snarl of frustration, Jordan threw her arms around her father. She backed away, hearing Sol's voice growing more insistent behind her.

"You stay alive," she roared at her father as she made for the terrace. "You hear me?"

Allan followed Jordan out and watched the two Arpaks take off into the early morning mist, answering the call. He spoke too late for her to hear. "You too, Jordy."

Strix warriors winged their way through the skies, making a beeline to whatever parapet or tower they had been assigned. Jordan and Sol were not manning the same station; they were not even in the same squadron. They had time only for a sobering glance before breaking apart. Jordan headed to the top of a tower that had been modified to support a machine gun nest with room for eight Strix behind it. Sol disappeared toward a tower west of hers.

Jordan landed on the stones, closed up her wings, and settled in behind the gun with the rest of her squadron, a mix of Nychts and Arpaks. Caje was there. He gave Jordan a nod as someone handed her a set of handmade earmuffs that smelled faintly like sheep. She secured the muffs over her ears and faced the dawn, eyes narrowed for dark shapes, mind ready to count enemy wings. Gray clouds laid a film over the horizon, beyond which nothing could be seen.

A few drops of rain struck Jordan in the face, and she heard a Nycht soldier suppress a groan. She looked up. The sky was heavy with cloud cover, but it was light in color, not dark.

"It won't come to that," she assured her comrade.

"How do you know?" came the response, muffled by her ear covering.

"Those aren't rainclouds, the sun will burn them off. You'll see."

The other Nycht grunted. The last thing a Nycht wanted was wet weather; it made for wet wings.

"We'll be home before lunch, Asil," offered a more optimistic comrade.

"Don't overestimate the guns," Jordan snapped. At least the wretched vibrations had stopped, and that awful popping in her ears. "That would be a mistake."

Caje stood behind the gunner, silent.

A hush fell over Rodania. For a breath, it seemed like any other quiet morning. Birds chirped, and a light breeze ruffled the hair and feathers of the waiting combatants.

When the shadows appeared, there was an intake of breath. They materialized like ghosts from a heavy fog. Jordan gave up any hope of counting the enemy; the approaching mass writhed like a cluster of worms, each harpy indistinguishable from the rest, so little was the space between them. This was not a dozen harpies––this was not even two dozen. There were hundreds of them. Maybe even a thousand.

The silence grew pregnant with dread as every eye took in the approaching horde. The harpies were silent––no screams or awful cries heralded this attack. The only sound was huge wings beating at the air, barely audible through the combatants' earmuffs, sounding not unlike waves crashing onto a rocky beach.

As the horde closed in, Jordan's keen eyes began to pick out distinct shapes. Black webbed wings, pinpricks of scarlet, horned heads. They seemed like extensions of a single shadowy abomination, moving on a crash course with Rodania.

Jordan's mouth was suddenly without any saliva.

The small but fierce Rodanian army was not ready for this. Not even close. This was death approaching.

Her thoughts flew to Sol, to her father, to Eohne, to Blue, and with a hot, racing anger, even to Jaclyn. Only the day before, Jordan had still been hoping to see Blue's shape in the sky over Rodania, coming home to her. But in the face of what was coming, she was now glad her reptilian friend was not here. *Fierce though he can be, how could he survive this? How can any of us?*

She took a breath and wrested her mind into place, shoving thoughts of her loved ones aside. The only thing she could do now was focus on not turning tail. She knew that if so much as a single combatant from her small group turned and dove from the tower, flapping to the southeast as fast as they could, she would follow.

Her fingers and lips trembled, and she pressed her mouth shut and uttered a prayer. *Does everyone else feel like their resolve is made of glass?*

She glanced at Caje's huge back. He had not moved, had not reacted to the incredible sight of the deadly numbers headed their way. Respect for the Nycht made Jordan stand a little straighter, feel a little stronger. Everyone dealt with the straining seconds in a different way; some fidgeting incessantly over a minor lace or fastening, others holding so rigidly still that they seemed made of wax. Others still leaned forward and stared at the approaching enemy as though willing them to close the distance faster and get it over with.

The Nycht gunner was crouched behind their single, light machine gun, knuckles white, waiting for the right moment. An Arpak reloader sat behind the gunner's elbow with a replacement magazine already in her hands. They were both as still as statues and had lumpy, handmade muffs over their ears.

The amorphous polyp of winged destruction had mutated into a jagged edged sphere sprouting two tendrils on either side. The flashes of red Jordan spied brought Caje's words crashing back to her memory: 'They're *organized'*.

Two pincering vanguards of agile male harpies broke away from the main body of the attack. One dropped fast, toward Lower Rodania, as the second spiked upward, driving hard for Rodania's highest island. Jordan had no time to marvel at the coordinated precision with which the harpies made this strategic move; the rest of the force was headed straight for them.

Jordan's mouth twisted with disgust, as the air curdled with the all-too-familiar stink.

When the Lewis guns began to fire, the clack-clacking sound seemed to fill the world. Spent shell casings flung themselves wildly sideways, and the Strix on the parapet pressed inward, away from the flying metal. In between firings, the booms of guns all over Rodania could be heard echoing in the distance. Jordan wondered what the poor citizens had been told to do in the event of an attack. She hadn't been involved in the communications strategy, if one existed at all.

The noise was incredible.

The Strix, unaccustomed as they were to this mechanical barrage, winced at the relentless sonic assault. The hapless loaders had their hands full keeping themselves and their crates of ammunition out of the path of the casings that tumbled and twirled, smoking and filling the air with another kind of stink––that of hot metal.

Jordan realized with a gulp that the Strix had fired too soon. The range was too great for an effective volley, but the sheer weight of the combined fire took three harpies out of the sky, their bodies tattered and bleeding, and several more joined shortly after. They plummeted like feathered bags of cement to the water below.

In spite of the auditory excess of the Lewis guns, a cheer could be heard as the Strix drew first blood. As if pausing to hear their own applause, many of the guns fell silent. Their magazines ran dry with a final, fatal *ping*, and there was a scramble to reload.

Her mind recovering from the battering waves of sound, Jordan realized the opening barrage had lasted less than two minutes. A quick glance at the ammunition beside the loader revealed less than half of what they'd started with. But the machine guns had begun to open up again, as the quickest loaders stepped clear and signalled the gunners to fire.

More harpies fell, but they were now close enough that the Strix could see their bodies writhe as the gunfire perforated flesh and wing membrane. One side of the approaching mob began to lose its cohesion, the harpies' innate aggression and cruelty weakening in the face of a furious and unexpected storm of bullets.

Some of the leading harpies crumpled in midair, tumbling toward the sea, while others wheeled wildly away with the grating cries Jordan had come to despise. Harpies died, but more and more of the guns fell silent as their magazines were spent. The sky was growing dark as though it were dusk, not dawn, as the harpies' wings blotted out much of the already diffused sunlight.

Caje's body was tense. He was watching, waiting for the right moment. When no repeating *clack-clack* came, it meant every one of the machine gun nests was out of commission. The Strix raised their eyes, their hands posed on the hilts of their weapons.

The Lewis guns had been no salvation; there were simply too many harpies. The sky was now black with them. The realization was settling over their ranks like a chilly, invisible fog.

All the hard work and preparation, all the trouble of going back to Virginia and retrieving the antique, seemed paltry now. Jordan clenched her teeth, and with great effort, threw off her despair with an angry mental shove.

When the call came, she was the first to react.

"To the air!" Caje bellowed in a battle cry that seemed too large for even his impressive frame. "To the air, you Strix!"

And with that, the stinking harpy horde was upon them.

CHAPTER TWENTY-NINE

Sol threw himself from the tower with a yell, and was immediately out in the open air, his wings powering him upward and forward. A potent gale of stink assaulted his senses as he climbed, and his eyes watered at the heavy, clinging odor. He gagged in spite of himself, succumbing to the noxious odor.

Bodies filled the sky––twisted, feathered, viciously armed bodies––until it seemed they crowded all dimensions. There were so many; *too many*. They outnumbered the Strix defenders at a ghastly ratio.

Through tear-blurred eyes, Sol spied a smaller, faster shape gaining altitude parallel to him. There was time enough to register Chayla's snarling grin. He'd forgotten in his fury that they were meant to stick together; already he was falling back into the habits of his solitary life.

His thoughts swung wildly to Jordan. His love was not ready for this, but then, none of them were.

A male, crimson crested and shrieking, came spiralling toward him, and Sol recognized the trick. The harpy would roll mid-flight and try to sideswipe him with its whiplike tail, so that the harpy following could lay its claws into him. Hatred for the flying monstrosities lent Sol speed, strength, and a frightening focus.

He matched the roll of the harpy, taking the beast through the chest with a spear. With a second spear, Sol stabbed upward, halting the follow-up attack. There was no time to savor his victory, though. More and more harpies filled the air——there seemed to be no end to them.

Time grew meaningless, and rational thought became a ponderous luxury. Sol's and Chayla's training took front seat as they reacted, and reacted, and reacted. It was an endless twisting, turning, deadly aerial ballet. A thrust here, a slash there, a dodge, a barrel-roll, a vault; on and on they fought, doing their best to stay close and watch each other's backs. Being moments and inches from death became the way life was lived. In the corners of his vision, Sol saw his companions fight, and he saw them die.

The world stopped making sense. His ears closed to all sound but his own breathing, and oddly enough, the distant grunts and cries of Chayla. The screeches and roars of harpies became a soft background drone. A harpy's throat could let a scream fly mere feet from his eardrum, and the sound seemed to come from somewhere far away. Yet Chayla could shout a warning across the battlefield, and it entered his ears as clear and crisp as springwater. Sol had never before observed the shift in psychology that happened in combat like this. He would have marvelled at it, had he the luxury of time.

The death and pain being dealt around Sol lit a white-hot fire within him, driving him to fight harder, faster, and fiercer than he ever had. He may be doomed to die; every warrior might share his fate, and all of Rodania may succumb to ruin, but with every ounce left of his life, he would wreak terrible damage.

Hurling one spear, and then the other, Sol pumped his wings hard to gain altitude. He snagged the spears jutting from a falling corpse, turned, and sent one into the belly of a bloated female. The harpy gave a shriek as her talons raked the air above Sol's head, blindly missing. As the stricken female swooned, the raging Arpak tore his spearhead free. He spun to meet another oncoming female who sought to gore him with her forward sweeping horns like a maddened bull.

Sol cleared her onrushing body, but the hag's barbed tail gouged a red line across his calf. He snarled at the burning pain, but used the momentum of the blow to fuel his torsion. The harpy struggled to turn her bulk, her demon-face twisting back with a rattling hiss. She caught a throwing blade in her eye for her trouble, and the beast shuddered and plummeted from the sky.

Sol turned from one stricken foe to hurl his spear at another. And so it went.

Looking beyond a fallen enemy, Sol saw Chayla smeared in blood, and with a nasty gash over one eye. She spun her single remaining hand-axe and unleashed a frenzy of hacking slashes at a passing female.

Sol barely had time to clear the taste of harpy filth from his mouth before he was drawn back into the raging current of war.

Jordan tried her level best to stay with her unit as they swept along one flank of the harpy flock, but the diving attacks by the agile harpy males made it impossible.

She had been heartened when a thrown knife had cut off the flightpath of an oncoming attacker. Now though, as more and more of the speeding demon-birds rushed over and through them, that one kill was such a meager thing.

The harpies came at them in rushes, a male or two at a time pelting toward them at breakneck speed. These were easy to ward off with thrown missiles or evasive moves. The Strix spun or parted to let the bolder harpies pass by, where rearward ranks could surround them and tear them apart.

At least, that was the hope. This had been one of the ploys Toth had taught them.

Jordan could hear a voice bellowing, doling out instruction, encouragement, and rebuke all in one thunderous blast. She could not see Toth, but she would recognize his voice anywhere.

How have we gotten so close? Toth's squadron had begun this battle a whole two kilometers west of her. She should have been encouraged by the power of his voice, but the insistence that it now carried struck at her heart. She had never heard him sound like this.

Contemplations of Toth were driven from her mind as she heard a different warrior at her shoulder; a redheaded Nycht with an impressive scar across her cheek.

"Head's up!"

Jordan's eyes swung about. She was treated to the harrowing sight of three large females rushing toward them.

There had been innumerable blessings in having her eyesight supernaturally enhanced since coming to this world, but as she registered these oncoming monsters, she found herself wishing for the comfort of a softer-edged, bleary world. Jordan could, unfortunately, pick out every vicious detail: the flex and sag in the enormous muscles of their shoulders and breasts, their wickedly curved horns, their cruelly hooked beaks, and brutally barbed talons.

Yet for all that, fear did not numb her mind like it might have before. She was facing the end of her life––a brutal end. But her head was clear, and her mind was fixed; she would go down fighting.

The trio of harpies charged, their horns lowered, seeking to scatter them. Jordan and the Strix had trained for this, and as one, they looped around each other in pairs. The harpies, having zeroed in on individual quarries, tangled with each other as they tried to respond. Croaking and snapping at each other, their charge stalled, and Jordan and her comrades fell on them like a pack of lions.

The entire performance unfolded over the space of a few heartbeats, and came to a crescendo as Caje led three warriors in a gloriously insane charge through the midst of Jordan's squadron, heading straight for a wave of oncoming harpies. Jordan watched in battle-shock as Nycht and Arpak screamed their bloody-fisted defiance, and were swallowed by the harpy horde.

Everything had fallen to pieces, but Toth refused to surrender to despair.

A short broadblade sword in each hand, he took turns hacking at passing harpies, and gesturing feverishly as he bellowed directions to the pieces of his army which still held some kind of order.

Caje and a band of Strix emerged from a clump of broken harpy corpses, their weapons stained with dark blood and trailing feathers like pennants. A single battle-mad harpy male flew straight at Caje, and was rewarded for his trouble with a flayed chest.

Jordan had been assigned to Caje's tower, and yet she was not with them. The Nycht leader refused to believe that meant the worst; it was nearly impossible to stay together in the chaos.

Toth had no time to watch his brother's wrecking crew, but he kept his eyes away from the battle line long enough to see Caje and his party smash through a cluster of harpies like a meteor. Each harpy was easily ten feet from horned head to taloned foot—many were larger, but they buckled beneath the brutal onslaught like kindling before the axe.

Mace, sword, and spear rose and fell, loosing their share of harpy blood. By the time Caje and his warriors were banking back toward Toth, corpses were pitching brokenly through the sky.

Toth scanned the battlefield for another target, another knot of resistance that just might buy them a little more time and hope. The deadly fury of the Strix fighting around the Nycht brothers gave an impression to all involved that the battle was being won.

They fought. Harpies fell.

But Strix who found a moment to raise their eyes and

look beyond their immediate surroundings endured a dismaying shattering of that illusion. The harpies seemed like the mythic hydra: for every head sliced off, four more took its place. The skies over Rodania were riddled with the enemy.

Toth watched this collective realization dawn in the faces of his combatants, and he fought all the fiercer to keep it at bay.

Jordan rammed her dirks into the back of a bucking harpy. She felt the creature's body sag, and, drawing her knees toward her chest, she kicked free of the dying monster and took to the air. Casting about, she searched for her comrades. Toth's plan had fallen to pieces under the sheer size of the harpy onslaught. There was only one directive any of them could follow now--kill as many invaders as possible, and try not to die.

When the mass hit, it was like being submerged in a stinking ocean. The air was choked with wings and bodies, and the reeking stench was everywhere. Every which way you turned, some snaring claw or gaping beak was bearing down. The battle felt like it had been raging for days. The sun hid its face behind thick clouds, giving nothing away.

Jordan had used most of her throwing knives, and then the longer blades had come out. She was not as good with those, but she was not fighting to kill. She didn't have the luxury of being that proactive. She was fighting to live, simply reacting to stay alive. Each thrust, each slash was to buy her another second, another inch of time and space, another moment in which her heart beat. Time and time again, her smaller, faster frame evaded death. The Strix and harpies were like sparrows to crows.

Jordan dodged right as a gaggle of males screamed by, then rolled a hard left as a hulking female barreled past with a snap so close, Jordan felt the wind from her beak.

Between defensive flying and striking at whatever came close, she searched the skies for her comrades. *How did I get so lost?* Rodanian villages and fields zoomed and tilted beneath her, the backdrop constantly changing. Her relentless surveying saved her life for the thousandth time as she spied a streaking form a split-second before it blindsided her.

As though they had minds of their own, her blades slashed, slipping between the creature's ribs. The harpy screamed and wrenched away, its breathing choked and labored. The Arpak fought to keep a hold of her weapons while the harpy writhed to get free of the blades embedded in her chest. Their struggle dragged Jordan, ducking and wincing, through tight ranks of harpies, until the creature finally tore itself free and sent the combatant spinning through the air, her blades gripped by aching fingers.

She reoriented and realized that she was suddenly flying very low, streaking through the midst of a Rodanian city. To a soundtrack of grating harpy screeches, Jordan dodged a bell tower, banked around a residential building made of gleaming black metal, and nearly rammed face-first into a red-crested male. His scream assaulted her ears as she spun, bringing her blades to bear——but the male flapped on, intent on some other mission.

Jordan let momentum carry her around, and rode a

thermal higher. She scanned in the dim light, homing in on a lone Nycht facing off with a female, and set off toward the pair.

She found herself in battle alongside the Nycht gunner who had crouched upon the tower with her at the beginning of the onslaught, what seemed like years ago. Together they brought down the female, then ducked for cover as harpies swept by in packs that would have overwhelmed them in seconds.

Without speaking, the pair finished off another crippled male as he limped along the street. Shutters were closed up tight and doors were barred against the apocalyptic events taking place outside.

In the middle of the street ahead they spied an Arpak, one wing clearly broken, lashing wildly with a blade, bravely deflecting two males harpies. Jordan and her comrade descended from above. The Nycht cut down one with his curved blade before it had time to look around, and Jordan leapt forward to strike into the other's back. The numbing shock of the impact shot up her arm. The harpy bucked, and she tumbled to the ground.

The pierced male hissed in rage; both of Jordan's hilts protruded from his shoulder. He lowered his jaw almost to the ground and gripped the stones with his talons, launching himself after her. Jordan rolled, and the beast snapped after her. Mad with rage and pain, he jetted forward, but Jordan reversed direction. His talons skimmed so close over her head that she felt them pull at her hair.

She scrambled to her feet, but she was now bladeless.

She grabbed at her empty sheaths with her eyes on the beast, feeling in vain for a leftover throwing blade.

There was a streaking flap of wings as the gunner threw himself between her and the harpy, his sword glinting in the dull light. There was a bone-rattling *crack* as he hit the monster hard, and together they rolled across the ground. Jordan danced at the perimeter, her eyes catching sight of her hilts as they flew by. There was a pinging snap, and the handle of one knife went clattering across the stones. There was a garbled screech; the harpy bucked and then collapsed. Everything became still, and Jordan could hear her own breathing, her own madly sprinting heartbeat.

Scrambling, crawling, not able to move fast enough, Jordan crossed the cobbled street to roll the dead harpy off the Nycht. The beast rolled away, and she met the empty eyes of the gunner with a sob. The dead warrior's vest leaked from half a dozen punctures where the harpy's talons had done their work.

She loosed a scream of anguish and frustration. Rage tore through her like wildfire, and she knew hate like she had never felt. It was a living, breathing thing, swelling in her heart and lighting every nerve. She thought she knew what hate was, but she was learning that it had only been an abstract idea. Her life had been absent of true hatred up until this battle.

She hadn't known the gunner, but she had fought beside him. His loss struck her so swift and so hard that it left her breathless and gasping. Hatred and a desire for revenge hatched in her like demon spawn. The harpies were something to loathe; that was a basic truth.

But whoever was behind them, as Caje had implied––this faceless, nameless force was the real object of her hatred.

Jordan silently promised the dead gunner that if she lived through this, she would not rest until the malefactor was found and made to pay.

She heaved another sob as a great, dull shadow passed overhead. Beyond where she knelt with her hands clutching at the Nycht's shoulders, great taloned feet settled some incredible bulk upon the paving stones.

Jordan dragged her eyes upward, her hands still on the gunner's vest, to see a huge, haggard female waddling in her direction. The monstrous animal cocked her head to the side, like a chicken, and glared at the injured Arpak that Jordan and the gunner had first come to aid.

The Arpak had collapsed, and was sitting with his back against a stone building nearest the road, his broken wing jutting awkwardly to the side. His face was ashen, but his chest was rising and falling. His eyes were on the hag, watching his death approach with nothing more than a weary acceptance. Jordan didn't know where his weapons had gone.

The Nycht gunner had saved her, and sacrificed himself. He hadn't shown an ounce of hesitation when he saw his comrade in trouble. Jordan's teeth clenched. In that moment, there was nothing more important to her than getting between that big female and the wounded Arpak.

The harpy lowered her heavy head and scraped a claw across the ground. The sound of talons raking on stones sent Jordan's skin crawling.

She cast about for a weapon. She spotted the blade of

her last unbroken sword, grabbed hold of it, and heaved. It did not budge, being locked in bone and slippery with blood.

She loosed a growl of frustration. She caught the glint of the gunner's curved sword where it lay on the ground, half hidden under the fallen harpy's black feathers. Jordan closed her fingers around the hilt, shoved herself to her feet, and tried to run. Her legs betrayed her, but she managed a stagger.

She was beyond any rational understanding of exhaustion.

Her very bones feeling leaden, she stepped forward on numb legs, hoisting her sword. Her wings were so slow to respond, so heavy. They trembled, and their quiver ran through her entire back.

"Get away from him!" she tried to scream at the hag.

When had her throat become so tight? Her mouth so dry?

The harpy ignored her, rearing her head and chest back to strike at the injured Arpak.

"Get. Away!" Jordan snarled through parched lips. She knew she wouldn't be able to cross the ground fast enough, so with everything she had, she sent the sword flying.

The harpies had pressed the Strix forces inexorably back over Middle Rodania, and that fact was driving Toth to desperate measures.

Calling on Caje as he had done near a dozen times before, he sent his brother and the dwindling wrecking crew of Strix to hammer at a pocket of harpy strength. This time, though, he had not read the tides of war correctly; he had not noticed until too late, a contingent of harpies composed of some of the largest, most battle-scarred females, coming up from below. They were suddenly frightfully close and tearing straight for Caje's crew.

When he saw them, Toth's guts turned to stone.

Screaming until his throat felt it would tear itself to pieces, he called to his brother's squad to fall back.

The wrecking crew of Caje's warriors fell on the enemy and wrought a terrible slaughter, and then lifted their faces to see death coming.

They died like heroes, but in the end, they died all the same.

Caught exposed and hanging in midair, most were slain instantly by the impact of talons punching through their leather-clad chests. Those few not instantly slain fought as best they could, but they were outnumbered and overwhelmed.

His heart twisting in his chest like a tormented animal, Toth watched as an immense harpy hit Caje hard and bore him down toward the city. The creature rolled mid-flight, and with a mixture of horror and pride, Toth watched his brother shove his entire hand down its crooked throat.

Like a tumbling rocket from a siege engine, the harpy and Nycht together struck a tower, smashing straight through the stonework, which crumbled in on top of them both. That terrific crash was Caje's death knell, and the chord that snapped the last line holding Toth in check.

Keening a scream of rage from the pit of his fracturing

soul, Toth set to work with his blades: stabbing, slashing, hacking, and gouging with wild abandon. He saw his brother's life end and knew a terrible emptiness.

He would fill that emptiness with blood, but it would never be enough. There was not enough harpy blood in all the world to fill this new and terrible void. Inside the manic winged barbarian, a sinister seed of guilt took root.

Emerging from the haze of blood and death, Sol and Chayla looked around with heads wobbling on sagging shoulders, and realized that Strix not from their squadron now tread the air beside them. All were bent with weariness; not one had escaped unscathed, though none seemed put out of the fight yet.

They looked to each other. If they'd had time, they might have shared the guilty looks of survivors who passed through hell. Instead, they watched a harpy horde descend upon Rodania.

They had merely slowed an inevitable assault.

Some of the Strix army may still have been caught down there in that churning mass that was chewing its way through the air, but there was a good chance that the unhappy few were all that was left. From the looks they shared, it was clear they thought so.

Sol dug deep and found words to fortify them. "We've not come this far to give up now."

Chayla loosed a wild, if breathless, laugh.

"Give up?" Her lip curled as those dark eyes narrowed at the scene below them. She brushed the blood from her facial gash off her brow. "Who said anything about giving up?"

The screams of the city rose to meet them as the last of the Strix army flew between the towers and buildings of Rodania, hunting and being hunted. Like a pack of hungry curs, they went from street to street, striking where they could.

Most civilians had been wise enough to get to cover. Some stupidly brave or lamentably foolhardy individuals had been drawn out to the streets to watch the defense of the city. They soon found themselves the target of descending harpies. They scrambled for shelter, and not all made it in time.

The Strix took down a squabbling trio of males clustered around a body before the harpies even realized what was happening. Yet, as quickly as they had felled those few invaders, the battle-worn band had to flee in the face of a mob of harpies that came pouring through the streets. Darting between buildings and spiralling around steepled roofs, or under galleried causeways, the Strix were fractured into a handful of desperate pairs and trios.

Toth may have been tired, and bleeding, and surrounded by a coterie of the same class of harpies who had killed his brother, but none of that mattered in the face of spilling just one more drop of blood. The cold fire had eaten up everything else inside him, until only this one, chilly ember remained to sustain him. It was fed on blood alone.

They had begun to coordinate their attacks, one or two harrying him while the others jockeyed for a position to strike a telling blow. He eluded them with nothing but speed, strength, and an utter unwillingness to let himself fall. All his evasion and counterattacks had dragged their battle over the rooftops of Rodania's middle tier.

In flashes, he caught sight of the harpies laying waste to the city, tearing into windows and perching on balconies in an effort to fish out the cowering flesh within. He thought he saw the occasional Strix straggler fighting on, desperate and doomed, but whenever he raised his head again, everything was harpies and the ruin they wrought.

It would be over soon. Despite the fact that he could not feel his limbs tiring and wings flagging, Toth knew that they were. Eventually, he would not be fast enough, and then he would fall, like the rest of the army he had commanded.

His death would be the final just penance for his failure to save Rodania.

Within the light of that cold ember of his brother's loss, he almost welcomed the thought. Then, in a flash of familiar color, he spied a pair of yellow wings fleeing a harpy.

Jordan, bloodied and bedraggled, was flying as fast as she could to stay ahead of a shrieking hag with half a sword protruding from the meat of her shoulder.

Fresh energy clawed its way up from the barrens of his soul. If he could get to Jordan, if he could just save her, then perhaps this was not all in vain. Maybe Caje would not have died in vain; maybe the emptiness would not be so vast.

Toth made to cut hard one direction and then roll back the other, but it did no good.

They had him ringed in.

Everywhere he turned, his attackers pressed in, sensing his sudden desperation to be away, his need to free himself.

Talons slashed, beaks snapped, and he could not get out.

And all the while, Jordan's pursuer grew closer.

Jordan could not keep this up. Her wings were stiffening as she fought to maintain altitude while weaving between the streets of Rodania. Only the lumbering size and clumsy movements of the old female had kept the Arpak beyond reach. The next moment, or maybe the one after that, would be all she would have left. Then it would have her. The hag's jaws would snap shut, and she would know no more.

An incredible, primeval roar set the air quivering over and through all of Rodania.

Having expected to hear the sound of her own bones crunching beneath a harpy's jaws, Jordan was struck dumb. She nearly fell out of the sky.

There was only one creature that was capable of that sound.

Dragon.

In spite of the looming spectre of death that was

coming for her, Jordan searched the sky. Her heart seized with an insane and giddy hope.

"Blue?" she called in a winded pant. "Blue?" It was all she could do to say his name.

Something huge set the clouds above to boiling.

Like a great shark breaching the waves, an immense draconian form descended upon Rodania.

Its proportions were incredible—–more vast and terrifying than anything Blue could ever dream to be. This juggernaut of scale and jaw was clad in brilliant crimson from snout to tail. Wings beat the air into gusts that sent both harpies and Strix tumbling. This dragon seemed too huge to sail through the air so gracefully, its horn-crowned head held high.

Some internal luminescence rippled through the creature's armored breast, like sunlight on river water. The beast bent its head and poured out its fiery displeasure in a torrent. The dragon's fire was a brilliant inferno of blue, with tongues of flame haloed in impossibly bright shades of turquoise and green, bleeding into white. Jordan winced against the sudden light, and watched the flames engulf an entire block of Rodanian real estate that was swarming with harpies. A hot blast of air, stinking of sulfur, thudded against her body, blew her hair back, and dried out her eyes.

Confusion made Jordan dip and lose altitude. *How can this be happening? How can a city that's already fallen be consumed in dragonfire?* It was too awful, an event born of some great, unfeeling cosmic whimsy.

But the joke had not yet run its full course.

The great red reptile was heading straight for her.

Both she and the harpy at her heels had faltered with the advent of the dragon. With a wild unhappy laugh of disbelief, Jordan put on what little speed she could manage as the harpy surged after her.

Perhaps she hopes to claim me before the dragon does?

The harpy was close enough that Jordan could hear her rasping snorts.

One more turn, she thought. *Just one last turn to spite her. I'd rather go to a dragon than a harpy.*

Her wings cramped painfully. It was an ugly, clumsy turn.

Her strength left her, and she lighted upon a tiled roof in what amounted to be a graceful collapse. Her limbs quivering with fatigue, Jordan looked up to watch the harpy that had been chasing her pass by overhead without another glance.

Almost casually, the dragon soared behind, its great jaws widening like the jowls of a universe. It unleashed a brilliant, multihued death upon the harpy, and the female became a spectacular torch of greasy feathers. The spiky fireball sailed a hundred more feet before striking the side of a stone tower in an explosion of burning feathers.

Jordan's mouth went slack with wonder as the red-scaled colossus gave a roar that set the tiles beneath her quaking. Arching its sinuous body, the dragon circled, and leveled an eye at Jordan where she knelt helplessly on the roof.

She waited for her own fiery death to come––her mind unable to fit the pieces together any other way. Her war-battered thoughts strained with fragility, and she noted numbly as she watched the leviathan wheel, how very much this dragon's eyes resembled Blue's; in shape, if not also in character. In fact, now that she was really looking, the dragon's entire head followed achingly familiar lines and aesthetics. This dragon was so very like Blue, yet dwarfed him in size.

A second roar rent the sky, this one higher in pitch.

Her neck creaking, Jordan watched as a dragon clad in scales of familiar blue and yellow descended from the heavens. He was far larger than when she had last seen him, though not nearly as immense as the red. There was no mistaking her reptilian partner.

"Blue," Jordan whispered.

She finally understood, and her relief was so great it seemed to break her in two.

Blue dipped his snout as though he'd heard her. He sailed beneath the red as she curved away from Jordan and toward the thickest mass of harpy flesh. Blue lifted his nose up as the red sent her snout down. The two dragons met in the briefest of touches. Jordan watched them part and then approach the harpy horde from either side. Tandem glows appeared in both scaly bellies, and dual blasts of fire lit the sky.

Jordan closed her eyes as hot tears tracked through the dirt on her face.

CHAPTER THIRTY

Blue and his mate cleared the skies of harpies with fire and jaws, inevitably leaving smoking wreckage behind them. The stink of harpy, brimstone, and sulfur hung over the city, thick and choking. As the last of the harpies fell in burning greasy fireballs, or turned tail and winged west, Jordan found enough energy to take to the skies.

Blue and the monstrous dragon were out of sight, buried somewhere in the clouds, or perhaps chasing off the last of the harpies over Rodania. Jordan was too tired to pursue them.

Her wings carried her in a slow, painful trajectory, over the city, back to where she'd started this insane battle. Smoke billowed from fires scattered throughout the countryside and in the streets of small towns. Rain began to fall, striking Jordan's cheeks in fat *plops*.

The carcasses of the dead, both harpy and Strix, peppered the landscape. With a grim satisfaction, Jordan noted that there were far more dead harpies than Arpaks or Nychts, but then again, there hadn't been that many Strix warriors to begin with--a paltry sum when compared to the horde they had fought.

Jordan landed on the tower, letting her wings droop behind her. The useless Lewis gun sat cocked at a jaunty angle, pointing at the sky, and the stones were coated with empty shell casings.

There were no other Strix in sight.

Have all of my companions died, then?

Jordan felt like she was being filled with cement slowly, from the pelvis up. *Is Sol alright? How do I even begin to search for my father, for Eohne, for Toth?* The event of near total devastation had not been discussed. She surveyed the skies for familiar winged shapes, her eyes stinging with the thickening smoke.

She squinted as the sound of wings reached her ears. Smoke and cloud cycloned as a shape emerged, and Jordan couldn't control the torrent of silent tears that came as she recognized the set of Sol's shoulders and the breadth of his wings. Relief made her breath hitch, and as he barrelled into her, they nearly fell with the impact.

"You're alive," she choked into his neck. Her fingers wound through his hair and squeezed, probably too hard. "You're alive." She gloried in the feel of him under her hands, his heat, the smell of his sweat, even the stink of harpy on him.

"Let me look at you," he said, setting her back.

But it was Jordan's eyes that grew horrified. "How much of this blood is yours?"

"Only a little," he said. He turned her, catching her

feathers in his face. "Your back? It's not cut?" His hands prodded and touched, sweeping over her frame.

"No. I'm mostly just scraped and bruised. Where are you hurt?"

"I'm fine. You're alive." He hugged her again, squeezing her so tight her ribs creaked. "I can't ask for more. Have you seen anyone else?"

Jordan shook her head miserably. "Can this really have happened? Can we have lost everyone?" She hardly dared to ask if Sol knew where Allan and Eohne were. "It was such chaos. I need…" She took another hitching breath.

"We'll find him, don't worry," Sol grabbed her shoulders. "Jordan, we won. Yes, it cost us dearly, but we *won*."

Jordan nodded. "Thanks to Blue and his new friend."

"Yes, thanks to Blue. Come on. Let's go for the training grounds. Some will likely go there. It's out of the worst of the smoke."

The Arpaks took flight, heading northwest to the small islands just beyond Middle Rodania. There were survivors there, but a sad few. Jordan was relieved to see Toth and one of the Strix from her own squadron. Being the strongest fighters of the bunch, several Nychts from The Conca were there as well.

Jordan and Sol greeted their fellow combatants with fierce hugs.

"Caje?" Jordan asked, looking for her fearless leader.

Toth only shook his head. His face was an expressionless mask. Jordan closed her eyes as grief climbed onto her shoulders once more. The big Nycht was gone. Jordan opened her eyes and reached for Toth, but his body language made her hesitate; the way he turned his shoulders a little away from her and brought his arm across his stomach. Toth didn't want comfort.

The Nycht looked to Sol instead. "Chayla?"

"I lost her toward the end. I thought maybe she'd be here," Sol replied. "There's still hope; she was alive when I saw her last, before we got separated in the fray."

Toth nodded grimly, then turned to Jordan. "Your father is safe, as is Eohne. I know you're worried."

"They are? How do you know?"

"I had Gillen deliver them to your apartment less than an hour ago, they are unharmed."

Relief flooded every joint, and Jordan's shoulders slumped. "Oh, thank heavens. Where were they?"

"In a chapel not far from my tower. To be honest, those of us fighting from the ground generally fared a lot better than our airborne combatants. Might be something to consider factoring into our battle strategy." A complicated expression crossed the Nycht's features.

Regret?

Jordan hadn't thought of the ground as being the safer place. She'd made an assumption that anyone with wings would automatically be at an advantage. She hoped they wouldn't have to test the new strategy for a long time.

Every Strix had an injury of some kind. Toth spoke to each combatant, examined each wound. The Nycht leader had already sent multiple wounded Strix winging toward the small field hospital that had been erected and staffed with Balroc's money.

"What now?" Jordan asked, looking back at the destruction.

Pillars of smoke were rising from the cities and fields of

Middle Rodania. Dragon roars could be heard in the distance.

"Right now," Toth raised his voice so all could hear, and the small cluster of battered soldiers closed in around him. "Arpaks, I want you to go home and get some rest, unless I've already told you to get to the field hospital. Nychts, we'll take first shift. The wounded need us, and there is no one more suitable for a night shift than a Nycht. At first light, we'll switch. Arpaks, we'll reconvene at the break of dawn."

And with that, as the last of that devastating day's sun leaked from the skies, the weary crew took flight. The Arpaks went home to rest, or to have their wounds tended, and the Nychts to find their fallen comrades and help whoever could be helped.

The fallen Strix soldiers numbered one hundred and ninty-three, while the critically injured came to sixty-eight. Citizens of Rodania managed to survive the attack with only a remarkable eleven deaths, and six critically injured. The city itself would take months to rebuild, if not years.

Commerce on Rodania ground to a halt, save for the necessities, while citizens and soldiers alike came together to help those in need and take stock of the damage.

Jordan recruited Blue to help remove harpy carcasses, and carry their stink far from the islands, dumping them in the sea for the fish to feast on. The fallen Strix were given a respectful cremation and burial, and the date for a solemn ceremony was set.

Days blurred together, and it seemed the work would never cease. Toth set the Arpaks and the Nychts on a rotation of daytime and night shifts. Someone was always working, yet progress still seemed slow.

In the mornings, Jordan and Sol dropped Eohne and Allan off in the main square near Juer's library, where they worked the daylight hours; Eohne at the field hospital, and Allan on a clean-up crew.

In the evenings, the odd little family would crash in Sol's apartment. The crowded bedroom remained a mess of mattresses, feathers, armor, and bodies at night. There had been so little time for their own lives, that the kitchen cupboards and tile floors remained broken from the harpy that had attacked Eohne and Allan.

No one complained of the close quarters, or the mess, but Jordan felt that one day soon—when the bulk of the cleanup was done, and Rodania no longer felt like it was in emergency mode— –their living situation would have to change.

Little by little, Rodania improved. More Strix joined the army, and Toth's ranks swelled. The citizens of Rodania lived in fear of another sudden harpy attack, and there was only one thing that seemed to quell the atmosphere of rising terror: the hulking shadow of the red dragon. She would not be seen for days, and then, as though a messenger sent for her, she would make an appearance in the skies over one of the islands. Word would spread like fire through prairie grass, and the Strix would feel safe again, for a time.

Jordan did not approach the red dragon, but Blue met Jordan and Sol every morning. He spent his days clearing harpy carcasses until there were none left to be found. When that was done, his appearances were fewer and farther between. Jordan didn't know if the bond they'd formed that day in Maticaw was damaged, or if it had simply evolved as Blue grew.

It was another thing she'd love to research if she ever had the luxury of time again.

"Where are you living these days, my friend?" Jordan asked her big blue companion, rubbing his snout. He was now the size of a small ferryboat, and blinked at her with an eye roughly the size of a laptop. "Have you taken up residence with a certain redhead in some secret lair?" Blue pressed his forehead to her shoulder hard enough to knock her sideways. "One of these days, when I'm not completely shattered with exhaustion, I'm going to follow you home. You know that?" She rubbed the smooth scales between his eyes. "At least no one will be chasing you out of Rodania anytime soon. They realize they might be signing their own death warrants." She kissed his snout. "Rodania owes you big-time, Mister."

The dragon gave his familiar whistle, spread his broad, leathery wings, and took to the skies. He climbed until he disappeared into the cloud cover.

CHAPTER THIRTY-ONE

The desire to sit and talk privately with Allan had been weighing on Jordan since her father had woken from his coma, but there had never been time. Each time Jordan made to call him aside, guilt that she should be doing something else would rush in to fill the space, and she'd push it off for another day.

She had gotten as far as telling Allan that she'd found Jaclyn, and that it had been a shock of elephantine proportions for her—–but Jordan and Allan had never been alone, and he would clam up in the presence of anyone else. These false starts at poorly timed moments had thickened the air with awkwardness, so Jordan let it drop until she and her father could be alone.

One day, the atmosphere in the city shifted. It was subtle, but palpable to every citizen, even the children. There was finally a feeling of hope wreathing the islands, instead of despair. Heartbreak and sorrow would take much longer to pass, but the collective consciousness seemed to agree: Rodania was scarred, but would survive.

Sol knew Jordan so well by now that, without her having to say anything, he pulled her aside one morning and told her to take an hour with her father. "It is well past due," he said firmly.

Another thing Jordan had meant to find time for was a conversation with Eohne about her plans. Thus far, the Elf had not mentioned returning to Charra-Rae, but they all knew it was inevitable.

Jordan pushed aside the thought and focused on her father.

She directed him to sit on one of the stools in Sol's kitchen, after Eohne and Sol had left for the day's work. Allan let out a long sigh and ran his fingers through his ginger hair. He'd known it was coming, and his expression was resigned. "This isn't going to be easy, Jordy. For either of us."

"I never thought it would be."

"What you told me about your mother, about Jaclyn," Allan crossed his arms over his chest, and his shoulders rose to his ears like he was cold. "It makes some sense to me."

Jordan's brows elevated almost to her hairline. "Which part?"

"Not the part about her running some trade office off the coast of Maticaw, I don't know anything about that. But what you said about her attitude, how you described her. It didn't come as a shock."

"It was a shock to *me*." Jordan crossed her own arms at the memory of their cold and brutal interaction. "Unless there was some secret Pig Latin going on between her and that crony of hers that I simply did not understand, she gave an order to have me killed."

"That is indeed a shock. As ruthless as I know Jaclyn can be, I would never expect *that* from her. It's unthinkable. I've only ever told you positive things about her, but the truth is..." Allan bit his lip, and his hazel eyes grew pained, "she never really loved me. I lied to myself about that for so long, because," he shrugged, "well, I loved *her* so much. You can't know what your mother was like when I first met her. She was magnetic. It wasn't just her physical beauty, it was her intelligence, her ambition, her charisma."

"I'm sure she can be very charming," Jordan said, her mouth flat. She remembered those beautiful brown eyes, the soft mouth belying a frightening kind of iron will.

"Charming is an understatement."

"How much of what you raised me to believe about her is a lie?"

Allan's shoulders tightened again, making him look small, and Jordan wondered at how the topic of Jaclyn could reduce her father in this way. Her anger burned like coals under the surface of her anticipation.

"Your mother and I did meet at a ribbon-cutting ceremony," Allan confirmed. "That part is true."

"For the new Children's Hospital?"

"Yes. She had recently won the Miss Virginia pageant, and she was at the height of her beauty and popularity. She was the sweetheart of Richmond. Everyone had fallen in love with her, and I was no different. I was the son of a well-liked senator, on my own trajectory for political 'greatness'." Allan's hands lifted, his fingers tense and curling, emphasizing the emotion of the time.

"People *wanted* us to be together as much as we wanted

it for ourselves; it was inevitable. Even my parents wanted me to marry her. I can't tell you how much that surprised me." Allan made a face. "They were such snobs, and Jaclyn had come from nothing; she was a nobody. Yet somehow, she had bewitched them. For her part, she appeared to have fallen in love with me just as hard as I had with her. It wasn't until later that I came to recognize the real reason she'd married me." The corners of Allan's mouth turned down, his brow creased.

"Money?" Jordan guessed.

But Allan shook his head.

"Not money. Power. Jaclyn may have come from nothing, but she had a money-making gene. She turned her pageant win into dollars with such skill and cleverness it took my breath away. It was like she'd been raised to be a president or a CEO. No, Jaclyn could make money without my help. It was power that she was most attracted to, and I had the best wagon she could have possibly hitched to at the time. She took to the high-profile life like a flower to the sun. She was like Jackie O, or––who was the Spice Girl?"

Allan snapped his fingers, searching.

Jordan blinked. "The Spice Girl?"

"Yes, the beautiful one who always looks perfect and never lets anyone see her eat or smile?"

"Victoria Beckham?"

"That's the one."

Jordan laughed. "I'm shocked at how easily that comparison just took my understanding of Jaclyn to new heights."

Allan chuckled. "Well, my apologies to Mrs. Beckham.

Maybe she's a nice lady, and is as different from Jaclyn as a horse is from a parakeet, but she gives the same high-profile consciousness and appearance. A girl doesn't wind up on the cover of Vogue without knowing how to play the game. You know what I mean?"

"I do."

"Anyway, we married. We went to Paris for our honeymoon, and it was as magical as one could wish for."

"That's where mom found the locket."

Allan nodded. "And the fellow that I met in prison, Marceau, he says there is a portal in Paris, so I wonder if the two are linked somehow. And the locket was empty, I can assure you."

"We've established that. The portrait happened later."

"Yes. So the first order of business was children. We both wanted them badly, and we started trying right away." Allan shook his head. "But something was wrong. We couldn't get pregnant. It stressed both of us out, which makes conception even harder."

"Did you see a specialist?"

Allan's shoulders sank. "We did." Allan took Jordan's hand. "It was me," his voice broke. "The problem was with me."

"But obviously you overcame this problem--"

Allan was shaking his head, his expression miserable.

"You...*didn't* overcome this problem?"

Allan's face spoke volumes, and his hazel eyes probed hers, watching, waiting for the truth to sink in.

"But..."

Jordan's head swam, and her eyes drifted shut as the room spun. *I should have known. The evidence was there, staring me in the face.* It was so obvious, she now felt like an idiot.

She began to breathe hard and fast.

"Jordy, honey." Allan put a hand on her back. "Here, put your head between your knees."

Jordan spread her knees and dropped her face between them, fighting back tears.

"No," she croaked out on a sob. "No. No. No. Dad…"

"Jordy," Allan's voice was breaking too. "I'm so sorry. Honey, it doesn't change anything; it doesn't change how I feel about you. You're my daughter. I couldn't love you any more than I do."

For a long time, Jordan fought to get herself under control. She'd assumed, when she had found her in that strange office, on that strange island, that Jaclyn's Arpak gene just wasn't expressed. After all, Sol had spent days on Oriceran without any visible wings; it was just as possible for her mother to have done so, especially if she had just returned from Earth.

The truth was far more brutal.

Jordan sat up, tears streaming down her face.

"Oh, Jordy." Allan searched his pockets for something, a tissue, a kerchief. He pulled out a dirty rag, one that had likely been used to polish a Lewis gun, frowned at it, and decided against giving it to her. "I'm so sorry. I know this is a shock."

Jordan wiped her face. "It's okay, Dad. You're right, it doesn't change anything." She smiled at Allan through her tears. "It's just going to take a little getting used to. So," she let out a shaky breath, "you never knew about Oriceran?"

Allan let out a startled laugh. "You thought I knew about this place?" Allan shook his head. "I had no idea."

"But you've taken to life here so quickly."

Jordan had been amazed by how much her father seemed to like life on Rodania——at least up until the harpy attack.

"Remember, previous to waking up in that bedroom," Allan jerked his head toward their crammed sleeping quarters, "I had been shut up in a prison, stuffed in a box on a ship, and tossed out of a boat by a man who looked and smelled like a rotten vegetable. Waking up here, with you and your wonderful and strange friends, was a kind of heaven by comparison. I was even useful right away. I think that did more to help me recover than anything else." He glowered. "I always felt so impotent as a politician. You know that."

"Yeah, I know," Jordan sniffed. "But go back. You couldn't get pregnant, then what?"

"Then Jaclyn and I began to fight something terrible. She felt betrayed. She was so angry with me, as though I was sterile by choice." Allan pinched the bridge of his nose and rubbed his eyes at the memory. "It was awful. She was awful. The fights got so bad that I left her alone at the house and went to my apartment in the city. We both needed to cool off." He blinked at his daughter through red eyes. "That's when she disappeared."

"The first time?"

"Yes, the first time. I tried calling her on the Monday morning after the weekend had passed. We hadn't spoken to each other for two days. There was no answer at the house. I figured she was still upset and needed more time, so I left it. I tried again on Tuesday. By Wednesday, I was really starting to worry, so I drove out that evening. That's when I discovered she was missing." Allan rolled his eyes up into his skull and let out a groan of exasperation. "I went out of my mind. I notified the police and took a leave of absence. The press caught wind and followed me around, asking stupid questions. I punched a journalist in the teeth outside the police station. I hired investigators and spent a ton of money. Even your grandfather, who loved Jaclyn and had bottomless pockets, questioned how much I was spending to find her. I had people combing every state; her photo was everywhere. I harassed Interpol, the police, my private detectives, every day of the week. It was a nightmare. Madness."

Jordan could picture it. Her father had an inner bulldog that would come out now and then. It had bared its teeth when Jordan was getting bullied in elementary school, and the school was doing nothing to protect her. There had been a nasty court battle; three kids got suspended, and a fourth was sent to another district.

Allan had been a force.

"How long until she came back?"

"Eighteen months, two weeks, and four days," Allan said without even pausing to think. "I don't know if you remember that old chalkboard I used to have on the wall in my war room?"

"The one covered in hatch-marks?"

"That's the one. Those hatch-marks didn't have anything to do with either of the World War timelines; they were marking off the days Jaclyn was missing. I was a shadow of myself then. I weighed about the same as a champion jockey, and lost a lot of hair."

"And when she came back, she…" Jordan swallowed. Her mouth was dry.

She got up and poured her and her father each a glass of water before returning to her stool. "She was pregnant."

Allan nodded, taking the glass Jordan offered. "Yes. She was pregnant." He took a couple of long gulps and set the cup aside.

"How far along?"

"Not very far, only a few weeks."

"I didn't know it at the time. When she came back, she was ravenous for me. Sorry if this part disturbs you," he said apologetically.

Jordan shook her head and waved for him to continue. Of all the things she was disturbed by, the idea of her parents enjoying some exuberant headboard gymnastics was the least of it.

"She made the agony of those months vanish with the intensity of her love. I thought," Allan swallowed, and the column of his throat moved. His expression hardened. "She let me think the babies were mine."

Jordan thought she'd misheard.

"Babies? You mean baby. Me."

Allan dragged his eyes to his daughter and they were ponderous with grief. "No, I mean *babies*." He took Jordan's hand again. "Poor Jordan, there is so much. Too much. I'm so sorry."

"Babies?" Jordan croaked.

"You were a twin."

Jordan's arms marbled with cold flesh as chilly fingers traced her skin.

"Are you okay, honey?" Allan put a warm hand on her shoulder.

"I need a minute."

"Of course." But he looked at her with a kind of terror, like she might vanish before his eyes.

Jordan went to the water closet and splashed her face at the sink. She looked at the girl in the mirror: her teal eyes, blonde hair, the shape of the bones under her skin. Those teal eyes were not Jaclyn's, nor were they Allan's.

So whose were they?

Her eyes narrowed. Her mind searched her memory for some masculine version of her countenance. There was someone there in the shadows of her experience, someone she had seen before. *But who?*

Jordan stared in the mirror for so long, and thought so hard, her head began to ache. She washed her hands to warm them, and then returned to the kitchen.

"What happened to my twin?"

Allan looked relieved to continue the conversation.

"I'll tell you what I know, but there's some other things to tell you first. When I learned Jaclyn was pregnant, I was shocked… elated, but shocked. And she did nothing to disabuse me of the belief that it was a miracle, *our* miracle. Part of me believed it, but as the pregnancy progressed, I couldn't dislodge a sliver of doubt. The doctor had already told me that I would never father children, that it was simply impossible. Doctors are wrong all the time, of course, so I clung to the hope that this was the case. He had just been wrong."

"In fact, he phoned me one evening after examining Jaclyn, specifically to apologize for having been wrong." Allan paused. "It didn't occur to me at the time, but now…"

"What?"

"I wonder whether she bribed the doctor to get him to admit his 'mistake'," Allan added air quotes with his fingers, "thus helping to conceal the truth. I wouldn't put it past her."

"That's supernaturally manipulative." Jordan pressed her palms to her eyelids.

How can I possibly be related to that woman, and not to the gentle soul in front of me?

Allan nodded his agreement. "I paid attention to the timeline and Jaclyn's state as the time passed. The math didn't work. She had to have been pregnant already when she returned."

"Did you confront her about it?"

Allan shook his head. "We'd been through so much already. Jaclyn returned with this story about being kidnapped and kept against her will, about being raped. My heart was broken already, and it broke again for her."

"But there was no ransom? No contact at all from this person she said held her hostage?"

"No. Nothing."

Jordan let out a ghastly laugh that gave Allan a chill. Jaclyn had orchestrated a deception so deep that its effects had travelled forward through time, even following them to an alternate universe. Even after more than two decades, Jaclyn's deception still cut to the bone.

"She had to talk to the police of course, and she spun a story like a black widow spins a web. It was convincing, and we believed her. What else could we do? She'd been gone for eighteen months, and she had to be *somewhere*. There appeared to be no motivation for her to lie; she loved her life in Richmond, and everyone believed she loved me. Why would she stay away if not because someone was detaining her? No one could have guessed what we know now." Allan sputtered with pure amazement, "that she'd travelled through some inter-dimensional portal to an alternate universe!"

The apartment was silent for a time. Then Jordan spoke with bitterness. "So you never told her you knew the babies weren't yours?" She was hit by an emotional aftershock, like a polo mallet to the forehead. *She had been a twin.*

"No. And when you were born, I fell in love all over again. There was nothing I wanted in my whole life more than a family. I was perfectly happy to take you as my own. As far as I was concerned, you were *mine*; not the offspring of some sadistic kidnapper."

"Was my twin a boy or a girl?"

"A boy."

"What happened to him?"

Allan took a deep, mind-cleansing breath. "After you were born, Jaclyn slipped into a depression so deep I feared it might only end in suicide. The doc diagnosed her with post-partum depression, but Jaclyn was broken. She went to a place where I couldn't reach her. No one could. Not even her babies could snap her out of it. I had to hire a nanny just to take care of you and your brother. Jaclyn seemed incapable of doing anything but crying, sleeping, and staring into the abyss."

"That's when you hired Maria?"

"Not quite. I hired her after Jaclyn disappeared the second time, and Maria was an absolute Godsend."

"What was my brother's name?"

Allan gave a sour chuckle. "That's a funny part in this story, if there can be any humor found in it. Your mother filled out your birth certificates at the hospital. You and your brother came quickly, and I was stuck in traffic. It was done by the time I arrived." Allan shook his head. "Jaclyn gave you your brother's name, and your brother, your name. Haven't you ever wondered why you have a boy's name?"

Jordan blinked at this, shaking her head. She had never questioned the nature of her name. It had always been hers, so why should it be strange? "It's not all that uncommon for a girl to be named Jordan."

"Maybe not these days, but this was twenty-five years ago. You didn't call a little girl *'Jordan';* especially in a respected, high profile, politically significant family. My parents were horrified."

"She gave me my brother's name?"

"That's right." Allan nodded. "And your poor brother got a girl's name."

Jordan gasped as a key slid home, and a mental lock clicked open. Her eyes widened. "Ashley."

Allan's face expanded with surprise. "How did you know that?"

"I met him," Jordan croaked. She folded her hands; her fingers felt like ice. It didn't matter that she'd washed them in hot water only minutes before.

The familiar masculine face she'd been searching for; it was Ashley's.

"Ashley was the mercenary who tried to kill me. Mom's lackey."

Her own twin had been the one chasing her through the pouring rain over the Maticaw harbor in the dark of night. Her twin had been the one to almost end her.

He would have killed her if it hadn't been for Toth and Blue.

She had suspected at the time that he was a young lover of her mother's, but the truth snapped into place like a puzzle piece, with all the feeling of 'rightness'. Jordan had thought there was something familiar about Ashley; it was her own face, only it was different enough to elude her. His eyes had been dark, Jaclyn's eyes.

"So." Allan let out a long breath. "Ashley is alive."

"She took him when she disappeared the second time?" Jordan understood what had happened. "She couldn't leave without her *son*." As irrational as it was after everything Jordan had learned about Jaclyn, the bitterness of rejection twisted the last word.

"No, sweetie, it wasn't like that. She loved you. She wanted you. I think she was just afraid that she couldn't care for two babies, wherever it was she was headed."

"She was depressed. How do you know she loved me?"

Allan spluttered. "She wanted you, she wanted kids. I believe that, if I believe anything."

Jordan shook her head. "You haven't seen her recently." She met her father's gaze. "She has no love for either of us."

Allan had no reply for this.

"What did you *think* happened to her and Ashley?"

"I thought she went back to her captor. I talked to a therapist about it; something called Stockholm Syndrome."

"When a kidnap victim empathizes with their kidnapper, even falls in love with them," Jordan nodded.

"Sick, I know. But that's the only way anyone could rationalize it. I don't need to tell you what a nightmare erupted when she disappeared for a second time."

Jordan shook her head. No, he didn't need to tell her. She'd been told in great detail how hard her family had searched for Jaclyn, how devastated they were by her disappearance.

"But how did you hide my twin from me my whole life? And why?"

"It was all to protect you, Jordan. I wanted as little of the tragedy to touch you as possible. It may have been a mistake, it may have been wrong… but that's what a parent does for their child—protects them—for better or worse."

Jordan took this in silently. How was she supposed to feel about this lie, even if it was to protect her? Jordan didn't know what it was like to parent a child, but she could imagine it. Somewhere, deep down, she understood, and did not despise Allan for it. The truth had a way of coming out, and now was its time. But she had another big question to ask, and braced herself for it to go unanswered.

"Do you have any idea who my biological father is?"

"If I knew that honey, I would tell you." Allan took her cold hand and squeezed it. "I hope you believe me."

Jordan nodded. "I do believe you, Dad."

Allan's face was soft with compassion. "I'm so sorry. I've made so many mistakes, but please understand that everything I did, I did for love of you."

"I know. And I will have more questions, of that I'm sure." Jordan got off the stool and looked at the blue sky visible beyond the terrace. "I'm not finished with Jaclyn," she murmured. "Or Ashley."

"What do you mean?"

She didn't answer at first. She needed time to process, but she knew without a shadow of a doubt that she could not simply walk away from her history, her blood-mother, without making her face what she had done.

Jordan set her jaw.

Sometimes, in order to move forward, one had to go back. Things had happened in their past to bring them to this present time and place––but things were happening now, too.

Jaclyn worked the Maticaw port, as bizarre as that seemed, and it appeared that she was messing with trade. Jordan had a twin; as unbelievable as it sounded, it was a fact. *What has Jaclyn told Ashley about me? Anything?*

The colors of the chessboard had changed, but the same game was still in motion.

"I mean," she turned back to the man she called her father, "this story isn't over."

FINIS

THE STORY CONTINUES

The story continues with book four, *Transcendent*, available at Amazon and through Kindle Unlimited.

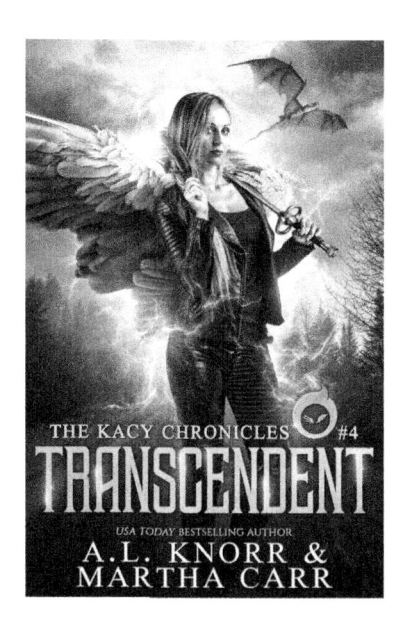

Grab your copy today!

AUTHOR NOTES - A.L. KNORR

WRITTEN DECEMBER 20, 2017

I know, I know! It's been a hallmark of this series to end on a bit of a cliffhanger, and the third book is no different. Rest assured that the final installment of The Kacy Chronicles; TRANSCENDENT, is already in production. I also have a few ideas for spin off stories, so when you get through Transcendent, I'll ask you for your opinion on these potential stories and will look forward to hearing your thoughts.

The end of every novel written is the end of another intense session of planning, writing, and learning. I never fail to learn so much from this process, and hopefully get a little better every time.

Some things in Jordan's story may have taken you by surprise, other's you may have guessed at, but my hope is that you thoroughly enjoyed being in the moment with our Strix friends and were swept away through an astral portal of your own.

As I pen these author's notes, I am sitting on a bright red overstuffed couch in a Venetian apartment. Rain sprinkles from gray skies on this fine winter day, and a hot tea sits on the table at my knee. Footsteps echo under the window as people stroll along the canal and voices murmur, perhaps telling their own story, as boats float along like river-ghosts. What writer could ask for a more moody, melancholic place to create?

As always, there is some anxiety that goes along with launching a new story. Will my readers like it? Will I disappoint them? Will their hearts beat a little faster at the battle scenes or the moments of love? Isolated as I am from you, I'll never know unless you tell me, and so I hope you do.

Thank you to my wonderful editors: Jen and Nicola. Thank you to my Street Team and Beta Team for your feedback. Thanks also, so much, to the JIT Team at LMBPN Publishing, as well as to Michael, Martha and Steve for all the support. I'll be cracking along to work on TRANSCENDENT, for as Jordan just told you, this story is not over yet.

I hope you'll come find me on Facebook, at my website, or over email. I am always thrilled to hear from readers!

Warmly,

A.L. Knorr

AUTHOR NOTES - MARTHA CARR

WRITTEN DECEMBER 19, 2017

So, apparently, I'm really a Texan now. My blood has thinned out and I've gotten used to 45 degrees being cold. You see, I thought it would be a good idea to go back to my old stomping ground of Chicago during Christmas time. The city really knows how to get in the spirit and I missed being able to see snow, visit the Kinder Market, go to the Music Box and see It's a Wonderful Life. I like to do so much Christmas, diving right into the lights, the parades, the scent of pine and the caroling so that by the time it's December 26th, I'm done.

Only thing is someone left open the giant freezer door of the world and the place was 20 degrees BEFORE the wind chill. And trust me, that close to Lake Michigan the wind chill can shave another 20 degrees right off the top and leave you at zero. Mind you, all my old buddies didn't seem to notice but I had a few moments where I really wondered what warm felt like anymore. That would have been a good time to know how to open a portal and go to Oriceran and the warm Dark Forest.

It was so cold that on Friday, FRIDAY, not SATURDAY, I asked Abby-Lynn if she'd like to do a short livestream on Facebook to advertise a sale going on with her books... for Saturday. I have no idea why Abs went along with this scheme except that she was in Canada (I think) where it's even colder. I'm telling you, there's a theme here. So, we told everyone the books were on sale that day and it wasn't until I pointed out to Magic Mike that the prices weren't changed and he said, "That's because today's Friday," that I had a clue. You have to laugh... and drink more hot water and lemon while wrapped in a blanket.

Still... I love Christmas, no matter how I can get it. For me, it's a reminder that joy and peace are always possible and it can begin with me. Enjoy Combatant, third book in the Kacy Chronicles series and snuggle up to someone close near a warm fire and think of me, back home, finally warm again.

PUBLISHER NOTES - MICHAEL ANDERLE

WRITTEN DECEMBER 20, 2017

Thank you for not only reading the stories, but allowing us the opportunity to share a bit of our lives here in the back!

Right now, I'm not looking out the window in a Venetian apartment. Although I was blessed to be in Venice this last June so I can imagine the image Abby is describing.

Rather, I'm in Texas looking out my back window. I see my dormant light-brown grass and down a row of eight homes on the left, and eight homes on the right. My house is sitting similar to the head of the table, looking at everyone else down the table which is the back of their homes as they recede into the distance. There is another home at the end, which is facing me.

Nothing very Venetian, I assure you.

I share Abby's concerns when new books come out. You would think that would go away after doing twenty-something of my own books and almost a hundred others, but it doesn't. It seems that my mind has the creative ability to come up with yet a NEW and exciting way to bite the ends of my fingernails off.

Unless I'm exhausted. In which case the book goes live and I'm collapsed somewhere, trying to come back to reality. When this happens, I start by peeking at the web page to see if I have a ranking yet. Then, are the reviews starting to come in? Have I really screwed up and went in a direction that you fans weren't expecting (and didn't like?)

I've done that once, and *OMG* was it a seriously horrible experience. I had to write a new series of four books (The Dark Messiah books) to fix that bad decision.

Now, I get to talk about Michael Anderle – *Author* plans for Oriceran. As you know, or might know, I started the effort to create Oriceran as a place to play a little when I was done with my first Kurtherian Gambit series.

Having just provided Martha a small overview, I'll share them with you here first.

My character in this Universe is called Mr. Brownstone. The series is "The Unbelievable Mr. Brownstone," and he is essentially a magical bounty hunter who uses his abilities to track down both magical and non-magical people who need to come back to justice.

Or not.

Will he decide a couple of times to just leave the reward and take care of the bounty, permanently? I'm not sure.

Yet.

During these efforts, he meets another bounty hunter who is not what she seems, and a little blind teenager who is the linchpin for his lonely existence. A loneliness he has to recognize before he can do anything to fix it.

I have three core character stories that I'm planning

and hope to have a twelve (12) book release for these characters in Summer of 2018.

GO ME! (*LOL.* If you don't yell for yourself, who will?)

So, that is part of my plans here in the next few weeks to get that kicked off as I work on the next two books in the TKG Universe.

I hope you and your family – whether they be typical or atypical, enjoy the end of the year.

If 2017 kicked your ass, then flip it off as we walk into 2018 with a new determination to at least smile 10% more. If for no other reason than you *can*, because it is a choice.

Now, if 2017 was awesome for you, then enjoy the HELL out of the results. Be pleased and don't let anyone bring your happiness down. Let 2018 be the next step going up to a brighter and better future for yourself and your family.

I hope we have brought you a few smiles, a few *'hell yeah's!'* and perhaps a tear or two this year with our stories. May we do it again in 2018.

Wishing you the best in life, love, and happiness.

Michael

OTHER SERIES IN THE ORICERAN UNIVERSE:

THE LEIRA CHRONICLES
CASE FILES OF AN URBAN WITCH
SOUL STONE MAGE
THE KACY CHRONICLES
MIDWEST MAGIC CHRONICLES
THE FAIRHAVEN CHRONICLES
I FEAR NO EVIL
THE DANIEL CODEX SERIES
SCHOOL OF NECESSARY MAGIC
SCHOOL OF NECESSARY MAGIC: RAINE CAMPBELL
ALISON BROWNSTONE
FEDERAL AGENTS OF MAGIC
SCIONS OF MAGIC
THE UNBELIEVABLE MR. BROWNSTONE
DWARF BOUNTY HUNTER
ACADEMY OF NECESSARY MAGIC
MAGIC CITY CHRONICLES

OTHER BOOKS BY JUDITH BERENS

OTHER SERIES IN THE ORICERAN UNIVERSE:

OTHER BOOKS BY MARTHA CARR

JOIN THE ORICERAN UNIVERSE FAN GROUP ON FACEBOOK!

OTHER BOOKS BY A.L. KNORR

The Elemental Origins Series

Born of Water
(including novella The Wreck of Sybellen)
Born of Fire
Born of Earth
Born of Aether
Born of Air
The Elementals

The Kacy Chronicles

* with Martha Carr *
Descendant (1)
Ascendant (2)
Combatant (3)
Transcendent (4)

Other books and Stories

OTHER BOOKS BY A.L. KNORR

Pyro (including the novella Heat)
Returning Episode II

CONNECT WITH THE AUTHORS

A.L. Knorr Social

To be the first to learn about new releases and special offers, sign up for A.L. Knorr's newsletter here: https://www.alknorrbooks.com/

Facebook: https://www.facebook.com/alknorrbooks/
Instagram: https://www.instagram.com/alknorrbooks/?hl=en
Twitter: https://twitter.com/ALKnorrBooks
Pinterest: https://www.pinterest.com/ALKnorrBooks/

Martha Carr Social

Website: http://www.marthacarr.com

Facebook: https://www.facebook.com/groups/MarthaCarrFans/

BOOKS BY MICHAEL ANDERLE

Sign up for the LMBPN email list to be notified of new releases and special deals!

https://lmbpn.com/email/

For a complete list of books by Michael Anderle, please visit:

www.lmbpn.com/ma-books/

Printed in Great Britain
by Amazon